I Remember

Noëlle Harrison was born in England and moved to Ireland in 1991. While based in Dublin in the early nineties she wrote and produced plays. She has written extensively on visual art in Ireland. Her first novel, *Beatrice*, was published in 2004, followed by *A Small Part of Me* in 2005. She lives in Oldcastle, County Meath.

Praise for *A Small Part of Me*

'Harrison is an intriguing and sensual writer, confidently charting out her own distinctive territory'

Sunday Independent

'The search for redemption and the simple heartbreaking love of a mother for her child imbue this novel with echoes that you won't forget'

Irish Independent

Also by Noëlle Harrison

Beatrice
A Small Part of Me

I Remember

Noëlle Harrison

MACMILLAN

First published 2008 by Macmillan
an imprint of Pan Macmillan Ltd
20 New Wharf Road, London N1 9RR
Basingstoke and Oxford
Associated companies throughout the world
www.panmacmillan.com

ISBN 978-0-230-70964-5

1 3 5 7 9 8 6 4 2

A CIP catalogue record for this book is available
from the British Library.

Typset by Intype Libra Ltd
Printed and bound in the UK by
CPI Mackays, Chatham ME5 8TD

For Corey and Helena,
brother and sister

The only way to forget is to remember.

Sigmund Freud

One

It was her eyes. Just the same as my brother Mattie's, the colour of wet slate; wood-shadows in a child's baby-face, markers of pain, or presentiment. They made me understand why I was meant to be lost in a foreign country, alone apart from her, needing me. Every time I looked at her eyes I knew I was right.

Everything happens for a reason, Mammy used to say before the 'accident'. *There is no such thing as a coincidence.*

I see my mother standing at the kitchen sink, her back turned to me, arms immersed in greasy suds, pausing, looking out the window at the scudding clouds, speaking dreamily and thinking maybe of her gods, only hers.

So clearly these images from my childhood return, like pools of light, sudden illuminations within a very dense wood. And in the darkest corner of the forest that is my memory – its tangled briars still confused – stands little Matilda Finch, with eyes like my brother's, and a name not dissimilar. She was my charge when I was eighteen years and two months old.

I remember the weight of her small hand inside the cup of my palm, and the silhouette of her face against the blinding Mediterranean sun, looking at me. Her head is tilted to one side. Her gesture says it all, for she points ahead and waits for me to take action.

We are gasping in the heat. Matilda from her condition, and I from the climate, unused to the stifling humidity, for all I have known are the chill, damp summers of home. We are in an unearthly land, halfway between heaven and hell. Water and heat become a hazy sheen, hovering above the flat salt plains. We are two tiny figments floating in this seaside mirage, two outcast angels swallowed by the barren landscape and the heavy sky. We are each other's guardians.

Our bare feet slither across the hot sand dunes, but now we have started we cannot stop. We walk relentlessly. It is the farthest Matilda has walked in two weeks, and we just keep on going. Away, and away, from a place which frightens us both.

Two

I am standing outside 5 Winchester Gardens, tan leatherette suitcase in hand, red bomber jacket zipped up high, my stomach still churning from the rough crossing and rain cascading from the sky. But I don't hurry as I open the wrought-iron gate, walk up the pebble path, up the stone front steps, and rap the royal-blue door with the big brass knocker. Instead I examine my new home. My eyes travel from the big bay window on the ground floor, up the storeys of the red brick house. I count four. Back home, we don't even have a staircase, not any more. I look up at the row of three tiny windows protruding from the slate roof, and hope my bedroom isn't up there. I would rather be down below. Even the basement would do rather than the height, the vulnerability of being way up there. I crane my neck and angle my face up into the sky. The rain pelts down upon my cheeks, yet oddly the sky itself is bright and blue. I see a corner of a rainbow tucked behind the silver roof of the house and descending through the branches of a large horse chestnut tree.

A good sign, Mammy said. *A rainbow always means luck.*

But I feel mounting anxiety. Suddenly I want to go home. I could. There is nothing stopping me. I could turn around and go straight back to the tube station. I could get the train and be in

Holyhead in time for the night crossing. I have enough money to get home.

I pause; lick my lips. Even the rain is different here. Back home it tastes of salt, clings to your skin, like a misty film, lacing your lashes and penetrating your wool sweaters, whereas this London rain is stinging me, slapping off my cheeks, ferocious as a tropical storm, I imagine. It is humid, and I am sweating underneath my pvc jacket. I wish I hadn't worn it now. When I had looked in the mirror in Lyons in Sligo it had seemed the height of fashion. Now I suspect it looks cheap, especially in my present surroundings. I have never walked down such a grand road. Not even in Dublin, the time I had gone up to get my passport.

I move forwards and stand on the first doorstep, looking down at my feet, soaking in my pumps. I can't go back. Not now. Even Mammy had said I should leave. There is nothing left for me at home. No jobs, and my childish world of fairies and woods, bogs and the sea, all my fantasies of living in the wilds up the side of a mountain in love with a young god of a man, all these dreams could never sustain me. Ever since I was nine I have been a prisoner of my past: my mother's daily conversations with the dead a constant reminder; my father's absence another. I could never build a life at home. All possibility of it was burnt to cinders the day our house went up in flames, the day of the 'accident'. I had to go.

I had two choices: America (staying with cousin Deirdre, and working illegally in an ice-cream parlour in Long Island) or England. My Leaving Cert. wasn't going to be good enough to go to college. I couldn't bear the idea of repeating a year and besides I really hadn't wanted to be a nurse anyway.

So why had I chosen this? Fiona's sister, Carmel, had done it for a year and by all accounts had great craic. Her employers' friends all had Irish au pairs, and on their days off the au pairs would get together for a big session. They met lots of boys; some of them even had English boyfriends.

Carmel had gone on holiday with her family. They had taken her to America, all expenses paid. She had even got to go to Disneyland. That was a couple of years ago but Carmel had never come back to Ireland. She had a good job in Selfridges department store now, was settled in London with a flat and a fiancé. She had a proper life, and was still great friends with her old employers. The children had loved her.

Fiona had told me all this the day we went shopping in Sligo, just after the Leaving Cert. I'd bought a bright pink-and-blue sweatshirt, with bat wing sleeves, with my savings, and Fiona had bought a pair of drainpipe jeans. They looked great on her. She was so skinny.

'If being an au pair is so brilliant, why don't *you* do it?' I said to her.

'Ah no, it's not for me.' Fiona shook her head, pulling the flake out of her 99 and licking it. We were sitting on a bench by the river, watching the ducks and being pestered by sea gulls. 'I *know* what I want to do.'

Fiona had always said she wanted to be a schoolteacher from as far back as I could remember. When we were younger she used to make me play terminally dull games of school, when I had to sit alongside her dolls and teddies as one of her pupils. She even made copybooks for her 'class' with her father's stapler, and had a little blackboard and chalks. It bored me to tears but Fiona was in her element. Never had I met anyone so suited to her calling.

'I suppose,' I replied biting the creamy peak off my ice cream. 'But don't you want to go somewhere else?'

Fiona stopped licking, screwed up her eyes, and looked thoughtfully at a swan gliding confidently upriver.

'No,' she said emphatically and then smiled at me, an ice-cream moustache framing her pink lips. 'You know I'm a home bird. But not you, Barbara, you don't belong here.'

Suddenly it stops raining. I stand with both feet on the bottom step of my new home, as the sunshine showers me and steam rises off the wet stone. Why do I feel such dread?

Trust your instincts, Mammy used to say.

And just as I have decided to turn around and walk away, to listen to my gut feeling, I notice something out of the corner of my eye. It is a movement behind the windows of the basement. The sunshine is so bright I can't see through the glass, just a reflection of the bustling clouds, and sunlight spilling across the sky, and me, looking at myself, looking in. As I peer over the stone balustrade – my fingers gripping its edge – looking at the bamboo plants shielding the basement windows, I am distracted. In that moment the front door opens, and it is too late, for now I have arrived.

Olivia Finch looks down at me. She says nothing, just stares. Her eyes are startled as if she is surprised but she must have been expecting me. I hurry up the steps, and now I am standing in front of her. I try to smile, but I can feel my lips wobbling with nerves and worry.

'The agency sent me,' I manage to spit out.

She nods, and then looks me up and down. I squirm under her critical glare. She doesn't smile at me. I am not used to this. At home we always smile; even in Dublin, strangers greet each other with a kindly smile. I am at a loss. I do not know what else to say or do.

'How old are you?' she asks me in an accented voice, and I realise she isn't English.

'Eighteen,' I practically whisper.

'Really?' She raises her eyebrows. 'You Irish girls look so young!'

She turns then and walks inside the hall. I hesitate on the

doorstep. She pauses at the staircase and puts her hand on the banister. 'Well, come on in,' she says, her face half turning, her gaze directed at the wall, where a large abstract painting hangs.

I step inside, my hair is dripping wet but I am afraid to shake it, afraid to spatter the pristine cream walls of Olivia Finch's posh London home.

'Close the door,' she directs.

I push it shut, and immediately we are cloaked in shadows. It is a relief to be out of the glare of the sunshine. The house is cool and smells of lilies. A huge vase of them sits on a glass table in the hall. The carpet is pale and plush. I am terrified my wet shoes will make dirty marks on it.

'Come,' she says, walking down the length of the hall and turning at the end at the top of another staircase.

I follow her down to the basement and into the utility room. The only sound is the whirr of the washing machine. She hands me a towel off the shelf. It is pure white and fluffy. I have never touched such a soft towel in my life.

'You got caught in the rain?'

I nod. 'Yes.'

'And it has been so hot,' she continues, 'so humid here. I can't bear to go out when it is like that. Even though it is hotter at home in France, but London is more uncomfortable in the summer. I was glad it rained. So much better for me, and for Matilda.'

She leads me into another room. It is the kitchen, immaculate like the rest of the house, apart from two cups of half drunk coffee on the counter.

'You want a coffee?'

I would prefer a cup of tea but I am too shy to ask, so I say yes, coffee would be nice.

She ignores the coffee machine on the counter, still bubbling away, and instead flicks on the kettle and takes a jar of Maxwell House out of the press.

'Sit, please.'

Olivia indicates a high stool, opposite the counter. I put my suitcase down on the floor and unzip my jacket. I don't want to take it off, for my t-shirt is clinging to my sweaty skin. I hope I don't smell.

'First thing,' Olivia says, opening a drawer under the counter top and taking out a packet of cigarettes. 'Very important,' she says, slipping the cigarette between her lips and searching in the drawer for a lighter. 'This' – she points at the cigarette – 'you must not tell my husband. OK?' She lights the cigarette and inhales deeply. 'He thinks it's not good for me or for Matilda. So I don't want to worry him. He thinks he is the boss.' She laughs suddenly, taking me by surprise. I press my hands into my lap, my throat dry with nerves. I want to say something: it is all a mistake and I have to leave, sorry but no. I can't stay. If I was different, more confident, sophisticated, I would be able to say something witty, show her I could be a good confidante, and maybe make the first move towards what? Friendship?

Olivia Finch stares at me. She smokes and she stares.

'You look so young,' she says again, shaking her head and pouring boiling water into a mug. She takes milk out of the fridge and passes it to me along with the coffee. She doesn't even bother to offer me sugar. I pour in the milk, my hand shaking, hoping she can't see, and take a sip of my coffee. It scalds my lip. It is bitter, and disgustingly strong. I wonder how I will manage to drink it all.

'So,' she says, inhaling. 'This is your first job as an au pair?'

'Yes, but I have had lots of experience minding our neighbours' children back home.'

'Yes, yes, I have seen the references,' she says, with a bored look on her face. She tips the ash of her cigarette out the open window, and turns round to face me. She is like a little doll, dressed elegantly, in a pair of tailored black trousers, high heels and white blouse. Her hair is in a dark bob, heavy fringe adding drama to her high cheekbones and large eyes with thickly mascared eyelashes. She looks the height of French chic and makes me feel like a country bumpkin.

'You will do fine,' she says, a little smile playing around her lips.

She puts out her cigarette, puts the end under the tap and throws the butt in the bin, returning the packet to the drawer. She opens the window wider and then comes over and picks up my bag.

'Is that all you have?' she asks, one eyebrow raised.

'Yes.'

'My God! It is tiny. I wish I could travel so light.'

She brushes past me. Her bare arms are cold, icy.

'Come,' she says, ushering me through the doorway. 'I will introduce you to Matilda, your new playmate.'

And she laughs again, but it's not a real laugh, for there is no joy in the sound.

When I first met Matilda I didn't like her. In fact I didn't like her for days.

Her room is the colour of primroses. The curtains are white and light, fluttering inside the room like angels' wings. They are drawn across the large window but still sunshine spills through their thin resistance, making patterns on the carpet and illuminating the little girl, who is sitting up in bed, a large drawing pad on her lap and coloured pencils scattered about her. She is bending over the paper, drawing with fierce concentration.

'Matilda,' says Olivia, walking over to the bed, and sitting on the end of it. 'This is your new au pair . . .' Olivia pauses, shakes her head and looks over at me. 'I am sorry, I forget your name?'

'Barbara.'

'Yes. Thank you.'

She turns back to the child and leans over her, putting her hand over the little girl's wrist, and forcing her to stop drawing. The girl looks up at her mother, and for a moment I imagine I can see the older woman flinching. She pushes the hair brusquely off Matilda's forehead and picks up her hands, examining the fingers.

'Look at you, you're a mess,' she mutters. And then speaking more clearly to the child she says, 'This is Barbara.'

Matilda looks up and regards me coldly. She sneezes and her mother takes a tissue from the box on her bedside locker, and wipes the child's nose. Matilda wriggles away from her mother's grip and stares at me. She looks completely unlike her mother, fair with bluey grey eyes. Immediately there is something familiar about her.

'Hello,' I say, stepping forward awkwardly to peer over the bed at the sketchbook. 'What are you drawing?' I try to sound friendly and upbeat.

The child ignores me, looks crossly at her mother.

'Mummy, I don't want an au pair. Why do I have to have an au pair?'

'Because Daddy says so.' Olivia pats her daughter's sheets and stands up.

'I don't like her, Mummy. Her coat is red, and she has red hair. Why can't you look after me?' Matilda's voice rises.

My cheeks are burning, I am mortified, but Olivia doesn't seem the slightest bit embarrassed.

'Because I need the help, ma petite!' she exclaims, hands on her hips.

'I don't want her,' Matilda whines.

'Don't be so selfish,' Olivia says, talking to her six-year-old daughter as if she is an adult. 'I can't cope on my own.'

I take a step back. This is a mistake, I should leave now, but my feet root me to the spot. I have never encountered such a rude child, or such a strange mother.

During my first week with the Finches I believed Olivia didn't possess a maternal bone in her body. In hindsight it all makes perfect sense.

'Mama,' Matilda says, her voice suddenly quiet, almost a whisper.

'Yes, my darling,' Olivia replies wearily.

'I feel sick.'

'All right, just a minute, there's a good girl.'

Olivia goes back to the bed and takes a china basin out from underneath it. She is just in time. Matilda vomits violently into the bowl.

'That's it, good girl.' Olivia's voice is softer, more gentle than before. 'I don't think that new medicine suits you. We shall have to tell Daddy, shan't we?'

I stand awkwardly in the doorway, not knowing whether I should leave or stay. Matilda's hair falls across her forehead in limp, dark blonde strands. I can see the blue veins through the pale skin of her face, and yet she isn't thin, or delicate looking; her cheeks are plump, if as white as snow. She looks at me, and her eyes are almost black, the pupils so large. I shiver . . . again that unsettling familiarity. It is as if I have seen her before but I can't think where. The child sits back against the pillow and closes her eyes. Her mother wipes her face with a tissue and motions for me to come over. She hands me the basin of sick.

'Please, can you get rid of this?' she asks me. 'Quickly.'

I dash out of the room, but I don't know where the bathroom is. The first door I try is a bedroom, surely the Finches', for it is huge, with an enormous bed covered with a purple counterpane and piled with lots of cushions, all blue and gold. The walls are white, but littered with art, mostly modern and abstract. I quickly close the door, afraid I might spill some sick on the pristine carpet, the smell of which is beginning to turn my already fragile stomach.

On my third try (after coming across a small study) I find the bathroom. It is all polished taps and slippery marble. I slide across the floor and pour the contents of the basin down the toilet. I flush and then wash my hands. I bend my head under the cold tap and drink some of the water. My throat is so dry. I rinse out the basin in the bath and then pause to look in the mirror over the sink.

My hair has almost fallen out of its ponytail. I pull it out and try to comb it with my fingers, twisting it back up into a bunch on the top of my head.

She has red hair. That's what Matilda said. Why doesn't she like red hair? I prefer to describe it as auburn, or chestnut. I smooth my eyebrows down with my fingers. I have never noticed before how thick they are. My eyes stare back at me, the colour of bog water Daddy once joked; or seaweed, Fiona said. One of my eyes is darker green than the other. I am uneven. I find it hard to look at myself for I seem so foolish, and so young, like Olivia Finch said. I feel like an alien, so out of place in this big, grand house. I don't belong here, and the little girl is a monster.

Yet I don't want to go home, not any more. I need to get away from our house in Culleenamore, from all the memories in the field next door, the ruins of a happier life, slowly buried in the weeds and brambles, but nevertheless constantly staring me in the face. There are the words my mother conjures up – every day for the past nine years – from Mattie, for she cannot leave go of him, not even for a day.

And the secret: it is my fault. Mammy is right, there are no such things as accidents. I have tried to hide this from her ever since it happened, and I thought there might be a time when she could forgive me, but as I grow older, begin to understand the depths of her grief, I know she never would. And so I keep silent, and my non-confession is like a gaping wound in my side, getting larger and larger, until the whole of me feels empty.

'Barbara.'

I start, nearly dropping the basin onto the tiled floor.

I open the door and Olivia Finch is standing on the landing.

'What took you so long?' she asks crossly. Without waiting for a reply she takes the basin out of my hand and places it on the floor outside Matilda's room.

'She's sleeping now so I'll show you to your room.'

I pick up my suitcase, abandoned earlier on the landing. To my surprise, instead of going up the staircase to the second floor, she opens the door next to Matilda's room, one I had not tried yet.

'I thought it best you were next door to her. She often needs help in the night,' Olivia explains.

I like the room. It is sunny and bright, and beautifully decorated. It is how I imagine a hotel room might be: snowy white sheets, smart wallpaper with tiny rosebuds on it, and pink lacy curtains.

'John decorated this room for Matilda, but she didn't like it. She doesn't like pink, or red. Not favourite colours of mine either. Pink is too sickly, and red' – Olivia pauses looking at my jacket, her lips curving into an unkind smile – 'well, red lacks subtlety. So I made her room yellow, the colour of summer. She prefers it.'

I go over to the bed and put my suitcase on it.

'If you want to come downstairs in a couple of minutes I'll go through your duties, and tell you about Matilda. Did the agency explain about her condition?'

She speaks quickly as if it is a subject she wishes not to dwell on.

'They said she had seizures, but not exactly what it is . . .'

Olivia laughs shortly. 'Yes that is the million dollar question. My daughter is not well, has never been well since she was very little. If we were in the nineteenth century you would say she suffers from "hysteria". Some days she is better than others. Today is not such a good day . . .'

She starts to walk out of the room.

'Come down in about ten minutes.'

The door snaps shut.

I walk over to the window. My room overlooks the garden and the large chestnut tree I saw earlier. The sky is cloudless now. Late-afternoon sunshine spills onto the lawn. The garden is as immaculate as the house. There is a small greenhouse at the back, along with a large shed. A pond takes up the centre of the garden, and there are luscious water lilies floating on its surface. The beds are bursting with different flowers, many I have never seen before. It looks like the garden in *The Tale of Peter Rabbit*. I half expect to see a little brown rabbit with a blue jacket, hopping across the lawn. The air is thick with flies and bees buzzing drowsily as the day begins to wind down. I see a man come out of the shed. He is carry-ing a trowel and a pot. I wonder if he is Mr Finch. He has dark brown hair, is quite stocky, and looks a little younger than Mrs Finch. As if he senses me looking down at him, he pauses and looks up at the house. I quickly step back feeling silly.

I take off my jacket, move forward again, open the window and step back, careful not to look out again. A slight breeze enters the room, but the air is hot, warmer than back home. I decide to change out of my t-shirt. I unzip my suitcase and rummage with desperation through my sparse wardrobe. Unhappily I notice that a lot of my clothes are red, and pink. I pull out a baby blue t-shirt, a favourite I have had since I was fourteen but cannot bear to throw out. I pull it on. It is a little tight, since it has shrunk and I have grown over the years. But its tightness is quite fetching I decide, looking into the mirror. I take my hair out of its ponytail and leave it down. I give it a good brush but it refuses to stay straight, espe-cially after getting so wet in the rain, and pings immediately into a series of waves and kinks. I wish I had perfectly smooth hair, like Fiona's. She looks the way boys like.

I have never had a proper boyfriend. Of course I've shifted a few boys, but I've never actually gone out with someone. Fiona and Murtagh have been going out for two years. Fiona slept with Murtagh when her parents were away last summer. I didn't ask her the details but she said it didn't hurt, not like they said it would, and that it was nice and made her feel special. Murtagh gave her a claddagh ring, and Fiona says it is a secret engagement ring, their secret and mine because I am the only one who knows. I like Murtagh. He always includes me in the things they do, and invites me with them everywhere, but sometimes I think Fiona minds so I say I can't go, and go walking by the sea with Solomon, and since he died, on my own.

I still get angry when I think about Solomon. They should never have put him down. But Mammy said we couldn't afford to take him to the animal hospital in Dublin, even though I offered to pay for it, all of my savings – communion and confirmation money – but she said even that wasn't enough for the operation.

I said, 'You wouldn't put me down if I needed an operation, you'd find the money somehow.' But to my mother Solomon wasn't as important as a human. To me, he was more important. I try not to think about my dog as the tears come boiling to the surface. I wipe my hand across my eyes. I miss him so much. More than I miss my mother, and my father. More than Mattie.

Immediately I feel sick with guilt. I sit down on the bed and catch my breath. This is a new beginning, I say to myself. An adventure, I whisper weakly, but somehow it doesn't feel like one. I wish I were Fiona, because to me it appears she knows exactly who she is, what she is going to do with her life and who she loves. I know nothing. I am at sea.

*

I walk into the kitchen and Olivia Finch is drinking wine with the man from the garden. I hesitate, unsure if this is Mr Finch, waiting for an introduction. The man looks at me and smiles kindly. I smile shyly back.

'Ah, there you are, Barbara.' Olivia offers the man a cigarette, and I know it could not be her husband. 'This is Gareth,' she says brightly. 'He is our gardener.' She puts great emphasis on the word gardener, and then chuckles. Gareth smiles at her and says hello to me. She lights his cigarette and then draws back and drinks her wine.

'Would you like a glass?'

I nod, wondering whether it is ruder to say yes or no. I have only ever drunk wine once or twice, and it was sweet and sickly. Myself and Fiona prefer cider, and Murtagh drinks Guinness.

'Will you pour Barbara a glass? Thank you, Gareth.'

'It would be my pleasure.'

Gareth sounds posh, and not the least bit how I should think a gardener speaks. He hands me a tall glass of white wine. It is so cold that the glass is misted over with condensation. I take a sip. It is delicious. I have never tasted wine like this before.

'Do you like it?' asks Olivia. She looks amused.

'Yes, it's lovely.'

'Don't get too drunk. You have to help me with the dinner.' She indicates a pile of vegetables on the draining board.

Gareth laughs. 'You lazy old thing, Livie. Leave the poor girl alone, she's hardly off the boat.'

'She's not on holiday, you know, Gareth, although you seem to behave like you're permanently on vacation.'

'Touché,' Gareth responds good-humouredly. 'Ignore her, Barbara. Sit down and relax for a moment before Madam slave driver gets her claws into you.'

I feel awkward in the middle of their banter, yet Olivia Finch's hard edges have softened and she is the least intimidating I have seen since I arrived.

'So,' says Gareth, pulling a chair out for me. 'You're from Ireland?'

'Yes.' I am blushing although I don't even know why. It is a horrible sensation but I can't stop it. It happens to me all the time.

'Where in particular?' He leans back against the counter, brown hairy arms folded across his chest.

'Sligo.'

He looks clueless.

'The north-west, not too far from Galway.'

Recognition.

'Oh Galway, yes . . . you know I have Irish roots,' he says to Olivia.

'You do? So that is where you get your silver tongue from?'

'Ha bloody ha, Miss Froggie.' Gareth tickles Olivia's arm and she wriggles away from him. 'My grandfather was from a place called Wexford. Do you know it?' He turns to me again.

'Oh yes. It's on the east coast. It's very nice, by the sea,' I say enthusiastically, my cheeks gradually cooling as the wine makes me feel a little more relaxed.

'I keep meaning to go there, on pilgrimage, one day,' Gareth says.

'You don't want to go to Ireland,' Olivia interrupts. 'Not with all those terrible troubles.'

Gareth sighs. 'Don't be so stupid, Olivia, you've more chance of being blown up by the IRA in London than in the south of Ireland.'

'Is that so?' She looks surprised.

'Christ, you really need to brush up on your current affairs. Well, now you've the perfect chance to educate yourself with a young Irish woman in the house.'

I redden again. I can't help it, for he has called me a woman, not a girl.

Olivia snorts and then glances at the clock on the wall.

'Come on, Barbara, give me a hand with this, will you? John is home soon. Are you staying for dinner, Gareth?'

'I've a hot date tonight.' He downs his glass of wine and puts it on the counter.

Olivia rips open the lettuce. She turns on the tap and fills the sink with water, throwing the leaves into it. Gareth stands behind her.

'How's Matilda today?' he asks quietly.

Olivia shrugs. 'Oh, you know, the same, not so good, not so bad.'

He pats her back, says nothing.

At that moment I hear the front door shut, and a voice calling from the hall. Gareth moves slowly away from Olivia.

'We're in the kitchen Finch!' he calls.

Olivia beckons to me. She is flushed. 'Can you come over here and chop these tomatoes?'

I stand up, a little giddy from the wine, and take the knife she hands me.

I nervously begin to chop up the tomatoes. I hear footsteps on the floor above, and then down the stairs. I can feel the tension coming off Olivia although Gareth appears perfectly relaxed.

'Where's Matilda?'

John Finch stands in the doorway, shirtsleeves rolled up, and in suit trousers. He pushes his hand through his damp, fair hair. My first impression is that he is very tall, and very thin, and tired. He has a long oval face, with a narrow nose. He smiles at me. His welcome is warm, unlike his wife's.

'Hello there. You must be the new au pair. Barbara isn't it? From Ireland?' He reaches out his hand.

I stop chopping the tomatoes and look around for something to wipe my hands on.

'Here,' says Olivia, handing me a towel.

I shake John Finch's hand. He has a firm if damp grip.

He asks me a few questions. How was the journey over? What time did I arrive? Have I met Matilda yet? Olivia explains about Matilda getting sick.

'I'll go up to her,' he says, moving towards the door.

'She's sleeping,' says Olivia, but John Finch ignores her and heads out the kitchen door. Olivia sighs.

'Here, have another glass of wine,' says Gareth, refilling her glass. She turns to look at him and takes a sip. He pats her arm.

'Everything will be all right,' he says.

I turn to the scallions and begin to chop them, bending down over the wooden board. The room is filling with the scent of garlic and some other herb from the oven.

'Will you not stay for dinner?' Olivia asks Gareth again.

'No, I can't let my lady friend down.'

John Finch appears in the doorway. 'She looks better than yesterday,' he announces.

Olivia ignores him, turning towards the sink and pulling out dripping lettuce leaves, before drying them off and putting them in the salad bowl.

'Are you off out gallivanting, Downey?' John asks Gareth.

'But, of course. It's a hot summer's night, what else would I be doing?'

'One of these days someone will catch you,' John says laughing, pouring a glass of wine. 'It's about time you got hitched, Downey. I have my best-man speech written already.'

'You'll be waiting a while yet.' Gareth smirks.

John picks up the packet of cigarettes on the counter and examines them.

'Olivia?'

'They're mine,' Gareth interrupts, snatching them off him, and as John turns round to open the French windows, Gareth winks at me.

'I'll be off. See you tomorrow, Olivia and Barbara.'

'*À tout à l'heure*,' Olivia murmurs.

'Be good,' says John.

We eat outside, it is so warm. The food is delicious, unlike anything I have experienced before. We start with salad, crisp and fresh, full of juicy tomatoes, olives and tiny scallions, and laced with a rich herby dressing, along with slabs of hot garlicky bread. This is followed by a chicken casserole, soft and tender, and bathed in a rich tomato sauce, with green beans and herbs. Time is taken over each course, and it is already getting dark when Olivia brings out dessert – little dishes of sweet vanilla custard, which she calls crème brûlée. At home food is plain and functional. When he was there, Daddy always gobbled his and left the room before Mammy seemed to have even finished her first mouthful.

Olivia says this is how they always eat at home in France. She tells me that usually I will have tea with Matilda at 5 o'clock but because I arrived so late today, I am eating with them, just this once.

John says little now. His early good humour has disappeared with his friend, Gareth. As Olivia drinks more wine she gets chattier, not friendly but more forthcoming. She explains that Gareth is an old school chum of John's; they went to Oxford together, and both ended up in the City, John in banking and Gareth as a stockbroker. But last year Gareth gave it all up and announced he was going to become a gardener. In fact he doesn't need to work at all and is extremely well off, but he is good at gardening and he loves it.

Olivia and John recommended him to all their neighbours and now he has a thriving business.

We are drinking coffee when it is mentioned first. The holiday.

'What time are the flights?' John asks Olivia.

'Do we have to fly?' asks Olivia. 'You know how I hate it.'

'Think of Matilda. All that way in the car and on the boat, it would exhaust her completely,' John snaps back.

'Do we have to go at all?'

John looks surprised. 'But you wanted to go,' he says sharply. 'It's your family we're visiting. Besides, I've booked the time off work, we have to go on holiday now.'

'We could just stay here.'

'Don't be stupid,' John replies tersely.

There is silence between them. I see two spots of red flare on Olivia's cheeks but she says nothing.

John turns to me. 'You're not afraid of flying are you?'

'No,' I reply, hesitantly, for I have never flown in my life.

'Good, you can look after my wife, then, and be her minder for the journey.'

John sees the puzzled expression on my face.

'You did tell her didn't you?' he asks Olivia.

'Oh,' she says absently. 'Maybe not. I was hoping you might cancel. I think maybe Matilda is too sick to travel.'

'She'll be fine,' John says emphatically, and then turning to me he says, 'We're going on holiday to stay with Olivia's family in the south of France, and of course you will be coming with us.'

It is not so much a question as an order.

'Oh.'

I don't know what to say. I feel nervous, afraid of going so far away from home, but at the same time I feel a rush of excitement. Never before have I been abroad, apart from England. The south of France. It sounds terribly glamorous. I can't wait to tell Fiona.

Olivia takes a swig of her wine and says something in French to John. He answers back in English.

'It will be fine, Olivia. We could all do with a change of scenery.'

He puts down his knife and fork, and wipes his mouth with his napkin.

'Have you been to France before?' he asks me.

'No.'

'Parlez-vous français?' asks Olivia.

I colour, shake my head.

'Well you'll learn quick enough. None of Olivia's family can speak English very well.'

'Apart from Pascal,' Olivia corrects him.

'Yes, of course, Pascal.' John turns to me. 'Pascal is Olivia's brother. He studied in America for a couple of years. He's fluent in English.'

He stands up and walks over to the flower bed, pulls a couple of weeds out of it.

'Gareth is slacking,' he says, and then adds, 'I tell you I can't wait to get out of stinky old London.'

He stands with his back to us as he speaks, as if he is talking to himself. Olivia sulks at the table. I sit, stuck to my chair, unsure whether I should get up, go back into the house and do the washing-up. I have lied, for I can speak a little French. I did it for my Leaving Cert., and it was one of my best subjects, but I am too embarrassed to say so, afraid Olivia will start talking to me in French and I will be unable to respond.

'Can you go and check on Matilda?' John asks me as he turns. His eyes are blue like his daughter's, but a completely different shade.

Dusk has fallen. The yellow walls are golden as light from the setting sun fills Matilda's room. It is too neat to be a real child's room.

Nothing is out of place. At home Mattie and I had revelled in our chaos, and I had never changed my ways, even now. I have a flash of my old room at home, how I last left it, and how Mammy will find it and tick her tongue crossly, although maybe feel a little sorry now I am gone. Clothes will be strewn everywhere, records and tapes lying about the floor, as I packed in a panic, afraid I might miss the bus to Dublin. I don't think I even made the bed. I close my eyes and I can see the pictures of Solomon on the wall – the one of him running on the beach at Rosses Point, leaping through the waves; and another in the garden, chewing an old tin of dog food gripped between his paws.

Matilda is sleeping. I can hear her breathing. I creep towards the bed, terrified she will wake up and cry. I see her drawing from earlier lying on the floral duvet at her feet. I pick it up and look at it. It is a drawing of a fairy, or an angel. It's very good for her age. The fairy's face is neatly drawn and detailed. She has green eyes and, surprisingly, red hair. Her wings are bigger than her whole body, and she appears to be flying above the sea. Matilda has drawn lots of fish in the water, and one little boat bobbing on its surface. It is a sweet picture and makes me like her, just a little.

The duvet is halfway down the bed, and Matilda's shoulders and chest are exposed. Even though it's not cold I pull it up, cover her bare arms, so that only her face is protruding from her nest. She looks like she is lying beneath a field of flowers. They are, of course, yellow. Her mouth is open, and she looks angelic, like all small children do when they are asleep.

I wonder again what I am doing here in Matilda Finch's house. I have no interest in children. As a rule I don't like them, and I don't think I get on with them that well. I have only ever babysat before and that was just to earn some extra money. I never actually liked doing it. I used to dread the children waking up, for they would invariably misbehave and never do what I asked them. It's like horses, Fiona would say, you have to let them know who is boss or else they'll act up. I could understand that a little because I love riding, but with a horse I feel an affinity, not so with children, even though we are the same species. Children sense my weakness, my inability to amuse. At least, she's not a baby, or a toddler. That would be worse, when you can't communicate with them at all. But my first impression of Matilda Finch is not favourable. I am not looking forward to pandering to this spoilt little girl.

And yet she is sick. The agency mentioned an illness, but no one has told me yet what it is that makes Matilda Finch unwell. I wait for her parents to explain it to me, but apart from telling me what medicine to give her and when, and Olivia's reference to her Victorian constitution, I am not told anything. She is the sick child and I am her carer. I tiptoe out of her bedroom and back down the stairs.

Later I wake and it is dark. I am in a sweat. I pull the covers off my bed and lie on the sheets in my nightie. The room feels airless. I get up and go over to the window, pull back the curtains and open it wider. It is a half moon, but the sky is clear and littered with stars. An orange glow seeps from the city into the night sky. I realise it will never be truly dark here, not like home. I go back and sit on my bed. I can't sleep, even though I was so tired earlier. After doing the washing-up and writing down a schedule of my duties with John (Olivia had been too tired, or had had too much to drink, to go through it with me), I had barely been able to stand by the time he sent me up to bed.

I sit on my strange bed, which feels so stiff and hard, unlike my soft, bumpy mattress from home, and look about my new room. I would have loved a room like this when I was a little girl, so feminine and pretty. I am sure the wallpaper must be from Laura Ashley.

I hear voices. I know I should ignore them and try to go back to sleep but the noise rises. I tiptoe to the door and pull it open. The landing is completely dark, but I can see a light on under the door of the Finches' bedroom. I stand at my door, looking across the dark landing at my employers' bedroom, listening to them argue. They are speaking in French but I can catch words: *Matilda, maladie*, my name, *Barbara*. Gradually I begin to understand what Olivia is saying. She doesn't like me; Matilda doesn't like me; I am too young; she has changed her mind and she wants me to go. And John Finch says nothing. All I can hear now is the French woman ranting. And then she stops in mid-flight, and I can hear the bass of a man's voice but can't work out what he is saying. There is silence. It is so quiet I am afraid to breathe, afraid to pull my door shut in case it squeaks and they hear me.

Their bedroom door suddenly opens and I pull my head back quickly, hold my breath, and stand stock still behind my door. I hear someone walk across the landing. They stop at my door. It is ridiculous but I am frightened whoever it is will come into my room, and find me standing here, listening. I know it must be Mr or Mrs Finch but there is an atmosphere in the house, which suggests something other. I think of the ghost stories Fiona, Murtagh and I would tell each other, when we were tipsy on cider and Guinness, sitting on the rocks at Strandhill and watching the Atlantic bashing the shore. Murtagh claimed he had seen the old woman banshee once, and Fiona's mother had seen the pooka when she was a little girl. It appeared as a wild white horse with flashing red eyes. But it can take many forms. I had seen something terrible too, an awful creature, half human, half beast, the night of the fire, but I never told that story, not even to them.

I am shaking behind my door. I am sure whoever it is can hear my fear, but then all that happens is the door is pulled shut. I breathe out slowly, press my hot forehead to the cool wood. Whoever it is goes into Matilda's room. Light splashes under my door frame onto my toes. They must have turned her light on. I can hear Matilda coughing. She is coughing and coughing, and she sounds like an old man. It is a terrible noise. I climb back into bed. I put my hands over my ears but I can still hear the coughing. On and on, it is such a desperate sound. Poor Matilda Finch trying to catch her breath, and it sends me back, as my eyes slowly close, back to the night that never ends, and the fire which burns eternally in my mind and in my memory.

Three

I wait for Olivia Finch to tell me to leave. Part of me hopes for it. But we sit through breakfast with hardly a word exchanged. Matilda is up today and sits at the head of the table. Her father has already left for work, gone before any of us had risen. Olivia sits to her right, and I to the left. The French woman drinks a cup of strong black coffee, intermittently dipping a croissant into it as she browses through the paper. From time to time she looks up to direct me.

'Warm her milk for her.'

'She can have Rice Krispies today.'

'Wipe her mouth.'

Matilda is quiet too. The energy involved in eating her breakfast seems to require all of her strength.

I wait for Olivia Finch's final directive: 'Pack your bag.' But it doesn't come. Whatever her husband said last night made her change her mind.

I wish I could leave but I feel I can't just walk out, not unless they ask me to go. If I did, I would be letting everyone down. Mammy would nod her head, 'I knew you couldn't do it.' My father wouldn't say it, but I know he would think it too. Fiona would be sympathetic, but disappointed in me. She wants me to be more like her, more sure. But two confident friends doesn't make sense. There can only be one leader.

I feel a sudden urge to talk to my childhood friend, and tell her about everything that has happened so far. She would laugh, I am sure, and make light of my night-time fears. Fiona would make me feel so much better, in a way neither of my parents ever could.

How would Fiona cope in this situation? Capably, I decide. She wouldn't trail Matilda's napkin in her milk, or spill coffee on the table, or put the wrong spoon in the jam pot. She would make Olivia Finch admire her efficiency, her deft ableness at all that is domestic.

'I am going out for an hour or two,' Olivia says to me. 'If you need me I will be at this number at twelve.'

I look down at the card she hands me. It says Dr Warren, with a trail of letters behind his name and an address in Notting Hill.

'I need to get something for the flight on Saturday.'

'This Saturday?'

'Yes, did John not tell you when we are going?'

'No.' I feel a flutter in my stomach.

'Where are we going, Mama?' Matilda pipes up.

'To France, of course.' Olivia stands up and picks her handbag up off the counter.

'To see *Maman et Papa*?' Matilda continues, a frown on her face.

'*Oui*, Matilda, to see my parents.' Olivia opens a small compact and examines her face. 'She always calls them *Maman et Papa*, because that is what I call them,' Olivia explains to me. 'It should be *Grandmère et Grandpère*, if you were being correct. I want Matilda to be bilingual, but it is hard, we spend so little time in France, and John likes me to speak English in England.' She sighs and takes out her lipstick, artfully colouring in her lips.

'OK, I'll see you later.' She snaps her bag shut.

'Mama, I don't want to go to France.'

'Don't be silly, it's our holiday.'

'I don't want to go.'

'You have your list?' Olivia ignores her daughter and turns to me.

'Yes.' I take it out of my pocket, crumpled from the night before. She opens a cupboard in the kitchen.

'All the cleaning things are in here. Matilda needs to rest after lunch for a couple of hours.'

'I don't want to rest. I don't like it.'

'You don't like much, do you, Matilda?' Olivia grumbles, before walking out the door. She doesn't even kiss her daughter goodbye.

I feel sorry for Matilda yet she doesn't even seem to notice her mother's lack of tenderness. She continues to pick away at her cereal, not even bothering to look up.

We kiss goodbye every time. No matter how much anger there is between my mother and I, we always embrace on the threshold, even if our hearts are raging. It has been this way since I was tiny, right up until Sunday last, when I left for Dublin. It's what makes my mother unusual, how affectionate she is with those around her, always touching, always caring. It's what makes her work even harder than it is for others who do the same thing. It's what makes my father stay away. He cannot carry her burden for her.

I wonder, does he travel all around Europe driving a truck, just to give himself some credence? I think about it, and decide he liked being away from us, because of the return. Like a hunter coming in out of the wind, he would visit us, a cape of foreign climes still around him, sweeping us away with tales of cities we could only imagine in our heads, and little gifts, tiny things to eat: little sweets from Germany, and chocolate from France, and my favourite of all, small hard almond biscuits from Italy, which Mattie hated so I had them all to myself. Did he blame himself, I wonder, for not being there that night? Does he think if he had not been driving a truck across England on his way to Dover, as the old house lit up like a

Christmas cracker, he might have been there to save us all – Mattie's life, Mammy's heart and my soul? Is it possible he could feel as much guilt as I?

'Get my paints.' Matilda's voice breaks through my thoughts.

'What's the magic word?' I say emphatically, determined to teach the child a little respect.

She stares at me, her grey-blue eyes narrow. She looks mean. I feel unnerved, ridiculously so by a small child.

'I don't have to say "please" to you,' she says smartly. 'You're only the au pair. You're a servant.'

'You always say "please", Matilda, when you are asking someone to do something for you, no matter who they are.'

'No, I don't.'

I get up from the kitchen table and start clearing away the breakfast things. She repeats her command, but I ignore her and look at the list in front of me:

Wash up breakfast things
Clean kitchen
Hoover hall and staircases
Polish hall and staircases
Prepare Matilda's lunch
Clear up lunch things
Wash Matilda's laundry
Hoover and clean Matilda's room while she has a nap in the sitting room
Hang out all the washing
Bring in laundry and iron Matilda's clothes
Have dinner with Matilda (Olivia will make it)
Help Matilda in the bath
Read Matilda a story
Lights out 7 p.m.

Please confine yourself to your room after 8 p.m., unless you are going out. We require you to be home by 10.30 p.m. at the latest. If we require you to babysit we will give you at least one day's notice.

Fiona had said that all Carmel did was look after the children, take them for walks in the park and meet other au pairs for coffee and gossip. She may have done some food preparation, but cleaning the house and doing laundry never came into it. She had been viewed as part of the family – their house was her home, and she would eat with the parents. Obviously my situation was completely different, but in a way I didn't mind. I would rather not spend any more time than necessary in Olivia Finch's company.

A wail emerges from the end of the kitchen table, and I nearly leap out of my skin. Matilda Finch is puce in the face. I realise she is furious, so angry she can hardly get the words out of her mouth.

'Paints . . .' she gasps.

I don't know what to do. I don't want to back down but I am frightened she will start coughing like last night.

'Matilda, calm down,' I start to say.

'GET ME MY PAINTS!' she screams. The child is actually having a temper tantrum, and at the age of six. It astonishes me.

'OK, just relax, please . . . Matilda.'

'And paper,' she shouts after me, as I leave the room.

I run up two flights of stairs, and into the child's bedroom, cursing all the way. It is just my luck to be lumbered with the child of Frankenstein. I wish I had a boy, a happy little fellow. No bother to anyone, an angel.

I rummage in the drawers of her cupboard, eventually finding a box of paints and a pad of paper. I notice a small apron hanging on the back of her door and bring that down with me too. By the time I have returned to the kitchen Matilda is a normal colour again. I look for newspapers everywhere I can think of to put on the table.

'Is this usually where you paint?' I ask anxiously.

'I don't know,' she says unhelpfully.

I put her apron on; tie it around her chubby frame. Despite her illness, Matilda is a large child, plump and ungainly.

In desperation I pull the sports page out of Olivia's newspaper from breakfast, praying neither she nor her husband want to read it, and spread out the paints, jar of water, brushes and the paper.

'Now, there you are.'

She says nothing to me, opens the pad and carefully tears out a sheet of paper.

'"Thank you" would be nice.' I say, sounding like a sulky teenager. But Matilda ignores me. It is as if she is entering her own little world. She begins to splash paint onto the paper. Her breathing has returned to normal, and she looks like any other little girl now, not like the screaming monster of a few minutes ago. At least she is preoccupied, I think gratefully, as I turn to my list and start my first job of cleaning the kitchen.

I have just finished mopping the floor and Matilda has spread her third painting out on the table when the patio doors slide open. Gareth appears.

'Good morning, Matilda!' he says cheerfully. 'How lovely to see you.'

The child actually smiles at him. It is the first time I have seen Matilda smile. She looks almost pretty.

'Hello, Gareth,' she says sweetly. 'Do you like my paintings?'

He stands on the threshold. 'I had better not come in. Barbara has just washed the floor.'

'Oh,' says Matilda. That is all, no demands or insults.

'Hello, Barbara. How are you getting on?'

'Grand, thanks.' I try to sound upbeat.

He looks at me, then takes his boots off and tiptoeing across the wet floor he flicks on the kettle. 'And where is her ladyship?'

'Mama has gone to the doctor.'

'Has she now, Matilda? How she does love the doctors.'

I redden. I don't know why.

'Would you like a tea or coffee, Barbara?'

'Thank you, I'd love a tea.'

'She should make your tea, Gareth,' Matilda pipes up. 'She's the au pair.'

'And I'm the gardener and you're a cheeky little girl who should be making tea for us all.'

Matilda shuts her mouth. She giggles. I am in awe.

Gareth walks over to the table and sees my list of chores.

'Christ!' he exclaims, picking it up and reading. 'No wonder none of the others stayed long. This is a bit much don't you think, Barbara? More than you bargained for?'

I shrug my shoulders. I am uncomfortable talking about it in front of Matilda, and somehow feel I shouldn't be disloyal to my employers so soon.

'My dear friends the Finches go through their au pairs as if they're going out of fashion.'

I shift awkwardly. Gareth notices.

'I'm sorry. I shouldn't have told you that.'

'Seven in seven weeks, Daddy said,' Matilda trills triumphantly. 'And I can remember all their names, Gareth.'

'Well, aren't you clever?' he says, pouring water into a teapot.

'Maria, Katin, Synnøve, Sally, Amanda, Donna and Susie . . .'

'Was Susie the girl from Australia?'

'Yes, she ate kangaroo.'

'I think she was having you on, Matilda.'

'She stayed one night.' Matilda screws her face up with concentration as she dips her brush into the water and mixes more paint.

'I am sure you will be staying longer, Barbara, won't you?' Gareth looks at me pointedly as if his question means something else. I feel confused and embarrassed. I hate all this focusing on me. I wish he would leave me alone, and go and talk to Matilda, look at her paintings.

'There you go.' He hands me a steaming mug of tea.

'Thank you.'

I sip my tea.

'So when is Olivia back?' he asks, pushing his hand through his thick hair.

'In a couple of hours.'

'It's a beautiful day. If you want to set Matilda up outside I can watch her while you get on with all those chores.'

'Do you think that will be OK?' I ask, attracted by the idea of being away from the little girl for an hour or so. To be alone with my thoughts, even if I have to clean the whole house, is preferable to pandering to spoilt Matilda Finch's demands.

'Of course it's OK,' he says, ruffling Matilda's hair. 'It will be good for her to get some fresh air. She has been cooped up in this house for far too long.'

We take Matilda outside and it is like walking into another world. We step out of the clinical, shadowy confines of the house, into a land of lush and sunny opulence.

'Oh my God, it's gorgeous,' I gush.

Gareth looks pleased. 'Well thank you – I do my best.'

The flower beds are bursting with blooms. Gareth tells me what they are – foxgloves, dog roses, dahlias, geraniums, sweet pea, the list goes on. They have no function, apart from their beauty, their ability to please the eye and the nose. The fragrance from the flowers around me is heady, seductive. I want to lie down on the grass and daydream. It is torture to pull myself away and go back into the dark, sterile house.

'Stupid, stupid . . .'

I mutter to myself as I vacuum the already immaculate staircase, heaving the cumbersome hoover up three flights of stairs. I think of Gareth. He must be at least fifteen years older than me, but I can't shake the look he gave me when I went into the house.

'Don't be too long now,' he called, crouching down beside Matilda as she sat at the garden table, painting away with such voracity. And he smiled at me. And I looked away, for I knew I was blushing.

I am in the utility room trying to work out how to turn on the washing machine when Olivia Finch returns. I hear the front door slam, and then her brisk footsteps down into the kitchen beside me. I hear the patio doors sliding open as she goes out into the garden.

I meet her in the kitchen, as she is ushering Matilda inside. She is furious.

'Look at her!' she says accusingly.

Matilda's apron has slipped down and her top is covered in splashes of blue paint. So is her face and even her hair.

Olivia grabs a wet towel and starts to clean her daughter's face.

'Ow, Mama, ow. You're hurting me.'

'She's not allowed to paint until after her nap,' Olivia says crossly. 'In the morning you must play with her. Talk to her.'

'I didn't know,' I say quietly, wondering how I can possibly do that and all the housework they want me to do. 'It will come out,' I add, watching Olivia scrub at the blouse.

Olivia stops what she is doing and looks at me distastefully. 'That is not the point.'

She pulls paint out of strands of Matilda's hair. The little girl starts to cough.

'Did you give her the pills?' she asks me.

'Yes, at midday, like you said.'

She nods. 'OK, take her upstairs and get her changed, please, ready for her nap. She can put her pyjamas back on. She always sleeps in the sitting room at the front of the house in the afternoon. There are blankets on the side of the sofa if you need them.'

Matilda troops out of the kitchen. Olivia catches my arm as I follow her.

'It's important you play with her in the morning,' she says, staring at me with her doe eyes. 'My daughter spends too much time on her own, and always painting . . . painting . . .' she sighs. 'It's not good for her. She needs to play with someone.'

I feel like saying something back, like what about you, her mother, or a child her own age? Wouldn't that be more appropriate? But it doesn't surprise me Matilda seems to be friendless. She is far too spoilt to put up with competition. Olivia turns around and walks out of the kitchen into the garden. It is as if she has washed her hands of both of us. And yet she walks heavily, and I see her hand shaking as she brings it up to her face to shield her eyes from the sunlight. I am curious.

Matilda is wearily climbing the stairs when I catch up with her. By the time we are in her room, she is exhausted and sits down with a bump on the bed, her chest heaving in and out. I don't make a fuss of her, and open her chest of drawers pulling out a fresh pair of pyjamas. They are cream with black polka dots.

'Did you see my pictures?' Matilda asks breathlessly.

I shake my head. 'No.'

She takes a deep breath. 'Gareth says they're good.'

She is so worn out that she lets me change her clothes without complaining.

'Bring my pictures in, it might rain,' she orders me, as I wrap a dressing gown around her.

I say nothing, not wanting a repeat of this morning's tantrum, but Matilda is different since her mother came home, more subdued, her tone a tiny bit more respectful. I wonder at her behaviour, her exhaustion, the oddity of compulsory naps for a six-year-old.

In the sitting room, I bring her over to the sofa and she lies down on it. I cover her with one of the blankets and then draw the curtains closed.

'I wish I could go to school,' she whispers out of the darkness.

'It's the summer. You don't want to go to school in the holidays?'

'I would like to,' she says longingly as if it is a place she has never been.

'Have you started school yet?'

'Yes.' She looks up at me, suddenly shy. 'But I got sick. Daddy said I can go back soon. When I'm better.'

I am upstairs in Matilda's room, dusting the dust-free surfaces, clearing away the non-existent mess. I kneel down to tuck in the sheet on her bed and notice a box of papers under it. I pull it out, and inside are drawings, stacks of them. They are all of angels, some on their own, and some with families. She draws them standing outside little houses with orange roofs, by the seaside having a picnic, or in trees in the wood. Her angels fly in the sky, just above the tops of mountains, and they sleep, lying back on their clouds, with blissful smiles upon their faces. On some of the sheets of paper she has written 'ONCE UPON A TIME' in thick print, as if she is copying it from a book. That is all she writes, nothing else. I wonder if she can read or write yet. It is then I have my idea. What I will do to make Matilda Finch like me.

Four

My first week with the Finches is achingly slow. Part of me yearns for home, yet part of me is glad to be gone, free from the past. I am anonymous. There is a thrill to thinking this, to knowing that no one in England knows about me or my parents or what happened to us. I follow my list of chores industriously, and when I fall into bed at night I see my mother's face, an amused smile playing on her lips. It is the expression she had when I first told her I was going to London to be an au pair.

'Yes, the cards told me you were leaving.'

She was standing with her back to the kitchen window, the bulk of Knocknarea behind her. Her bright red hair framed her pale pixie face. Her figure was a sharp abstract outline against the lush green mountain. 'Six of Swords, crossing water, a short journey. It will be an opportunity to leave your worries behind.'

'Stop it, Mammy.' I put my hands over my ears. 'I don't want to know.'

'An au pair.'

She said it slowly, putting her hands on her hips. I could see the smile on her pale face as the clouds moved across the rain-laden sky and her face became a grey shadow.

'Yes, I saw the Page of Cups, so a child is involved.'

I walked out of the room, slamming the door. I was in a fury. How dare my mother read cards for *my* life. I did not want my future mapped out. I did not want to believe in fate.

Each day I am an observer in the Finches' lives. I hear John Finch go to work very early in the morning, but always, always going into his daughter's room to kiss her goodbye. Olivia usually rises after myself and Matilda, going out the front door with hardly a word to either of us. She is cold and distant and shows so little affection for her daughter it shocks me. And yet when Gareth appears Olivia thaws so completely she could be a different woman, one with a heart. Gareth is very friendly, but sometimes I feel as if he is laughing at me. It makes me feel awkward so that I blush when he talks to me, and stutter in reply.

Every afternoon I sit in Matilda's room, on her flowery bed, and stare into space. She is sleeping downstairs, and the house is as still as death. Sometimes noises rise through the window from the garden – Gareth using a saw, or the lawn mower, or he and Olivia talking. But they never break my reverie. It is at this time I can feel the weight of the hole in my heart. It is so black and yawning I fear it will never be filled. Sometimes the sense of my loss is so powerful I begin to cry. I lie down, belly first, and push my wet cheeks into the yellow buds and delicate green sprigs on Matilda's duvet cover. My hands reach down to the floor, but no soft muzzle is pushed into them, no kind lick across my knuckles. Solomon is gone. I bury my face in Matilda's pillow and sob for I have never felt so lonely in my life.

Thursday is my day off. I ring my father.

'I'm here,' I tell him. 'I've finally come to London.'

He is surprised but yes he is free to meet me for lunch. He's tight for time so I go to him. I have to take the Circle line, and then the Bakerloo line up to Harrow & Wealdstone, the last stop. He tells me to take a right out of the station, and to meet him in the pub on the corner. He says, we'll have a proper ploughman's lunch.

He is already there when I arrive, a pint of Guinness in front of him; leaning over the paper. He folds it as he sees me approaching, and tucks it down by his side.

'Hello, Barbara,' he says grinning sheepishly. He has a few more wrinkles since I last saw him, but apart from that he looks just the same. The Irish rogue: dark eyes, laughter lines and wild hair.

'My God, you've grown up haven't you? Bloody hell, you're a young woman now.'

'Hi, Dad.' I sit down awkwardly. The pub is a bit dingy. I wish we were meeting somewhere nicer, like a restaurant, even a café.

'Do you want a drink? Now you're legal.' He chuckles.

'No thanks.'

I have to be back by six. The Finches are going out to see a play, and the last thing I want is to stink of drink.

My father lights up a cigarette.

'So,' he says, inhaling deeply. 'How's your mother?'

'OK.'

He nods. 'That's good. Do you want a mineral or something, Babs?'

'No. Dad, can we go somewhere else?'

'Sure we can, just let me finish my pint. What would you like to eat?'

'I don't mind. Pizza would be nice.'

He nods, sips his Guinness but he is in no hurry.

'So how's the au pair thing going?' he asks me, rolling another cigarette.

'OK.'

I don't expand, not because I don't want to tell. I'd love to be able to confide in someone. But there's no point telling my father. He wouldn't be any good at all. He never had much to do with child rearing in our household. Describing the Finches to my father would be like describing aliens. He wouldn't know what to make of them, just think they were rich *eejits*.

'I'm going to France,' I say.

He looks interested.

'France. Very nice . . .'

'The South of France.'

'Oh la la . . . that's great, Babs, really great. You'll love it.'

'Where did you go in France?'

'All over . . . Paris, Lyons, Bordeaux . . . but I didn't really see it properly. You never do when you're on the road, and under pressure to get to somewhere to pick up stuff, and then under more pressure to get it back. I saw a lot of roads, laybys, service stations and cafés in ports, but not much else.'

The door opens and we are showered by bright sunshine. I am dying to get out of this smelly old pub. I'd love to go for a walk in the park with my father, but he continues to nurse his pint.

'When are you going?' he asks.

'Saturday.'

'Jaysus, that's soon. Does your mother know?'

'Yes, I rang her last night.' I pause. 'She says hello.'

'Does she now? That's nice of her,' he says sarcastically. 'And did she have any pronouncements for me, any psychic information I should be aware of?'

I sigh. 'No. You know she can't help it, Dad.' Strangely I want to defend her.

He says nothing but he looks angry. My father thinks he played second fiddle to my mother's gift. For that is what she calls it. Or a curse.

One day, one terrible dark day, when we saw my little brother's white coffin dropped into the black earth, and everyone was there – all the neighbours and everyone from our townland, those we knew and those we didn't, friends and enemies, all alike united in the ring of grief around us – mother said it was a curse.

'I knew,' she whispered, as she dropped a tiny snowdrop into his grave. 'I knew,' she repeated, and her voice broke. 'It is a curse.'

And then she wept openly, as some woman, a neighbour, maybe Fiona's mother, put her arm about her shoulders and whispered comfort to her. But Mammy put her head up to the sky, shook her fist at it.

'No more,' she cried out. 'I knew, I knew.'

I looked at her in astonishment, my eyes rimmed with red. No, you don't, I wanted to scream at her, you don't know it was me. I killed my brother. It was nothing to do with fate. I could have changed what happened. This truth made my whole body shake. And the arctic January wind, which swept through my body, pierced my heart, made me a trembling statue unable to move, rooted to the spot beside my brother's grave. Mammy walked away, in a shroud of women dressed in black whispering to her, trying to help her contain her grief. My father stood opposite me and stared at the whole scene. He looked frightened, as if this was news to him. He walked around the edge of the grave, unable to look at it. He took my frozen hand.

'Babs?'

I shook my head, dazed and numb. How could I tell him what really happened?

I look at my father now, nearly ten years later, and I can still see that frightened look – the scar behind the smile – so that the twinkle in his eyes I remember as a small child is gone forever.

I push back into the stained seat, watch him order another pint, and a coke for me, two packets of cheese and onion crisps, and a bag of roasted nuts. The door opens again, and I notice the sunlight is gone and clouds have gathered.

Five

I am flying. My heart rushes into my mouth as I look out of the tiny round window. John Finch insisted I sit in the window seat once he found out I had never flown before. Olivia is next to me, white as a sheet, and staring glassily ahead. Matilda is behind me, with her father. She keeps kicking my seat, but I don't care, I am too pre-occupied by what I see outside. First when we took off, the houses, streets and cars becoming midget, like a teeming little ant world, and then once we broke through the clouds, away from mankind, an Elysian field of white down, bright blue sky, dazzling light, a place where gods and angels could dwell. Looking out of the window I feel as if I am floating on the fluff of dreams. I am nowhere near nervous and frightened, and I wonder how Olivia Finch could be.

We had been leaving the house, were waiting for John and Matilda upstairs, when Olivia offered me some valium. I shook my head; I knew what it was. Mammy was given it after the fire.

'Are you sure?' she asked, fidgeting with her bag. 'It makes a big difference. I always take it.'

'No thank you.'

She nodded, and I saw her scrutinising me. I was in my red jacket, clutching my leatherette suitcase.

'Wait there,' she said suddenly, running up the stairs.

A taxi pulled up outside the house. At the same time John and Matilda came down the stairs. He was carrying a big suitcase, as well as a pink satchel for her.

'What have you got in here, Matilda? It weighs a ton.'

'It's just my painting things, Daddy.'

He smiled. 'Of course.'

Matilda stopped at the bottom of the stairs. 'Why does *she* have to come?' She gave me a glare.

'Because she's your au pair, Matilda. Now don't be so rude.'

But he spoke softly, giving me an apologetic wink.

I blushed, wishing I could say what I felt. *Believe me, you horrid little brat, I wish I wasn't going anywhere with you, especially the south of France.*

But I remembered Fiona once saying a spoilt child doesn't come out of nowhere, it is the parents' fault the child is the way it is.

I watched John Finch so gentle with his daughter, and decided he was probably too soft, but then, why wouldn't he be to compensate for his wife's hardness. It was Olivia's fault Matilda was the way she was. I would try to tolerate her, at least until I could put my plan into action, the one where I got Matilda to like me.

Matilda looked out the window.

'The taxi is here,' she cried. 'Mama! Mama!'

Olivia came running down the staircase, a denim jacket slung across her arm.

'Here,' she said, thrusting it at me. 'I can't bear to see you in that awful red thing a moment longer. It will make me sick if I have to look at it all the way to France.'

Of course I went scarlet, I was so embarrassed.

'I couldn't,' I said politely.

She shoved it into my hands. 'Please,' she said. 'I don't wear it, it is far too big for me. I was going to give it to charity anyway.'

'Go on,' said John, smiling benignly. 'Olivia has a mountain for a wardrobe.'

She flashed him a look. 'Come on,' she said impatiently. 'Put it on for God's sake.'

I took the red pvc jacket off and placed it on the chair in the hall. I put on the denim one. It fitted perfectly and felt lovely. I could tell it was really expensive, although it looked casual, but there was something classy about it, something which was lacking from the rest of my motley collection of clothes.

Olivia smiled at me; she looked almost friendly. I wondered whether it was the effect of the valium.

'Very nice,' she said. 'It suits you.'

She swivelled me around so I could see myself in the hall mirror, and I was pleasantly surprised when I looked. The denim jacket hugged my figure, so that my waist looked smaller, and the colour was great against my red hair.

'Thank you,' I gushed. 'I love it.'

'You're welcome,' she said, as John shooed us out the door, to the waiting black cab.

I pull the jacket about me now. It is cool in the aircraft. I finger the silver rivet buttons, and the little label, which says *Levi*. I can't wait to tell Fiona. Maybe this is the beginning of Olivia and I becoming friends, like Carmel and her employer? I put my hands inside the pockets and then fiddle with the breast pockets as well. Inside the left one there is a small piece of paper. I should take it out and give it to Olivia, next to me, but for some reason I don't. I finger it, and then leave it there.

The air hostess comes round with the drinks trolley. Olivia has a glass of white wine.

She turns to me. 'Go on, have a drink, we are on holidays.' She is smiling hazily and looks stoned, the same droopy eyelids Murtagh gets sometimes when he's smoking dope.

So I order wine as well.

Things aren't so bad after all, I think, as I soar through the sky, sipping a glass of dry white wine and peering out the window at the world of air and light. Finally I am getting to see some of the world. I feel different in my new denim jacket, as if I have a new skin on. Maybe I can live in the future, I think, forget about the past. Maybe I can become someone else.

Shadows from the clouds create patterns onto the wings of the plane and look like water reflections. I feel the fluidity of my emotions and the fragility of my mind. As we approach Marseilles I notice how parched the landscape is. I see stripes of red and gold rock, with stubbly brush. And then I see the city, sprawling between the rock and the sea. The Mediterranean sea sparkles below me. It is azure, with dots of white yachts twinkling in the distance. The waves, which crash and pound on our beaches, are small little gasps here, gently rippling onto the white sand. This sapphire Mediterranean goes straight to the heart of me. The image looks familiar as if I have been here before. Yet even from the sky it smacks of a different lifestyle to the one I have been used to.

It is late afternoon by the time we land in Marseilles. As soon as we walk into arrivals there is pandemonium. Olivia's mother and father rush forward, grabbing Matilda and embracing her, while gabbling to their daughter in French. John looks over at me and smiles apologetically. 'You better get used to this lot. They are crazy.'

Olivia's father takes my hand first, and surprises me by kissing me on both cheeks. 'Welcome, welcome,' he says in English. His eyes are dark brown and mischievous, like a little boy's. His wife comes up behind him. She looks more like Olivia, petite, dark, but her smile is friendly and her eyes kind.

'*Enchanté*,' she says, again kissing me on both cheeks.

'This is Barbara,' says John. 'She is Matilda's new au pair.'

Matilda has been gathered up into her grandfather's arms and showered with kisses. I wonder why she didn't want to come to France. Her grandparents clearly adore her. I feel sad for a moment because I never knew my grandparents, but then this is the new me, the one with no family.

We all pile into a big old Mercedes. It's a squeeze; the two men in the front, Matilda on her grandmother's knee and myself and Olivia in the back. The sun is slapping off the tarmac in the car park, and I can taste the heat in the back of my mouth. I am sweating in my denim jacket. I take it off and lay it on my lap. The last thing I want to do is ruin it.

Everyone is talking in French, even little Matilda. I say nothing, although I understand little pieces of what they are saying. My name comes up, and Matilda says I am stupid and from Ireland. Her grandmother tells her off, looking over at me apologetically and her grandfather shakes his head but neither John nor Olivia react. I see Olivia's eyelids drop. She is obviously exhausted from the tension of the flight, or still dopey from the wine and valium.

From the airport we head straight out onto the motorway. I become disorientated and dizzy from looking at all the cars speeding along on the wrong side of the road. I look out of the window at the craggy mountain range, so different from my verdant home mountains, and at the arid landscape. The heat shimmers between me and rows of dark green cypress trees lining the road. White houses with blue shutters and terracotta roofs flash past.

Finally we turn off the motorway and the landscape changes. The mountains grow more and more distant, and the sky gets bigger and bigger. The land flattens. I can see lagoons of blue salt water, and marshes rich with golden, green, red and black reeds. There are birds everywhere, taking off, circling above us. And then I see them, the pink flamingos. They stand in a huddle, on one leg each in the pools of sea water, their necks arched, beak to beak, making hearts out of air. I can hardly believe my eyes. I remember Mattie then, for a painful instant, and how he adored the scene in *Fantasia* with the pink flamingos. He even had a pillow case with pink flamingos on it, flying across a bright blue sky. I imagine how excited he would be to see them for real. To think it makes my eyes water, and I quickly turn away from the others and rub my eyes dry.

'This is the Camargue,' John explains, turning round in the passenger seat. He looks over at Olivia, who is fast asleep wedged between myself and her mother. Matilda on the other hand appears full of beans. She is the most vivacious I have seen her since I met her. Her grandmother chats away to her, teaching her new words in French.

'She seems better,' I hear Olivia's father say in French.

'She can be like this for a few days,' says John, 'and then, bam, she has a fit and she is down again.'

The two men say nothing for a while. Then Olivia's father hisses, so quietly I can hardly hear, 'What is *it*?'

'They don't know, Hubert,' says John. 'Nobody can tell us.'

The sun is setting as we pull up in front of a large house with saffron walls, and sea-green shutters. A dog runs out from behind the house, and my heart lifts, for he looks exactly like Solomon. He could be his twin.

'Rafi, Rafi,' Olivia's father calls, as he gets out of the car door and pets the animal.

The dog greets us all. Matilda doesn't seem to like him and shies away when he tries to lick her. I crouch down and rub him behind the ears.

'You like dogs, Barbara?' Olivia's father asks me in English.

'Yes, I love dogs,' I reply enthusiastically as Rafi rolls over on the ground and demands a tummy rub.

There is more commotion, cries of 'Pascal' from Matilda, as a man emerges from the house. He looks to be in his early twenties, has thick black hair and an angular face with a long nose. He is not particularly good-looking but his eyes are startling. They are sapphire against his dark skin. He smiles broadly.

'Hello, my English princess,' he says, bending down and picking Matilda up. She laughs with delight.

Everyone kisses again, and then I am introduced.

'This is Pascal, my little brother,' Olivia says.

Pascal looks at me, and there is something in the way he does it which makes me blush. He kisses me on both cheeks. 'Hello, I am very pleased to meet you,' he says in English.

'Barbara has never been to France,' says John.

'Well, I hope you love it.'

Pascal's eyes stare straight into mine as if he wishes to say something else. I blush and look away.

We eat and drink for hours, sitting outside, initially bathed in orange and purple light from the setting sun, and then in darkness, our faces illuminated by the light of candles. It is still incredibly warm, and I am able to sit in my shirt, without a jacket or cardigan. Everything smells different from home. The food in front of us is pungent with aroma. Tonight I eat things I have never eaten in my life, and surprise myself by how much I like them. We start with a kind of fish soup, called *bouille*, a traditional dish in Provence. With John's help as interpreter Olivia's mother, Celeste, explains what is in it – crabs, eels, whiting, John Dory and hogfish! I have never even heard of hogfish. I try it gingerly, only to discover that it is delicious and I decide that *bouille* will become one of my favourite meals. It is rich, yet not too creamy, a divine combination of fish, garlic and tomatoes.

'Fennel, thyme, orange peel and a pinch of saffron,' John is saying. 'It's the herbs which make it.'

'It's gorgeous,' I say, nodding and smiling at Celeste, who beams at me proudly.

This is followed by duck, which although equally delicious is harder to enjoy. I cannot stop thinking about the ducks on the river in Sligo, how happy and carefree they are.

'But these are a different type of duck,' John assures me.

Everyone is smoking cigarettes and drinking lots of wine. I feel relaxed, and older, as if I do this every day.

Matilda is allowed to stay up. She can sleep in late, her grand-father says when John protests and says he should take her up to bed. Olivia doesn't pay her daughter much attention. Instead she is locked in animated conversation with her brother. I watch and listen.

'This must be very boring for you,' says John at one stage. 'We should speak in English not French, but Olivia's parents can't really speak good English. I hope you don't mind.'

'It's lovely here,' I say, sitting on the grass and stroking Rafi, who has followed me around since I arrived.

'It looks like you've made one new friend,' John says, leaning over and patting Rafi on the head.

Eventually it is agreed that I should take Matilda up to bed. I am told I am sharing a room with her. The idea horrifies us both.

'*Maman*,' Matilda bursts into tears and pulls at her grandmother. 'I don't want to share with her.'

I say nothing, embarrassed by the child's obvious dislike of me. John starts whispering to Hubert, Olivia stares stonily at her daughter, and Pascal looks at me curiously.

'*D'accord, d'accord*,' says Hubert impatiently, after John has spoken to him. 'Barbara would you mind sleeping in the attic?'

'No, that's fine,' I say, relieved I don't have to share with Matilda, despite my hatred of heights.

'Oh, Papa,' protests Pascal. 'That is a bit cruel.'

I am confused.

'It can get a bit hot up there,' John explains.

'That's all right,' I say quickly.

'Are you sure?'

I nod, suddenly tired, suddenly wanting to be on my own.

'I'll put Matilda to bed then.' He looks over at Olivia, who waves her arm.

'I shall come up, too,' she says, standing up and swaying.

Her mother looks at Olivia and frowns, but she says nothing.

'Barbara,' says Pascal, 'let me show you to the attic.'

Pascal carries my suitcase all the way up to the top of the house. He is right. The attic is a furnace. He opens the window wide and then closes the shutters. The lights are still off in the room.

'If you want to turn on the light, the switch is here,' he says. 'But close the window, otherwise you will be eaten alive by mosquitoes. You have very pale skin so they would probably adore you.' He smiles at me. 'Beautiful Irish skin.' I say nothing. The heat in the room is making me perspire, and I am dying of thirst.

'The bathroom is on the floor below, remember. Directly beneath. *Bon nuit*, Barbara.'

He grins at me, hesitates. I can see his white teeth in the dark. He reminds me of a dog. It makes me want to burst out laughing.

'Goodnight, thank you,' I say in English, trying to sound dismissive.

'Goodnight then,' he says again. He pauses at the door.

'That noise you can hear are the cicadas.' He waves towards the window. 'It is the sound they make as they quiver in the leaves. It makes summer sing.'

He leaves and I breathe a sigh of relief, and then go and open the shutters. The noise of the cicadas is even louder now.

One advantage of being in the attic is that I can see all around me. Other than the lights of another house a few miles away it is completely dark. But certainly not quiet. Apart from the cicadas there are all sorts of strange, foreign noises: the heat cooling down, making the house creak, the trees sighing with relief. I strain my ears and I imagine I can hear the sea. I peer across at the dark landscape. Is that the glint of the ocean lining the horizon? It reminds me of home. I cannot wait to dip my toes into the sea.

I have been lying on my bed, with no clothes on, just a single sheet covering me, still sweltering and unable to sleep, when I hear a cry. I hear it again, more loudly. It is coming from beneath me. I get up and put a big shirt on. It is an old one of my father's that he left behind one time. God knows why I packed it but it comforts me. I open the hatch of my attic and climb down the ladder. I need to get a drink anyway.

The crying is quite loud now, and it is coming from Matilda's room. I pause on the landing, wondering whether I should go into her room, as the door opposite opens. It is Olivia. She stands like a sylph in an ivory negligee, staring at me.

'You can go,' she mutters, and then steps back inside her room.

I am astounded. What mother lets a practical stranger go in and comfort her crying child?

I push Matilda's door open, and the little girl is sitting up in bed, crying her eyes out. I am expecting a torrent of abuse, but instead she looks up at me with pleading eyes. 'Where's Daddy?' she asks.

'I don't know. Will I go and find him?'

I walk towards the bed and she shivers.

'Do you feel sick, Matilda?'

She nods her head.

'OK, wait a second. I'll get your mammy.'

'No,' she almost screams. 'No.'

'I'll get Daddy, then.'

'No,' she wails. And then she starts retching.

I look frantically around me for something for her to be sick in. I grab a china washbowl off the dresser and shove it under her nose. The poor child empties her stomach. I put my hand on her forehead expecting it to be hot, but it is as cold as ice.

'It's all right.' I stroke her hair, as the little girl is sick again while crying all the time. I feel awful for not liking her, for thinking her a spoilt brat. Doesn't she have good reason to be the way she is?

Eventually her stomach is emptied and she sits back against the pillows, sighs.

I put the bowl down on the floor.

'I'll go and get your daddy now.'

'No,' she says quickly.

'But Matilda you're ill, I must tell your parents.'

'No,' she says again.

The colour is coming back to her cheeks and she looks almost normal. I touch her forehead and it is warm, a normal temperature.

'I will have to take the medicine. I don't want to take it.'

'But the medicine makes you better.'

'No, it doesn't. Mammy loves the medicine but it makes her sick.'

I feel a strange sensation, as if there is someone else in the room, as if someone is standing behind me and has their hand on my shoulder, but when I turn there is no one there.

'You'll be better soon.'

I tuck Matilda in, wondering whether I should tell John Finch she has been sick.

'I'm never better,' Matilda bleats, a large tear trailing down her cheek. Suddenly I feel like crying too. In the shadows of her room, her blue-grey eyes are appealing to me. And it takes my breath away. They are Mattie's eyes, my Mattie.

'Why do I have to be sick?' Matilda asks me.

Her words echo across the dark room, which feels like a cave, an entrance into the unknown. It is as if I have swallowed a large stone, as if I weigh a ton, and I am rooted to the spot. Something is wrong. Something is terribly, terribly wrong.

Six

Everything goes back to my summer in the Camargue. I have not returned to France since. Yet I cannot escape those memories, how that week – just days – changed me, and pushed me along a path I have never been able to retrace. For years I have tried not to think, living by instinct and need, just surviving, and wondering how I have. But now, one hot stormy summer in London, I find I am standing too long staring out the window in the kitchen, leaning against the wet draining board, hypnotised by the monsoon-like rain. The weather reminds me of the day I first arrived at the Finches all that time ago.

Liam comes and goes, saying nothing, but I know he is worried. It is too much to bear on his young shoulders.

'Mum,' he says, chewing his lip, looking nervous. 'Mum you're going to be late for work.'

And he pours me a steaming mug of tea and forces me to take it between my cold hands.

I slowly wake up, sip the tea. I want to tell him, I'm not depressed, I am just thinking. I am sifting through my memories. Liam hands me a plate of hot buttered toast, slightly burnt. He reminds me again that I am going to be late, and then, swinging his bag over his shoulder, he kisses me on the head, as he always has done, even though I am the parent and he is the child.

'I'm working late tonight,' I tell him. 'There's sausages and bacon in the fridge.'

'Don't worry about me, Mum.' And he saunters out the door, with all the feigned nonchalance he can muster.

As I slide through the day, in a job I have done for so long I only need to be there in my body, not in my head, I see pictures flashing across my mind: the rain in my garden, dripping off the overgrown bushes and onto the tin roof of the shed; the black plastic bags of old toys I keep meaning to give away but are shoved under the bushes in the corner, covered in pollen and dead leaves; my robust rose bush, unpruned but still bursting with yellow blooms . . . and I think of a house in France with yellow roses crawling up its ochre walls and shutters, the colour of faded turquoise, wide open in the heat. The dark interior is full of shadows while the terrace outside is bright and empty, sun-bleached paving stones, chairs grouped around a marble-topped table, but no one there. Someone is walking behind me. I see their shadow cast across mine. It is in front of me, yet when I turn around, quickly so I can catch them, they are gone, and the place is empty. No one is home.

My garden is big. I am lucky. Although we shan't be here much longer for the house is up for demolition. That is why everything is a little bit old-fashioned in my house. We don't have a proper cooker, and manage using a two-ringed portable stove or plug-in electric pans. But that does us, for we are only two, and Liam eats out a lot of the time now he's at college. We don't have central heating, and use gas heaters in the sitting room and bedrooms. The kitchen and bathroom are unheated. The windows are old and draughty, and in the winter they ice up from the inside. But I like it all the same, and I will miss it when it is gone. I can't bear to think of the large bay window in the sitting room being knocked out, or the black-and-white tiles on the kitchen floor being ripped up.

My garden is a tangled mess. I was never much of a gardener and Liam has no interest, but the advantage of its wildness are the animals, which have made it their home. We have foxes right down the end. I have seen them a couple of times, and heard the vixen at night. And there are so many birds: sparrows, thrushes, blackbirds and a pompous robin in charge of them all. I worry what will happen to all my creatures when the bulldozers move in.

The grey rain makes my garden emerald green, glistening and jewel-like, the colours of home. I think of bog irises, the same yellow as my roses. I see an image, the side of a ditch, a clump of yellow irises, petals unfurling like palms opening up, and dark reeds shielding them from a big cloud-filled sky. And then I realise my picture is not home, it is France again, it is the Camargue. I look at the ditch, and I see a child's flip-flop. Dark blue. Against the green reeds, the yellow flowers, a blue note. It is Matilda Finch's flip-flop. I see it lying there, I remember why that is, and my heart starts to race so that my hand is shaking as I try to press the keys on my cash register. My heart keeps pounding, my breath is short, and I wonder how I can do it, carry on as if everything is normal, delicately fold up the silk pink camisole and wrap it in tissue before putting it into one of the fancy paper bags, sealing the top with one of our stickers – Odette's, for even the name of the shop I work in is French.

I was married fifteen years and I never told my husband about my summer in France. It was rarely on my mind then. I had too much to cope with in those days: our relationship, a baby, a toddler, a little boy, needing to be looked after and protected from my husband's dark moods. He never hit me but in truth how many times, over the years, was I raped? *How many times Barbara?* I was flailing from each day to the next, at first confiding in Fiona. But she lost patience with me. She couldn't understand why I wouldn't leave, said she didn't know me any more. I was no longer her Barbara, the feisty Irish girl who hadn't been afraid to leave home and start a new life somewhere else, who hadn't been afraid of having a baby. I shut down. And then I shrank. My heart was so bruised, it curled in on itself and all I could do was stay alive, stay alive for Liam. How could Fiona understand for she didn't know about my hunger for punishment?

In the end I didn't leave him, he left me. I had freedom thrust upon me three years ago, when my husband grew bored of me and found someone else, a younger girl, to impregnate and to chain to his rage forever. And then I was alone, and it was like taking tiny baby steps all over again.

Mammy knew, like she had known everything. She told me not to marry, but we were madly in love. I thought I needed him. If she had lived longer maybe she would have given me the courage to leave him, and long before the damage was done. But we were only a few years married and Mammy was dead. She died young. She always said she would.

The only way to forget is to remember.

Last night I picked up one of Liam's college books, and this is what I read. The book was about Freud, someone I have always been suspicious of. Everything he says is too neat; life is not so tidy. But then, when I read this sentence, I knew what he meant, and I suddenly realised what I have to do. Go back. Walk down the flat straight roads of the Camargue. I need to lift one bare foot up after the other and feel the hot sand squeezed between my toes. I need to walk across the salt marshes – the *sansouire*, scattered with grasswort, dried up and cracked into mosaics, a desert of hardened mud – and I need to stride through the sea meadows, the reeds swishing across my thighs. I look up at the pink flamingos flying, and they are like Mattie's puppet friends, coral and black wings beating up and down, loping across the wide, bright sky in a long undulating line, like a great kite's tail. I look in front of me and I see the black bulls. They are the dark herds moving me back to the dawn of time. I see them wandering the flat expanses of land scattered with pools of briny or fresh water, between the river and the sea. One bull stops grazing. He looks at me, and I feel the old thread of fear. His eyes bulge beneath pronounced arcs, his head is long and black, and he is crowned by splendid crescent-shaped horns. He is lithe, agile and strong. He is a primitive force, a raging auroch. He bays, and then he comes for me.

Remember, remember, remember.

The bungalow back home in Ireland was sold after Mammy died, but the field is still mine. Always has been. The ruins of our burnt-out cottage remain. Sinking deeper and deeper into the undergrowth. I can go home now and build again. Like a Native American, I will circle my land, say the prayers I should have said, and talk to my dead brother. Come back into the family, Mattie – I will invite him and let's make this our home. And if I am back at the beginning again maybe I will find what I have lost.

Seven

I wake late. My head is still in the clouds of my dreams, strange flying dreams, filled with copper-haired angels and pink flamingos. Already the heat of the day is toasting me in my tiny attic. I look around the space. It is jammed with boxes and bits of old furniture. In one corner of the room there are a stack of canvases, all facing into the wall. I get out of bed, go over and turn one of them around. It is a portrait of a young woman. But not a typical portrait. The artist has mixed pencil with paint, so that the woman's face is drawn in pencil onto the canvas, and yet her hair and clothes are painted in thick textured paint. It could just be that it is unfinished, but something tells me this is the way it is supposed to look. It takes me a couple of minutes to realise it is a portrait of Olivia, when she was younger. She looks so different. She looks happy.

I sit down on top of a large cardboard box and listen. The house is silent, as quiet as back home. It makes me realise how noisy it was in London, with cars and buses passing by every few minutes, footsteps on the pavement, voices, children, dogs. The quiet makes me uneasy. I dress hastily and go downstairs to wash in the bathroom. The shutters and window are open, revealing an immaculately blue sky, with not a wisp of a cloud. The bathroom looks out of the back of the house, onto the terrace where we ate last night, a few small trees and a dusty arena. I can see stables from here as well, but they are all empty, their doors open wide.

As I descend the last staircase down to the ground floor I hear voices coming from the kitchen, and smell coffee and cigarettes. I stand outside the door, nervous and unsure, my shyness practically suffocating me. Shouldn't I have got up earlier and helped with Matilda? Maybe she was still in bed. I hadn't thought of that. Maybe she is sick again.

'You can go on in.'

I turn around in surprise. Pascal is standing right behind me in the hall. He is wearing jeans, a red shirt, and carries a black cowboy hat in his hand. I am mortified, my cheeks turning deep crimson. How long was he standing there for? He smiles, his teeth gleaming in the dark hall, and hanging the hat up, he walks towards me.

'*Bonjour*, Barbara,' he says softly. 'And how did you sleep? I hope it wasn't too hot?'

'Fine, thank you.' I look down, unable to hold the gaze of his dancing eyes.

'*Bon*,' he says, opening the door and stepping back for me to pass.

'Well, you must be hungry.'

The kitchen door swings open and we walk into a large cool room. The ceiling is beamed, and the floor is made from red terra-cotta tiles. I wonder how old the house is. There is a big table in the centre of the room. Olivia's mother is bringing a basket of croissants over to the table, and the rest of the family are sitting around with bowls of steaming coffee in front of them.

'I cannot believe it,' she is saying in French. 'For the first time in my life I have burnt the croissants, and we have a guest.' She waves her hand towards me.

'They look lovely, Celeste,' John says. 'I am sure they are as delicious as always.'

He pats his stomach.

'I always put on so much weight when I come to visit.'

Olivia glances at her husband disdainfully and sips her coffee. She is still in her dressing gown, her hair scraped back and her face unmade up, yet she still looks beautiful, fragile, breakable. But unhappy, so different from her portrait upstairs.

'Papa,' she says, 'pass me the cigarettes.'

It is Hubert who is smoking, puffing away, next to his granddaughter, no one saying a word. John glares at Olivia as she reaches over and pulls a cigarette out of the box.

'You want one?' She turns to me and Pascal. I shake my head, not sure whether she is addressing me or her brother.

'No, no, I must eat first,' says Pascal, pulling a chair back for me and then sitting down next to me. I am acutely aware of the heat of his body, and his brown arms so different from the skinny, freckled white arms of the boys back home. Pascal's are bare to the elbows, muscular, covered in dark hairs. He leans forward and takes a croissant out of the basket before offering them to me. His movements are relaxed and familiar and strangely I don't feel shy. I don't even blush.

I am sitting opposite Matilda. I look over at her. She is chatting with her grandfather, seemingly happy and animated, no sign of the previous night's distress. Should I mention it now? Last night it seemed the right thing to do, not to tell Olivia or John that their daughter had actually been sick, but now, in the morning, I am confounded by my irresponsibility. How could I let myself obey the commands of a six-year-old child? What if she tells them now? What will they think of me then?

'Would you like some café au lait?' Pascal asks me. 'Or tea maybe? I know you English prefer tea.'

'She is Irish, Pascal, not English,' John corrects him.

'*Pardon.*' Pascal grimaces, apologetically. 'Big mistake. I know, I know, there is a very big difference between England and Ireland. But still you both like the tea?'

'Thank you, tea please,' I say self-consciously.

'What kind?' Madame asks her son in French.

'My mother wants to know what kind of tea you would like.'

'Just regular tea.'

'Which is?' He smiles at me patiently. 'Camomile? Or *menthe*? Or is it the English Breakfast tea?'

'The English Breakfast tea,' I say hesitantly, not quite sure what I will be getting.

'Yes, that's what you want,' John joins in. 'I would recommend the coffee, though, Barbara. It's different from what you would drink at home.'

He picks up his bowl and takes a large slurp.

'It's a lot of coffee.'

He laughs. 'Yes it certainly is.'

I look at Madame buzzing around the kitchen, and at the men sitting at the table, letting her do everything. It's just the same as home. Only women like Olivia Finch get waited on. I get up and go over to collect my pot of tea off her. She smiles at me. Her eyes are kind, and gentle, and her face is a perfect heart shape. She looks younger than her years. She nods, says *merci* twice. I say *merci* back. Then she turns back to the sink, which is full of tiny half-moon shells. She catches me looking at them.

'*Tellines*,' she says, pointing at them.

I nod, wondering what she is going to do with all those little shells, for they hardly look edible, and go back to the table with my tepid pot of tea.

I bite into my buttery croissant, which though slightly browned, is far from burnt and melts into my mouth. I have never eaten a croissant like it before.

'You like?' Celeste asks, hands on her hips.

'Yes, thank you. *Bon, bon*,' I say.

Hubert and John sink into conversation about politics, and Olivia begins to talk to Pascal about London.

'Sometimes I hate it,' she says. 'But then I don't think I could live anywhere else now. It is so boring here. I don't know how you stand it.'

'I'm not here all the time, you know, Olivia,' Pascal replies good-humouredly, yet there is a slightly defensive edge to his voice.

'Yes, you are an odd cowboy,' she says. 'One minute riding across the Camargue on your mount, the next at the easel.'

'But that is where I get my inspiration, Olivia, out on the *san-souire*.'

'But you don't paint landscape, Pascal.'

'Yes, but the place . . .' – he pauses, dipping his croissant into his coffee – 'it makes me think of elements in people, some of us are land, some the wind, and the sky, and some are water, fresh or salt. All of these elements are in the Camargue.'

Olivia laughs. 'So what am I, little brother?' she asks sarcastically.

'Don't you know? Why, salt of course, but in a lagoon, land-locked and trapped,' he replies candidly.

Olivia's eyes darken, but she tosses her head and drinks her coffee as if she doesn't understand what her brother has just tried to tell her.

Matilda is playing with her food. She dips the end of her croissant into her hot chocolate and circles it on the oilcloth on the table as if she is drawing pictures. No one stops her.

'So who wants to come to Nîmes with me?' Pascal asks suddenly. 'I have to pick up a canvas off Chloë.'

'Can I go?' asks Matilda excitedly.

John looks worried.

'It might be a bit hot for you, Matilda, you should stay inside and rest.'

'But that's boring. Please, Daddy. I don't feel sick at all. Not one bit.'

'Oh let her go, John. Barbara can go with her in case she feels unwell. And Pascal will look after her. He knows what to do if she has a fit.'

Silence descends on the table. Olivia's words are brutal. Her mother stiffens as she sifts through her shells, her father looks embarrassed, and John's face clouds, but it is Pascal who speaks.

'Olivia, not in front of her,' he hisses.

Olivia gets up from the table impatiently.

'Well, I don't care what you all do today, I'm going back to bed.'

And she prances out of the room. I can see quite clearly where Matilda gets her spoilt daughter routine from. Hubert shakes his head and lights another cigarette, patting John kindly on the arm, while Celeste stands quite still, her gentle eyes cast down to the floor.

'*Merde*,' Pascal growls, and then noticing his niece, wide-eyed, staring after her mother, he leans across the table and flicks his napkin at her.

'We shall have fun this afternoon, *n'est-ce pas?*'

She giggles and he winks at her.

It is decided that Pascal, Matilda and I are going to Nîmes. Hubert is going out on one of the horses to check their herds, or what they call *manades* of bulls. John is going with him, primarily to birdwatch but promising to help out if he can.

'Never trust a man who spends hours watching small feathered creatures taking off and landing, hour after hour,' Pascal jokes.

'I'm not that bad. You forget I only get to see pigeons and sparrows most days. There's hundreds of different species here. I might even get to see an eagle, or a kingfisher today. That's something else now.'

'If you say so, John.' Pascal chuckles.

Olivia's mother is staying behind to prepare things for the dinner. She is making some special dishes from the region, in my honour.

I wait for Matilda to protest at my inclusion on our trip to Nîmes, but she surprises me by saying nothing. Instead she looks at me, with those steady grey eyes of hers, watching like a cat, with a special knowledge, our very own place of recognition. We are conspirators now, whether I like it or not.

Pascal drives fast. The roof is down on his 2CV and blows our hair. Matilda appears truly excited by the expedition.

'So later, or tomorrow, I will take you to Aigues-Mortes,' Pascal is saying, 'which is the closest town, and we can walk the medieval ramparts. But today we are going back in time to Ancient Rome.'

'Are we going to the amphitheatre?' Matilda asks, rubbing her hands with glee.

'But of course, I can't bring Barbara to Nîmes and not take her to the Arènes.'

He turns his head slightly towards me to explain.

I look over at him, at his rich dark skin and the slightly unshaven chin. He is a man, not a boy like Murtagh, and the thought of that makes my heart pound and I wonder how I look to him. Ashamed of my white legs, I am wearing my jeans and a sun top. It is extremely hot, and my legs are sweltering in the jeans. My face is flushed from the heat, and already I can see more freckles springing up on my arms and hands.

'Here,' Pascal says, reaching across me into the glove compartment, his arm brushing my thighs, and takes out a green cap. 'Put this on, otherwise, your face will burn.'

'Thanks.' I push it onto my head and try to shove my thick hair up into it. It is a relief to get it off the back of my neck.

A narrow bridge takes us across a small river, and then we drive the straight white road across the flat plains of the Camargue. The landscape reminds me of Connemara for the sea meadows are similar in colour to the bogs, the sky as immense and wide. The difference here though is the heat, bouncing off the road, shimmering around us, as we head north.

Nîmes is a big city with a mixture of wide and narrow streets. We drive past sun-bleached, shuttered buildings, bustling cafés in boulevards, Salons de Thé and Glaciers. People buzz around the hot streets. The place seems so vibrant, and yet relaxed and open, so different from Sligo. Pascal drops us off at the Arènes, a perfectly preserved first-century amphitheatre. I find it astonishing that something this old is sitting in perfect condition in the middle of this big town.

'I just have to call into a gallery and pick up a painting my friend Chloë was trying to sell for me. I think I have a buyer in Aigues-Mortes.'

'Are you an artist?'

'Well, I try,' he says. 'But my father would rather I forgot all about it. and concentrated on what I was born to do.'

'Uncle Pascal is a cowboy,' Matilda interrupts.

'I am not a very good *gardian*,' he says apologetically. 'That is what we call the Camargue cowboy. He is a *gardian*.'

'A guardian angel,' Matilda mutters, as we get out of the car, in front of the Roman ruin.

'I'll meet you here in an hour,' Pascal says quickly, and then drives off, leaving the two of us standing in the heat, dizzy under the blazing sun. Matilda takes my hand. It shocks me, but then there are lots of people about, she has probably been taught to do this.

'How are you feeling?' I ask.

'OK,' she says.

We walk towards the entrance. I have never seen a proper Roman ruin before. The amphitheatre appears perfectly intact.

'They fight bulls here,' Matilda tells me as we pay and go inside.

I don't like this place. The tunnels are spooky and I feel tense. I can't stop thinking about the terror and death which inhabited them, the fear of the gladiators before they stepped out into the arena. We go up some steps into dazzling sunlight, and stand looking out at the oval of the sandy arena. I look behind me at the high stone ledges.

'Do you think you could climb those?' I ask Matilda.

'Yes, I can, I can.'

We clamber up. They are steep, and I wonder why. Weren't the Romans supposed to be shorter than us? At last we are at the top, looking out over the rooftops of Nîmes. My heart beats a little faster. It feels good to be in a foreign place, standing in the proper heat, and looking at French people drinking coffee or wine in a streetside café below us, or looking across at the terracotta tiles, at balconies bulging with greenery, and shutters of different colours and sizes. I don't feel so gauche any more. I am infected by a new freedom, a willingness to embrace everything in this country and become a different Barbara, coffee-drinking, and chic.

I suddenly remember something, and opening my bag I take out Matilda's bottle of pills.

'This is a little late,' I say. 'It's past noon already, but if you take them now I don't think it will matter.'

Matilda looks at me sternly.

'I'm not taking them,' she says.

'Don't be silly, Matilda,' I coax. 'You have to take your pills. If you don't, you might get sick and we can't risk that, not here.'

'No I won't,' she replies quickly in a beat.

'But your daddy told me if you don't take the medicine you get dizzy and you can . . .'

I don't want to go on, but John Finch had been quite graphic in his description that morning of the first time his daughter had gone into a seizure just two years ago, and how their lives had been turned on their heads ever since in their efforts to find out the reasons for it. Epilepsy had been ruled out, and allergies. It was as if Matilda was prone to some kind of hysterical seizure, which at its most extreme caused her to writhe around on the ground, but with the help of medication was reduced to episodes of vomiting. I finger the two red pills in my hand, understanding why Matilda hates red, and pull a bottle of water out of my bag.

'Come on, Matilda . . . please, you know you have to.'

She sits down on the stone seat and stares down at the arena.

'Why did the gladiators kill each other?' she asks me.

'They were made to. They had no choice because they were slaves.'

'If they all refused to do it then no one would have been killed.'

'Someone would have killed them, probably Roman soldiers, or animals. They would have been thrown to the lions.'

Matilda shudders.

'I won't get sick,' she says again, confidently.

'Matilda,' I plead. 'Please . . .'

'Barbara,' she says, looking at me suddenly, her pewter eyes boring into me. She appears older and wiser than her six years. 'It is the pills that make me sick. They make my mama sick and they make me sick. Mama wants to be sick, but I don't want to, I don't want to . . .'

She begins to cry, big gulping sobs. I don't know what to do. I shift on the uncomfortable stone. She folds into my side and I put one of my arms around her. I look at the pills in the palm of my hand, and then I slip them into my jeans' pocket. I am confused.

My suspicions from the night before return to me. Was Matilda's illness a fabrication? And if so, who was making it up? I make a decision. It is rash, and probably very foolish, and it could get me into so much trouble, but I decide to do it anyway. My instincts tell me to do so, and at the end of the day I have absolute faith in my mother's odd philosophies. I will wait, and see what happens if Matilda doesn't take her pills.

We sit side by side, looking at swifts swooping in the sky and drifting on the wind.

'Did you know that swifts never land?' I tell Matilda.

'Even when they sleep?' she asks me, her eyes opening wide.

'Yes, even when they sleep. They are always aloft. When a swift sleeps, we call it sleeping on the wing.'

'But how do they build their nests if they never land?'

'They fly and build their nests as they're hovering but if they land on the ground, they can't get up again.'

Matilda screws up her eyes.

'Are you teasing me? Is it really true?'

'Of course. I saw my father pick up a swift that had fallen on the ground once. He had to throw it into the air again, like this.' I stand up and demonstrate, and Matilda giggles. 'And then it flew away.'

'I wonder what it feels like,' Matilda says, 'to always be flying.'

'I suppose you might feel like the wind, constantly flowing, never stuck anyway. You probably feel free.'

Pascal returns an hour later, carrying a painting under his arm.

'Come on, let's get an ice cream.' He looks at Matilda. 'You look well, Matilda.' There is colour in her cheeks and the little girl is smiling. Suddenly I am her friend. I had planned to play schools with her, just how Fiona used to play with me, but now I see I don't need to do that to make her like me. All I had to do was trust her.

'I climbed up to the top, Pascal.'

He looks genuinely shocked.

'Really?' he asks, and then turns to me. 'Was she all right?'

'Yes, no problem, she's fine,' I say confidently.

We eat ice creams sitting out in the square, looking at everyone walking by. I close my eyes and feel the heat prickling my eyelids. I lean back into the sunshine. It is wonderful to be so far away from home.

'Can I see your painting?' Matilda is asking Pascal. I open my eyes. Pascal looks a little embarrassed.

'OK,' he says reluctantly. 'Chloë wants another like it; so it can't be that bad.'

'Is Chloë your girlfriend?' Matilda asks cheekily.

'Not at all. She is a grumpy, middle-aged art lover who happens to run a very good gallery in Nîmes.'

Matilda giggles. Pascal turns the canvas around. I immediately recognise the style of the portrait of Olivia I looked at that morning, yet this picture is even more adventurous — a mixture of charcoal drawing, paint and fabric. It is a painting of a flamenco dancer. Her head is in profile, her neck arched and imperial, and she twists her torso and hips in a red dress. At the bottom of the painting he has attached red fabric onto the painted dress so that it emerges from the frame of the painting. Words are written at angles across the background; they are in French.

'Ugh,' says Matilda. 'Her dress is red.'

'Do you like it?' Pascal asks me, and he looks a little nervous, almost shy.

'Yes, I love it,' I reply enthusiastically. 'I have never seen anything like it.'

'Thank you.'

Matilda falls asleep on the way home. I am edgy, watching her constantly, waiting for her to be sick, or have a sudden fit, but she appears completely normal, just tired out as any child would be after a fun day. Pascal drives me around Arles on the way home.

'I love this town,' he says. 'It is a special place for artists. Vincent Van Gogh spent a lot of time here.'

'It's so pretty,' I comment, as we drive down winding cobbled streets, past narrow shuttered houses, with balconies cascading with foliage and sleeping dogs on their doorsteps. I see another arena, smaller than the one in Nîmes.

'Do they bullfight in here as well?'

'It is not like it is in Spain,' Pascal explains. 'We don't kill the bull. In fact it is more like a game than a fight. It is a chance to show off our agility skills.'

'How so?' I say hotly, for I have always hated bullfighting.

'We call them bull runs. It is about enticing the bull to chase you so that you can take the attributes – the *cocarde*, that is the rosette, and the strings and two tassels – from the bull's head. The men who do this are called *razeteurs*, or handrake holders, and they wear white and have a special hook. It is quite dangerous, you have to be swift-footed and quick-witted.'

'Have you ever done it?'

'No, I am too slow.' He smiles. 'Besides, I don't like to tease the bulls. But my father used to when he was a young man and the Provençal traditions were revived. Also some of our bulls have been *cocardiers* – the stronger, bolder ones.'

On the way out of Arles we drive past a restaurant, with a vine-strewn terrace, tables and chairs outside.

'My favourite restaurant,' Pascal tells me. 'You must go there while you are here.'

He pauses. I say nothing, reddening, stiffening with shyness, sensing what he is about to say.

'I will bring you if you would like to go,' he adds, and then briefly takes his eyes off the road to look at me. Our eyes lock and I can't look away. His face is so inviting to me, already familiar although I have only known him one day. His eyes are a joyous shade of blue, unlike the damp blue eyes of Matilda Finch, of my dead brother Mattie.

'Yes, I would,' I whisper.

He looks pleased and turns his attention back to the road. I feel effervescence off him, a natural kinship so that when he takes his right hand off the wheel and places it on his leg, right next to me, I am tempted to touch it. I want to push my fingers through his, to feel the texture of his skin. No one has ever made me feel like this before. He reaches a roundabout, and is forced to replace his hand on the steering wheel. I sneak a look at him as he takes the exit for La Camargue. He has an unusual face, angular with high cheekbones, but to me he is the most handsome man I have ever laid eyes on. It seems incredible he might be interested in me. But although I am inexperienced, I know this much: there is something beginning between us, as yet as delicate as a gossamer thread.

I wonder about Mammy and Daddy, and how it was for them. She always described their meeting as something magical, as if she was pulled towards him like a magnet and had no control over whether it was right or wrong to fall in love with him.

'He was such a looker,' she told me. 'There was a wildness about him like a wolf you wanted to tame. And he made me laugh. No one was as funny as your dad.'

I find it hard to fit that description to Daddy now. The sad-faced man, sitting in a tweed jacket, bending over his pint of Guinness, dappled by the tawny light of a London pub.

But there was love between my parents. A big love, which broke ground rules and survived censor, which made my mother an outcast.

I close my eyes and try to imagine Mammy when she was my age, the year she met Daddy. There she is in my mind's eye, standing in her father's back yard, wearing a pair of bright red flared trousers, matching the flare of her red hair. It is raining. But still she stands waiting. The lights from her parents' pub illuminate her against the grey stone and concrete, and as my father carefully angles the truck into the yard she appears like a bright angel amid the November gloom. The blood runs to his head, and all he can think is that he needs her. She will save him, although in fact she, and all that she brings, will become his downfall.

This is how it happened, how my mother fell pregnant with me. For one instant the sun broke through the clouds and it stopped raining. Everything was dripping around them, the eaves of the old shed roof, and the drainpipes and the leaves on the sycamore tree. She wrapped her legs tightly around him and he couldn't stop. It was wrong. And yet perfect.

Eight

I cannot look John Finch in the eye, for I cannot stop thinking about the little red pills burning a hole in my jeans pocket. He is in a good mood, his trip with his father-in-law rewarded with the sighting of a purple heron.

'Very rare,' Hubert says, as he dips bread into the garlicky oil at the bottom of his bowl.

We have been eating *tellines*, scooping out the insides of the tiny shells Olivia's mother had been preparing that morning. It seems remarkable to me that these little organisms are edible, but they have a delicate flavour, not all that different from cockles. Celeste asks, through John, if we eat similar shellfish at home. And I say no, not really, thinking briefly of our fish and chips nights when Mammy is too drained to cook, and I am sent out on my bike to pick up two portions of battered cod, and one of chips between us, and when my father was there, a portion of onion rings. For all her great gifts, Mammy is not a good cook.

We move on to beef, one of their own, Pascal explains. It is another local dish, *taureau de gardian*. The beef is served in a rich, red-wine sauce. It melts in my mouth, and I am almost speechless.

'You like my mother's cooking?' Pascal smiles at me, leaning over and filling my glass with more red wine.

'Yes, it's delicious,' I enthuse, and Celeste, recognising my tone, smiles at me, her humble brown eyes shining in the candlelight.

Matilda is still up, eating with us, and she appears the most energetic I've ever seen her. She springs between her father, her grandfather and her uncle, taking it in turns to sit on their laps and taste their food. Olivia picks at her food, but she is cheerful, telling John that Gareth called this afternoon, and is going to arrive tomorrow, a surprise visit.

'Don't worry, *Maman*, I know we don't have a bedroom free. He can sleep on the couch. It is just a flying visit. He is on his way to St-Tropez to visit friends.'

'What about the garden?' John asks, a worried expression on his face.

Olivia cocks her head and raises one eyebrow, looking at her husband questioningly.

'There's a heatwave in London, everything will die if no one waters the plants.'

'My God, John, you're so . . .' Olivia shakes her head and pulls a piece of bread off the baguette. 'He is getting his new apprentice to water the garden. He is so busy he took someone else on, remember?'

'Oh yes.' John nods, and looks down at his plate.

We are sitting out the back by the swimming pool. The air is humid and thick with mosquitoes, but we have special candles burning to keep them away from us, determined to enjoy the last hour of sunshine. I can see the stables from here: a small row of wooden stalls. There are three horses, all of them varying shades of white: from pure white to dappled grey. They flick their heads, whinny occasionally and look in our direction. One in particular is looking at me. I long to get up and go and talk to her, stroke her strong head, and look into her black eyes with their long fair lashes. The sun is setting resplendently and the landscape is on fire. I feel the heat of the day sink into my bones, the rich food warming my belly, and the wine making my heart pump.

'Barbara,' Olivia suddenly says. 'Can you clear the plates please?'

I start out of my relaxed reverie and stand up awkwardly, beginning to reach out to take Pascal's plate. He puts his hand over mine, stopping me.

'Olivia, Barbara is not our servant.'

'Well, actually Pascal, she is.'

Pascal looks over at John, but he is distant now and looks away, unwilling to contradict his wife.

'Barbara,' Olivia snaps, and clicks her fingers.

I start to collect the plates, my cheeks burning with embarrassment, but Celeste gets up from the table and helps me, and I hear Hubert admonishing his daughter, telling her that an au pair is not a servant but part of the family, and did she not remember her own au pair when she was a little girl? Olivia is furious.

'John, will you tell my father and mother that this is none of their business. Barbara is our au pair and if we want her to wash up the dishes then that is the way it will be. She is not part of the family.'

Pascal takes the plates out of my hands and smiles apologetically at me.

'Barbara, please ignore my sister. Sometimes she can be a terrible bitch. You must forgive her. She does have a good side.'

'John!' Olivia snaps angrily.

'Barbara, can you take Matilda up to bed,' John says turning to me, speaking hastily.

'Of course,' I reply, glancing at his weary face. He looks exhausted, older than his years, his forehead deeply lined and with dark shadows under his sad eyes. I feel terribly guilty. I have deceived him by not telling him about last night or about Matilda's red pills. I will tell him tonight, I resolve.

*

'Where are you from again?'

I look at Matilda's reflection in the bathroom mirror, her head bent as she leans over the sink and rinses out her mouth. She looks up and catches my eye in the reflection.

'Ireland.'

I wipe her face with a towel and we go back into her bedroom.

'What's it like?' she asks, as she climbs into bed.

I think of home. I am surprised by a deep ache inside me as I see Culleenamore Strand, rivers of seawater at low tide running through the orange, red and black sand, and the landscape of undulating green fields and blue mountains in the distance, Ben Bulben just visible from our bungalow, its almost right-angled cliff dropping to the sea.

'I live close to the sea, and the mountains. There is a mountain called Knocknarea, right behind my house, and on top of it is the grave of a very famous Irish queen called Maeve.'

Matilda looks interested.

'Do you have a boat?'

'No.'

'Can you swim?'

'Yes.'

'So can I. Uncle Pascal taught me.'

'The sea is very cold where I live. We don't go swimming often.'

I hear the roar of the Atlantic surf in my head. I see a picture of myself and Fiona standing on the stones at Strandhill in the lashing rain, before Solomon died, his lead gripped in my wet hand. We are watching Murtagh surfing with some of his friends, laughing at their mishaps, cuddling into each other in our raincoats to try to keep warm and dry. I let Solomon off the lead and he runs towards the ocean, as if he is trying to protect us from the angry surf. He barks manically at the crashing waves and at the surfers.

'Do you have any brothers or sisters?'

'No.' And then before I can stop myself I add, 'I used to have a little brother. He died.'

Matilda's eyes open wide. She stares at me, and I am sinking in the blue waves of her eyes.

'I had a brother too.'

I feel a cold finger running down my spine. I turn away, shaking slightly. The room is filling with dusky shadows, but it is so incredibly hot and stuffy. I go to the window and open it wider, trying to gulp in fresh air, but the atmosphere is dense and humid. My heart is racing and I am scared. How could I be frightened of a little girl?

'Do angels exist?'

I turn around. Matilda is sitting up in bed, staring at me. Her lank hair falls about her pale oval face, and her large grey-blue eyes are fixed on me. I recognise John Finch in her expression, yet there seems to be nothing about her which is like her mother.

'I believe they do.'

'But are they real? Have you seen one?'

'I think you have to feel an angel, rather than see one.'

She lies back down on the bed, closes her eyes.

'My brother is an angel,' she says sleepily. 'He is a tiny little baby angel, playing with all the other baby angels on their clouds.'

I want her to stop now. We shouldn't be talking like this. Within the last twenty-four hours Matilda has changed in my eyes from a spoilt, demanding little girl, to a creature altogether different. She is not normal. I almost wish back the brat I detested my first week as her au pair, because at least things were simple then. Now I begin to feel the lines blurring between us, the coincidences are too strong; and her need for me. It is almost physical. I can smell it, like burning timber, like hot brick, like the smell of Mattie needing me.

I go over to the dresser, pick the bottle of pills off it and shake them.

'Matilda,' I say quietly. 'We forgot to take your pills again.'

'I know,' she whispers with her eyes closed.

I unscrew the lid and take two pills out. I look at them, shining like two tiny red eyes in my pale palm.

'Don't tell,' she says, and in an instant she is asleep, her mouth open wide, snoring softly. I stand over her watching, wondering if she is away with the angels now, playing in the land above the clouds.

John Finch is standing outside the room when I come out. I nearly jump out of my skin with fright.

'Sorry,' he apologises, 'I didn't mean to scare you. I was just coming to say goodnight to Matilda.'

'She's asleep.'

'Already?'

I nod. He shifts from foot to foot, looking uncomfortable.

'Barbara, I do apologise for Olivia's behaviour.'

I colour, shake my head.

'She is a little out of sorts at the moment. You see . . .' He pauses. 'She has been through quite a lot recently, and she hasn't been well . . .'

He laughs shortly. It is a bitter laugh. 'I suppose I am the only member of our little family in full health.'

'Matilda is getting better,' I say optimistically. 'She has so much more energy than when I first arrived.'

John looks glum.

'That's only because of the medication. If we take her off the pills she will have a seizure within less than twenty-four hours. So yes, she is better if she takes her medicine, but you see that still makes her a sick child. She still has to have special care.'

I look down at the floorboards on the landing. Why can't I tell him what I have done? It is on the tip of my tongue, when he suddenly turns away, his hand on the doorknob of Matilda's room.

'Goodnight, Barbara,' he says, before creeping into his daughter's room.

I go back downstairs, preparing to do the washing-up, but Celeste has done it in my absence and the party are now all sitting outside, drinking and smoking cigarettes. Pascal offers me one, and surprising myself I take it. I have never smoked, only the odd spliff with Fiona and Murtagh, because I was never interested in cigarettes. But now I feel the need. I sit back in my chair and stare into the dark landscape, inhaling and exhaling, tasting the bitter tobacco in my mouth. I catch Olivia looking at me. Her eyes narrow as Pascal turns to talk to me.

'Can you ride, Barbara?'

'Yes, I'm not great but I love horses.'

He smiles. 'I thought you might. Tomorrow would you like to go riding?'

'I'd love to.'

Olivia shakes her head. 'Pascal, Barbara is here to mind Matilda.'

'Yes, but surely like any other job she has time off?'

Olivia says nothing. I can see she has had a lot to drink. She sways in her seat and then gets up suddenly.

'I'm going to check on Matilda,' she announces.

'John is with her,' Pascal says.

'Oh yes, of course. Darling Daddy is looking after her.' She sits back down again with a bump.

Only Pascal and I understand her sarcasm. Hubert begins talking to his daughter in French, while Celeste gets up, picking up the empty bottle of wine.

'Would you like to say goodnight to the horses?' Pascal asks me.

I nod, and we get up together. Pascal tells his parents he is going to give the horses some hay, and we walk away from the others towards the stables.

'This was just an excuse of course,' Pascal says, smiling at me, and touching my arm lightly.

We walk around the side of the stables.

'For what?' I ask innocently.

'For this,' he says and kisses me lightly on the lips.

I don't step back. I don't turn away. I touch my lips with my fingers, blush and look into his eyes.

'You're beautiful,' he says, taking his hand around the back of my neck and pulling me towards him. He kisses me again. And for a moment I forget everything: Matilda's red pills, John Finch's sad face and Olivia Finch's hostility. I forget home, Mammy's predictions, the empty space where Mattie should breathe, and I even forget Solomon. The pleasure in this one moment cradles me, it is intoxicating and it is liberating.

Nine

I have very few memories of Mattie. I was nine when he died. He was four. Four years is not a very long time. And yet it is a lifetime for my brother. Four years my father tried to blank out, and my mother went over again and again. My memories get confused over different things that happened in our childhood. How old was Mattie when Daddy brought us the Pinocchio puppet from Italy? Or when Mammy took us to visit her parents, only the once, and they slammed the door in her face? Or when we went to Rosses Point, and Solomon swam with us in the sea?

I remember Mattie getting into bed with me in the middle of the night when he was scared. He would climb in and bring all of his cuddly toy gang with him, so that sometimes by morning we would be falling out of the bed, a row of teddies and cuddly animals lined up all along the pillow. Sometimes he wet my bed, and I used to get very cross, but always forgave him when he started to cry. I'd take the sheets off the bed myself. I even put them in the washing machine.

If I concentrate hard, really hard, I can conjure up Mattie's scent, and how his body felt next to mine. His bony knees, tucked up into the back of my legs, and his thin arms wrapped around my body, clinging on, as if I was taking him somewhere, as if he were the turtle shell on my back, and we were floating in the sea, among Technicolor fish and pink coral, swimming down to the moon's reflection all the way at the bottom of the ocean. We were so close we dreamt the same dreams. How many times did I try to re-create the magic of these moments when Liam was a little boy? Always I can see Mattie in my son, even when he went past the age of four, even now as an adult, I can see how Mattie might have turned out if he had lived.

I possess discs of memories. They are like gold coins I take out of the treasure chest in my mind and examine. There was Mattie's first day in school, when I took him into baby infants, and he was squeezing my fingers so tight I nearly cried out. I feel guilty now when I remember how much I wanted to get away from him, and back to my friends in third class, and how forlorn he looked, like a lost puppy, when I left him sitting at his desk in his crisp new uniform, shiny plastic lunchbox in front of him.

There are earlier memories when he was a baby, and I used to play with him, as if he were a little doll, as if he was my baby. I dressed him up in my old baby clothes, little pink shawls and bonnets, and popped him in the big pram, which I wheeled up and down the road in front of the house. Solomon would be at my feet, a puppy then, dancing on his paws, sprightly and energetic, but always my keeper.

I remember the time I was minding Mattie the afternoon I discovered what Mammy did. He must have been about two by then, and I was seven. I thought I was a proper little grown-up. Mammy was in the front room, with one of her 'visitors', and we were in the kitchen, eating soda bread and rhubarb jam, and watching TV. We were watching the English channels. I loved *Blue Peter*, although Mattie preferred the cartoons. He was too young for *Blue Peter*.

It was a bleak March day with a black stormy sky. The back door was banging with the wind, and the chimney was howling, the fire flaring up and throwing sparks onto the floor behind the guard. When I looked out the kitchen window the dark clouds had turned Knocknarea a deep emerald green. It was like a menacing giant at our back door. I was trying not to think of Daddy on the boat being tossed across the Irish Sea. I wished he were coming back, not going away. *Blue Peter* was over. Mattie was sitting on the floor watching *Paddington Bear*, and Mammy was still not finished yet. I was bored. I could hear voices through the door so I did something I had never done before. I crept up to the closed door, bent down and peered through the keyhole. Of course I couldn't see anything at all. So glancing at Mattie, and telling him not to move, I went out the back of the house to walk around to the front and peek in the window. I didn't put a coat on and the wind cut through me like cold knife blades, but now I was on a mission, and I wasn't about to give up. I glanced up at Knocknarea. From where I was standing I could no longer see Maeve's cairn, just the heavy bulk of the mountain at my back, but I knew she was there.

'The Queen of Connacht is always watching us,' Mammy said, 'searching for her bull.'

'Tell me the story again,' I would beg.

And Mammy would sit on the end of Mattie's bed, and she would tell us the old Irish legend of the Tain Bo Cuailnge (The Cattle Raid of Cooley), when Queen Maeve and King Ailill invaded Ulster to steal a great bull.

'They were having an argument,' Mammy explained, 'over which of them was richer. In the end they were equal apart from Ailill's great bull. Maeve learnt of a greater bull in Ulster so she tried to take it by force. She got the bull but it caused a major war, much bloodshed and suffering. Ultimately her invading armies were defeated by the great warrior Cúchulainn.'

I lapped up the words and Mattie sat upright in wide-eyed wonder.

'Queen Maeve wasn't a very nice person,' Mammy continued. 'She was very cruel to her subjects. That's why they buried her in the northernmost fringe of her kingdom.'

Mammy said she had chosen to live in this place because she didn't believe Maeve was as black and cursed as others said. She said the mountain was special. It had power.

'We are halfway between two heavenly realms,' she claimed. 'The heavens of the sky and the heavens of the sea. Here all the angels pass by.'

It was true, our stone cottage and little green field next door were halfway up the side of a mountain, and in front of us was just one narrow tarmac road, bushes, hedgerows and three fields dropping down to Culleenamore Strand, with its silvery trails of sea and sand, and behind that blue mountains. Every day we looked out at the sea. Now I realise that Mammy was giving us a gift to grow up in such a beautiful place, but when I was young I found it frustrating to be so far from my friends, out in the middle of nowhere. And when it was stormy on a day like this one, even if you were inside you felt exposed, unsettled, as if something bad was going to happen.

The wind blew my hair across my face, and I pushed it behind my ears as best as I could as I bent down below the front window. I was just the right height. I put my hands on the sill and pulled myself up so that my eyes were level with the bottom of the window.

Mammy's back was to me. And the woman she was with was facing me. And that was a terrible thing because of how she looked. One eye was black, and then on her other cheek, there was a terrible mark. It was red and raw in the centre, and circled by a dark grey rim, almost black. It looked like someone had pierced her cheek with a hot arrow. The woman was crying, but silently, no noise, she was just shaking, like *she* was out in the wind not I, and my mammy was holding her hand. Then Mammy leant forward and licked the woman's cheek, right on the hot hole, and she licked again and again. I dropped down onto the ground in shock, shivering with the cold and with disgust. Why was my mother licking that strange beaten-up woman's face? I wanted to look again, but I knew I shouldn't leave Mattie for too long. *Paddington Bear* was a very short cartoon. Sure enough, by the time I was back in the kitchen, rubbing my blue hands together and stamping my feet to get warm, Mattie had been up to mischief. He was such a curious child, always looking and poking and hurting himself in the process. This time he had decided to explore the contents of the coal bucket. His face, hands, torso – whole body in fact – were covered in black coal dust, only the whites of his eyes and his teeth appeared clean. He was grinning at me and licking a piece of coal.

'Mattie!' I screeched, whisking the coal out of his hand. 'That's dirty. Oh Mattie, you're very, very bold.'

Mattie smiled at me impishly and began running around the room, coal dust flying onto the covers of the couch and on the floor, and just about everywhere.

'Choo! Choo! Choo! Choo!' he called. 'Paddyton! Paddyton!'

I expected a slap from Mammy, but when she came into the kitchen her face brightened, as if she had been in a very dark place and the sun had just come out.

'Matthew Joseph Delaney, you little rascal!' She crossed her arms in front of her chest and she laughed.

'Well, Madam,' she said, turning to me, 'where were you when all this was happening?'

I crimsoned and looked away, out the window at the grey, racing sky and Knocknarea, my only witness.

'I see,' she smiled. 'Were you spying on me?'

My mother had an uncanny habit of reading my mind. Some things were impossible to hide from her; some she never noticed at all.

'No,' I lied, kicking my foot into the coal dust on the floor.

The expression on Mammy's face changed from good humour to a frown. Her green eyes darkened, and the shadows beneath her eyes looked even darker. She handed me a broom.

'Well, you had better clear this up, and think about cleaning up your mouth too. Lies are filth, Barbara.'

Her look was fierce and I crumbled under her glare.

'Sorry,' I whispered, tears welling in my eyes.

She took the broom out of my hand and began sweeping the floor.

'It's important to always tell the truth Barbara, no matter what. Once you start lying, it is hard to stop. Remember, your lies will always trip you up one day.'

I nodded.

'You shouldn't spy on me when I work. Often the people who come to me are very weak, like fragile glass. I have to protect them.'

I felt ashamed then, for staring at the woman with the burnt face and black eye, and finding her ugly.

We took Mattie upstairs and bathed him, and I remember that well. The fun the three of us had so that in the end we were all a very pale shade of grey. It took weeks to get the coal grime out from under his fingernails.

'It will do him no harm,' my mother said. 'I ate coal when I was pregnant on you.'

'You did?'

I am confounded.

'Yes, and oranges non-stop on Mattie. I do think the oranges were better for me!'

*

Later, my mother and I watched Mattie asleep. I could see the curl of his hair on the back of his neck, and his round downy cheek, the in and out of his little chest, all in the warm glow of the nightlight.

'You'd think he was a little angel, wouldn't you?' my mother said, sitting down on the end of my bed. I pulled her down towards me and hugged her tight.

'What is it, Barbara?' she asked me.

'Why did you lick that woman, Mammy?' I whispered into her ear.

My mother pulled back and said nothing for a moment. She looked beautiful in the soft light of the bedroom. Her cheeks were still flushed from bath-time and her eyes were glinting in the dark like a cat's. She looked like an elf princess with her neat ski-slope nose, her pointed chin and sparkling eyes. Her dark red hair was half tied up and half undone, with curling tendrils stuck to her forehead. She put her hands on her lap, neatly slotted one over the other, and thought for a moment.

'I shall tell you this, Barbara, but please don't tell your friends at school, or Mattie, not yet.'

I waited breathless, completely captivated by what she was about to say.

'I have a gift. It is the cure for burns. I have always had it since I was your age.'

'What is a cure?'

'It is something I have in me, which means that if I lick some-one who has been burnt, I can heal their burn and eventually the mark will go away. It depends how bad the burn is. If it is very, very bad it might not heal.'

'What kind of burn did that woman have, Mammy?' I said, remembering the circle of hot pain on her cheek, and how the woman winced when Mammy licked her.

My mother paused. She sighed and laced her fingers together, and then she said very slowly, 'It was a cigarette burn, Barbara.'

I knotted my brows, confused. How could you burn your cheek with your own cigarette? Why would you want to do that? I touched my cheek with my hand, and suddenly it dawned on me. The woman hadn't burnt herself. Someone had done it to her.

I put my hand to my mouth, opened my eyes wide in horror. My mother stroked my head.

'I know, Barbara, sometimes humans can do terrible cruel things to each other.'

Should my mother have told her seven-year-old daughter this? I don't know. I always felt more grown up than I was, and at the time it seemed perfectly natural she might tell me. But now, when I think back, what would my father have said to know my mother was telling me such things? Wouldn't he have thought me too young to be made aware of such violence and abuse existing in the world? Or would he have cared?

I never forgot that poor woman's face, her wet eyes, her silent sobbing; and what a broken thing she was, like a little bird which had flown smack into a window pane, and had dropped like a stone onto the ground, dazed, just breathing, unable to get up and fly away. I remembered her face many times years later when I sat alone in my husband's house shell-shocked and crumbling, unable to catch hold of myself. I was disintegrating, just as that poor woman was. And although outwardly I had no scars to show for it, I was burnt inside, a big black stinking hole in my heart.

For all her 'visitors' for the cure and for readings with the cards, my mother was a lonely woman. She had no friends. She wasn't like an ordinary mother. Did the other women even consider her a sort of witch? Were they unsurprised when dark forces ripped her own family apart, for had she not courted tragedy by letting such power work through her? Sure, the cure was one thing.

Everyone accepted it as being the work of God, but the tarot cards, they were something else. As I got older I began to notice how the women would shun her in town, and then at night creep up to the house, knock on the door and beg her to read their cards. How many times did my father ask Mammy to stop? He said the tarot were bad luck. And he was right, because our family was struck down by the worst luck possible. For what can be worse than one sibling killing another?

Ten

I cannot sleep. I lie in the bed, replaying my kiss with Pascal over and over again. I can feel his strong hand on the back of my neck, his fingers pushing into my skin. His cheek is pressed against mine, its roughness alien, its smell intoxicating. Pascal smells earthy and rich, and very slightly of horses. There is a hint of tobacco off his breath, but I like it, and his lips taste of salt, from the Camargue marshes. I close my eyes and see him standing before me – his black hat on his head, covering his thick hair, shading his cobalt eyes – and smiling at me, inviting me in. He is a real cowboy. I put my hand to my heart, sure I can feel it pumping in my chest, bursting to break out. Is this how it feels to be in love? Can you fall in love this fast?

I long to speak to Fiona and tell her about Pascal, our kiss, the way he looks at me. I want to know what she thinks I should do; I want to ask her about sex. I push my hands down between my legs and finger myself tentatively. I have a sensation of falling, and falling open, like a leaf uncurling to the sun, and I decide it is time now. I think about my virginity, and how much I want to get rid of it. It stands in the way of me becoming a proper woman.

Now I wish I had gone all the way with Finbar Kiely. He had been willing, with a packet of rubbers in his back pocket, got from his cousin up north. We had drunk a flagon of cider together, listened to Fiona and Murtagh in the tent next door, looked at each other, and in a hazy giggle decided to do it as well. But either we were too stoned, or too drunk, we couldn't get the rubber on right and then we couldn't stop laughing and Finbar said to give it a break and have another joint. After that we were too wrecked to try again.

Maybe it was just as well. I hadn't fancied Finbar. He was a redhead like me, with pale freckly skin and fat hands. I was just desperate to catch up with Fiona, who I was slowly losing to her boyfriend, and sex, and a world I didn't know about.

What will Pascal think of my virginity? I decide not to tell him, in case it puts him off me. I pull my sheet up over my skin, feel it billow over my naked body, and sigh as I let myself drift off into a fantasyland. I see Pascal and myself together, years from now, a happy couple forever and forever. I picture our wedding day in the South of France, nothing too fancy. Hubert and Celeste would be there, bestowing paternal adoration on us, while my parents wouldn't come. I could imagine neither of them being present in my glamorous French idyll. But Fiona and Murtagh would be there, waving us on. Fiona would be smiling at me, a mixture of happiness and envy, for now I had the perfect man. Pascal and I would be married in a ruined church on a rough peninsula jutting out to sea, like a French version of Killaspugbrone Church back home. Afterwards we would ride off together across the sand, my long white silk shift trailing against the horse's flanks.

I imagine Pascal naked; I imagine touching his body. The thought makes me shiver with desire. I see our house. A traditional Provençal *mas*, solid and golden, with big blue shutters, and three dogs dozing in the sunshine. I see myself waving to Pascal as he heads off to herd the bulls on his white horse. My other arm cradles our baby. The sun blazes down and the land is shimmering in the heat.

A crust of white salt lies between the arid marshes and the bright open sky. I stand and wave at him, until he is a little speck in the distance, riding upon a white line.

A drop of rain falls on my forehead, and then I see Matilda. She is standing in our yard and pointing at me. She has not grown at all. She is still a pudgy six-year-old girl, with flaxen cheeks and straggles of mousey blonde hair. Her eyes are the colour of rain-clouds and she looks like she is about to have another tantrum.

'Oh go away, Matilda,' I say crossly. 'I don't look after you now.'

More rain spatters onto my head, and I press our baby close to my chest, covering his downy crown with the blanket.

Matilda won't budge. Her finger shifts for she points to some-one standing behind me, and at the same time I feel a shadow cast about me and a chill creeping through my body, like two cold hands pressed around my heart. I turn and Olivia Finch faces me. She is taller, thinner, with black skin the colour of charred wood. But it is still her, just a dark version of herself, as if she has burnt. She walks towards me, expressionless, and takes the baby out of my hands. The skies open and rain begins to cascade out of the sky. I reach out to Olivia to retrieve my baby, but when I touch her arm it is as hot as a poker, and I cry and jump back, scalded and para-lysed by shock.

Olivia takes Matilda with her other hand and leads her away from me. The rain doesn't bother her, as she walks steadily across the sandy arena turning to mud, and through the gate on the other side. They go in between the rows of leafy green vines, lines of rain obscuring them, the sky almost white with water, out and across the marshes, where the reeds are black and the water is pink. Olivia Finch takes my two charges. She leads them through the brackish lagoons, across the dunes, off out to sea.

'Come back,' I call, hysterical with grief. 'Come back.'

But Olivia has taken them both, Matilda and Mattie, all over again.

The noise of the birds wakes me. It is early yet but I don't want to go back to sleep and return to my nightmare. I get out of bed and, wrapping my sheet about me, I walk over to the window and look out. Early-morning mist swirls above the landscape, a lattice of lagoons, marshy reeds and dry desert. I can sense it is going to be very hot today for I can see steam rising off the earth, and there is a heavy stillness in the air. I peer into the distance. I can see a herd of black bulls like a dark cloud at the edge of the flat plain, moving across the horizon in front of a silver line of sea. I wonder if it is Hubert's *manade*. Everything I am looking at appears as in flat planes, as if I am looking at a two-dimensional picture, so different from the landscape at home. Here I am in the belly of the earth, whereas at home we are up high, touching the sky.

My heart quickens as I notice a group of flamingos in one of the lagoons. They are huddled together, sleeping on one leg, their necks tucked into their wings so they look like large lollipops in the water. I watch as several of them put their other legs down, stretch their necks and strut in a line. To my delight they gradually gather speed and begin to run in long strides, beating their wings and taking off, bringing the whole flock behind them as they rise up into the sky in one wavy line. They appear weightless like the daddy-long-legs in our bathroom on a summer's night. They are an improbability for surely their wings are far too small to carry their long necks and heads and their pole-like legs? The flamingos join together in tight formation, moving as one. Now I can see the magnificence of their pinkness in the pink dawn. They are the colours of sunrise and night. Their wings are bright and dazzling fuchsia pink, edged dramatically with black. They surge across the sky, a strangely silent spectacle, as they fly past the house, their formation breaking up and gradually disappearing in one loose V into the distance.

I hear a horse whinny, and wonder if Pascal is up yet, mucking them out and feeding them. I feel a little strange now, after my dream. As if we have shared an intimacy, although in reality we have only just met.

Sometimes you can meet someone who you have known in a previous life-time. There is recognition.

This is what Mammy believed. She said she 'recognised' my father, and that their destiny was to come together in 'this lifetime' as she called it. This was how she explained the immorality of their match.

I wonder if I had 'recognised' Pascal, or if he had 'recognised' me? I am not certain because his face is so attractive to me I find it hard to make the distinction. With Matilda there is recognition, the way her eyes are like Mattie's.

I shake myself and try not to think about my mother, for her opinions always confuse me. I get dressed quickly and sponta-neously ditch my jeans for a dress, the only one I have brought with me. It has spaghetti straps and falls to just below the knee. In fact it is an old sundress of my mother's, which she gave to me. It is green, grass-green as she calls it, a shade she claims looks well with our red hair.

Green and red are always a good combination. They are the colours of anger and healing, working together.

How do anger and healing work together?

There is no mirror in the attic, so I look down at myself, trying to ignore my white legs in last year's flip-flops. I pick up my watch. It is half past six. I wonder what time Madame gets up to make croissants. I like Olivia's mother. Although we are unable to com-municate with each other, her behaviour towards me is kind — a quality distinctly lacking in her daughter.

I climb down from the attic and peek into Matilda's room. She is still fast asleep, little snoring noises coming from under the covers. I close the door quietly and tiptoe down the stairs. The kitchen is dark and shuttered. I open the back door and step out onto the terrace, momentarily blinded by sunlight. Rafi rushes up to greet me, thrusting his wet nose into the palm of my hand. I squat down and rub him behind the ears and under the chin. He licks my hands and arms, lies down on his back, begging me to rub his belly. I laugh softly, rubbing with all my might. It feels so good to touch his soft fur, flip his velvety ears back and forth, to stroke another dog again after losing Solomon.

My chest tightens as I remember my old faithful. Why could Mammy not let me try to save him?

'It's his time, Barbara,' she said. 'Let him go.'

'How do you know? How do you know?' I screamed at her.

When I think about Solomon I get angry and I find it hard to forgive my mother. It was one good reason to leave home. It became unbearable living in the house without Solomon. At least when Mattie died the cottage was destroyed too, and we had to live somewhere else. I breathe in sharply. How can I compare my little brother to my dog? But I can't help it. Solomon grew up with me.

I sniff and wipe my nose with the back of my bare arm. I have no tissue with me. I stand up and Rafi flips over and stands to attention watching me. I walk across the terrace and round the side of the house. He doesn't follow me but lies down on the paving stones already warmed by the morning sun.

The horses are hungry but I have nothing to give them. They push their muzzles into my chest, trying to nibble my green dress, as if they think it is a big giant apple. But they are gentle creatures. I can see it in their sable eyes, and I can tell they are well looked after. They are smaller than most horses, but strong and sturdy.

They make me think of how horses once looked in ancient times. It seems apt they belong to this preternatural landscape.

My favourite is Pedro. He is more dappled than the other two, but this imperfection makes him more attractive to me. I twist my fingers into his luxuriant mane and whisper to him.

'Do you ride, Barbara?'

I nearly jump out of my skin. John Finch is standing behind me. He is wearing a loose white shirt and old jeans. He is barefoot and unshaven. He looks exhausted, as if he hasn't slept a wink.

'A little.' I blush, continuing to stroke Pedro.

'I am sure Pascal will take you out.' He winks at me. 'He has taken a little shine to you, has he not?'

I can feel my face heating up, my cheeks reddening. I don't know what to say.

'Of course who could blame him. You are as pretty as a picture in your green dress. His artist's eye will not fail to notice that.'

'Thank you,' I mumble, mortified by his flattery.

John Finch sighs, his smile suddenly gone, and in retrospect artificial. He sits down on a mounting block and shakes his head.

'What I would do to be young again!' he exclaims.

'But you're not old,' I protest politely.

'I feel old.' He rests his chin on his hands and stares at me. 'I hope you aren't finding it all too hard and strange being Matilda's au pair. I know she can be difficult at times, and of course, she is sick a lot of the time, and then there is Olivia to deal with . . . Sometimes I feel she is more of a child than Matilda.'

I say nothing, continue patting Pedro, and let him push his muzzle into my palms.

John Finch is no longer looking at me, his eyes take on a distant gaze and there is a gleam in them of energy, even anger.

'She is not interested in me, or Matilda.'

His voice is flat, and then he shakes himself as if he remembers I am there, listening to his admission.

'Never fall in love with someone who cannot love you, Barbara.'

He gets up suddenly and pats Pedro as well, his hands brushing against mine momentarily. I don't want him to talk to me like this, as if I am his oldest friend, when in fact I have barely known him more than a week, when he is my employer.

'I'll try not to,' I say glibly, attempting to lighten the mood. I wish he would go away, yet I am too shy to walk off myself.

He says nothing. I am aware of how close he is standing next to me, and step away to the next horse-box and start to stroke Lilly, one of the other horses.

'God, I'm tired,' John announces. 'I can't believe Matilda had another seizure, not after she was taking that new medication.'

I freeze, my hand shoved into the horse's mane.

'She had another seizure?'

'Yes, in the middle of the night.'

'I didn't hear anything.'

'Just as well. I wouldn't want you to witness one of Matilda's fits. Although you probably will at some stage.'

He sighs wearily. 'I don't understand. I really thought those new pills would work.'

My throat goes dry. I am stricken, how could I have been so stupid? My hand is shaking as I stroke Lilly. I take a deep breath, summoning all my courage to make my confession to John Finch.

'The pills . . .'

But before I can say another thing, Pascal comes striding over and interrupts me.

'*Bonjour*, did you muck out for me then?' Pascal kisses me on both cheeks and I blush furiously. He looks even better this morning than he did last night. He is wearing a blue shirt, which matches his blue eyes and stands out against his dark skin and hair.

'No fear,' John says. 'Why don't you leave them out in the field in this weather?'

'*Le moustique*, they irritate them, drive them nuts. How would you like being left out in a swarm of mosquitoes?'

John begins to amble back towards the house.

It is too late now. I can't tell him about the pills, and I make a decision not to. The Finches would be furious to think I caused Matilda to have a seizure, and they would probably sack me. I don't want to leave. Not now I have met Pascal. From today I will be tough with Matilda, and do what I am supposed to do. I can't believe I have been so irresponsible.

'Would you both like some coffee?' John calls over.

'*Maman* is already on to it, but she might appreciate your help John,' Pascal replies.

John's tall thin figure disappears around the side of the house, and we are left alone. Pascal touches my shoulder lightly, and I look down at the ground, overcome with shyness.

'I see you got bitten, last night.'

I twist my neck, craning my head, and see the red mark on my shoulder.

'Oh, I didn't even notice.'

'I have some of my mother's herbal cream for it. I will give it to you when we go inside.'

'Thanks.'

He opens the stable door and goes into the box with Pedro, pats him on his rump.

'So who do you want to ride later?'

'Can we still go? Am I allowed?'

Pascal laughs, his eyes sparkle and make me smile back.

'Of course, just ignore my grumpy sister; everyone else does.'

'I don't mind. They're all lovely.'

'I'll give you Lilly, then. She is very gentle.'

I go over to Lilly's box and pat her forelock. She looks at me dolefully, tries to nibble my arms.

'She's hungry.'

'I know. Will you help me bring them out to the field? I have some hay for them there.'

Pedro sidesteps and pushes Pascal against the door; he pushes him firmly back.

'Sure.'

Pedro whinnies.

'I am sure he understands the word hay,' Pascal says, and then leading Pedro out of his box he looks at me, his eyes travelling down my body.

'Although it's a little dusty and you might get dirty. Also your feet' – he points at my bare toes in the flip-flops – 'I wouldn't like Lilly to step on your little toes.'

I look at Lilly's hooves and notice how unusually broad they are.

'Her hooves are very wide.'

'Yes, all Camargue horses have these hooves, to keep them sure-footed on the soft wet grasslands.' Pascal brings Pedro over to me. The two horses snort at each other and touch muzzles.

'Oh look, they're kissing,' Pascal chuckles, 'in a purely maternal way. They are mother and son.'

We are standing just inches away. So close I can smell his scent, the same as how I dreamt it. We look at each other and I feel the red heat from my heart travel up my chest, my neck, covering my cheeks. For a moment I can say nothing and there is silence between us.

'You go on in and have your breakfast,' he says, breaking the spell.

'It's OK, really, I want to help.' I look away from him, at the horses.

'You'd better not. My sister will be cross enough I am stealing you away this afternoon. You had better go in and look after *la petite Matilde.*'

He smiles broadly at me and I glow. His words 'stealing you away' play over and over again in my head as I walk back towards the house.

'I like your dress,' he calls out behind me. 'You look like a summer meadow.'

I am intensely aware of my body inside the dress: my nakedness beneath the thin cotton, apart from a pair of white bikini briefs. I am untouched. The thought makes my breath quicken and my senses sharpen. I know he is watching me, every little part of me, as I go inside.

Matilda feels better. She wants me to play with her, although Olivia has instructed me to do their laundry, despite the protestations of Celeste.

'We are paying her a wage, *Maman.*' Olivia is emphatic. 'It gives you a chance to relax and put your feet up by the pool.'

Olivia pushes her reluctant mother out the back door and into the sunshine.

'Look,' she says, sweeping her arms up to the bright blue sky. 'It is a beautiful day!'

Olivia looks stunning in a slinky black bikini, with a glittering gold-embroidered sarong wrapped around her waist, copper bangles on her wrists, and black and gold beads around her neck. Her hair is hidden under a thick black hairband, she is wearing large sunglasses perched on the end of her nose, and bronze lipstick. Her face is protected from the sun by a large sunhat, although she is already turning a deeper shade of honey brown. She doesn't appear to have a scrap of fat on her body, nor a hint of any stretch marks although she has given birth, not just once, but seemingly twice.

'But Mama, I want Barbara to play with me,' Matilda protests.

Olivia takes her sunglasses off and looks sternly at her daughter. 'Barbara has her duties, Matilda.'

'But I'm bored,' Matilda whines. 'She's my au pair. She has to play with me.'

'*D'accord*. But just for a little while. We are going into Aigues-Mortes after lunch, so if Barbara hasn't finished her jobs by then she has to stay here. Is that clear, Barbara?'

'Perfectly,' I say as politely as I can, although resentment wells up inside me.

How could a sweet man like John Finch be in love with such a complete bitch? It is beyond me, how this woman came to be so horrible. Her parents seem nice, especially her mother, and her brother's adorable. Was she just born nasty? I could almost forgive Matilda's demanding behaviour, for who would want a mother like Olivia Finch?

When we get upstairs, Matilda opens up her pink satchel and pulls out a large notebook and a pencil case. She unzips it and spills out a selection of coloured pencils. It is lovely and cool in her bedroom, unlike my furnace in the attic above. I lie flat on my back and feel the cold wooden floorboards pressing into my back.

'What are you doing?' asks Matilda.

'Floating,' I sigh. 'By Jesus, it's hot.'

Matilda comes over and pulls my hair out from under my head. She is surprisingly gentle. I close my eyes and let her stroke my hair, her fingers occasionally brushing against my damp forehead. Section by section, she fans my hair out above my head. I can hear her picking up her pencils, and the sound of them scratching the surface of the paper.

'What are you drawing?' I ask.

'An angel. Her name is Mary, and she looks like you.'

'That's nice.' I sigh, letting my body relax into the floor, feeling as if I am sinking to the bottom of the sea, my body weightless, my thoughts suspended.

'Your hair isn't red,' she says.

'It's not?'

'No, it's gold hair.'

I look up, and she is leaning over me, her eyes are smudges of grey pastel. They jolt my heart.

'Like the shiny gold circle above an angel's head,' she continues.

'The halo? Well of course, Matilda, haven't you worked out I'm your guardian angel?'

She looks serious.

'You have to be dead to be an angel.'

I sit up, leaving strands of ginger hair caught between the floorboards. Matilda starts to pull them out.

'Can I keep them?' she asks.

'OK, if you really want to.'

I look over at the picture she has drawn. It is very similar to all of her angel pictures but this time the angel is wearing a grass-green dress like mine.

'It's very good.'

She screws up her face.

'She doesn't look real,' she complains.

'I think she does.'

She twists the gold thread of my hair around one of her fingers.

'I'm bored,' she moans.

'What would you like to play?'

'I don't know. It's your job to think of a game.'

I ignore her rudeness and cross my legs, leaning over and picking up the notebook.

'We could play schools.'

'How do you play that?' she asks sulkily, but I can see a pinprick of interest in her eyes.

'Well, one of us is the teacher, and the other one is a pupil, and then we use all your dolls and teddies to be the other pupils. We pretend we're in school and make up lessons.'

'But I only have Jemima with me, I've no other dolls.'

'Never mind, that's enough. We can make-believe the other children. Do you want to be the teacher or a pupil?'

She pauses, chews her lip.

'A pupil.'

'OK, I'll be the teacher then.'

We rearrange the bedroom. I bring a small table over into the centre of the room to be the teacher's desk, and line up cushions against the wall for the pupils' chairs. I tie my hair up on top of my head to make myself look more like a schoolteacher and Matilda fills her satchel with books and pencils. I help her put her arms through the straps so that the satchel sits on her back as if she really is on her way to school.

'Now,' I direct her, 'you sit over on that cushion there with Jemima next to you, ready for school, and I'll go outside the door. When I come in you have to stand up, and say very politely "Good morning Miss . . ." What shall we call me?'

'Umm, Miss . . . Black.'

'OK, Miss Black.'

'Or Mrs Black. Aren't schoolteachers usually married?'

Matilda looks a little uncertain, but I can tell she is excited as she fidgets on her cushion.

'Not always.'

'My teacher was a Mrs. She was called Mrs Green.'

'OK, well I can be a Mrs too.' I go towards the door. 'So when I come in you stand up and say "Good morning Mrs Black" loud and clear. And you have to be very, very well behaved otherwise I might give you lines.'

Matilda grips Jemima to her chest, her eyes glisten, reminding me of my little urchin Mattie. I have never seen her so delighted.

We play schools for well over an hour, by which time we have gone over some simple sums, our ABCs and a little reading. Poor Matilda struggles with everything but it is not surprising since she has missed so much school. Then I decide we should write a story.

'Now children,' I say in my Mrs Black the schoolteacher voice. 'I would like you to write a story around one of your pictures, which you did in art last week. Matilda, you can use that nice picture of the angel. Jemima, you can write about the picture of the dog you drew for me.'

Matilda puts her hand up.

'Yes, Matilda.'

'Please, Mrs Black, what kind of story can you write about an angel?'

'That is up to you, Matilda. You have to use your imagination.'

'But I can't write very well. Will you write it for me?'

'Well, that is not standard, Matilda Finch, but seeing as you have worked so hard all morning I think I can give you a hand.'

Matilda looks pleased.

'I am always thinking of stories,' she tells me. 'But they just go round and round in my head. I can only write "Once upon a time" and then I get stuck.'

'You don't have to start with "Once upon a time". You can start a story with any sentence.'

She looks thoughtful.

'The stories Daddy reads me always start with "Once upon a time".'

'That's because they are fairy tales, but not all stories are fairy tales. They can be lots of different things.'

'My story is an angel tale.' She jumps up, clasping her hands. 'That's it,' she says joyously, 'an angel tale.'

I let my hair down and we both climb onto Matilda's bed. She hands me her notebook, and I take a pencil from the pencil case.

'OK, are you ready to begin?' I ask.

She gives a little cough and a sneeze. I hand her a tissue.

'Are you feeling all right?'

'Yes, yes,' she says impatiently, 'Come on.'

And so this is Matilda Finch's angel tale. This is what she told me.

Once upon a time there was an angel called Mary. She had hair made of gold. She lived in the clouds with all the other angels, and in particular her little baby brother angel, called Marcus. One day Mary and Marcus went for a walk and they got lost. They fell out of their clouds and landed on the bed of a little girl. They didn't realise until they landed on earth how small they really were because they were both very small, about the size of two mice. The little girl was sitting in bed, but it wasn't night. She was surprised when she saw the two angels land on her bed.

Who are you? she asked.

We are angels from cloudland and we got lost. Mary told her and her little baby brother angel, Marcus, started crying because he was so frightened.

Why is he crying? asked the little girl.

Because he doesn't like earth, said Mary Angel. It frightens him.

Why? asked the little girl.

Because he died when he was a baby on earth and will never grow up.

Oh, said the little girl, I know what you mean. I am never going to grow up too.

Why is that? asked Mary.

Because I am a sick child, said the little girl.

Why are you sick? asked Mary.

Because my mama is sick, and so I am sick too. She tells my daddy to give us little red pills and he thinks we will get better, but she wants us to get sicker and sicker because then he will love us more.

I see, said Mary, and she understood completely.

You will like it in cloudland when you become an angel, she tells the little girl.

We play a lot, and have lots of fun, and no one is ever sick, not even a cough or a sneeze.

Mary Angel flew around the room to show the little girl what fun it was to be an angel. And her little brother Marcus stopped crying and flew too, and the little girl thought what fun it would be to fly.

Do you have to be good to become an angel? asked the little girl.

You always have to do what your mama tells you, said Mary Angel.

Even if your mama is bad?

Yes, no matter how bad your mama is.

Are you my guardian angel? asked the little girl.

No, said Mary Angel. There are no such things as guardian angels. Adults just make them up so you're not afraid when they turn out the light at night.

And then Mary Angel remembered the way back to cloudland and told the little girl she had to go.

The little girl cried and asked her to stay because she was so lonely. She had no brothers or sisters and she was all alone.

No, we have to go back, said Mary.

Can I come with you? asked the little girl. I am bored of sitting in bed being sick, my bottom is sore and I have pins and needles in my legs. I want to get up and fly with you.

You can't, not yet. But do as your mama says and you will become an angel. Bye.

And Mary Angel and Marcus Baby Angel took off, and they flew around the room once and then they were gone, back to cloudland.

The End.

Matilda flops back onto the pillows, exhausted. I am shaking uncontrollably. Part of me wanted to stop her. I didn't want to hear what she was telling me, but her story was spilling out of her mouth, as if she couldn't keep it in any longer. I feel horror creeping through my bones. It must be at least 30 degrees outside, but I am a block of ice, my throat dry, my teeth chattering. I put my arms about myself to try to calm down. I go over her story again, looking down at the page I have written it on, as my writing gets messier and messier with alarm. Matilda has more or less told me her mother is making her sick, on purpose. That is what she is telling me, isn't she? I look up at the ceiling, appeal to it. Help me, I silently pray.

'Matilda,' I ask quietly, 'what is the little girl's name in your story?'

'Matilda, like me,' she replies chirpily.

I take a deep breath.

'Why did you get sick last night?' I ask her quietly. 'You said the pills were making you ill and you stopped taking them. So why did it happen again?'

'I told Mama,' Matilda replies, piercing my heart with those eyes she shares with Mattie.

'What did you tell your mother?'

'I told her by mistake. I said I felt better because I hadn't taken the pills and she was very cross. She said you were bad not to give them to me.'

'And then you took them?'

'Yes, she said I should. She said Daddy would be cross.'

My heart is pumping fast, and my face is burning. I lean over the bed and take Matilda by the shoulders.

'Matilda, promise me you won't take any more of those pills if you can help it.'

'But Mama stands over me while I take them.'

'I'm going to tell your daddy that you shouldn't take them.'

She looks surprised.

'But you're not a doctor.'

'I know, but we'll ask your daddy to take you to a new doctor.'

'I hate doctors, they're nasty men. They're not nice men like Daddy and Papa and Uncle Pascal and Gareth.'

Her face brightens.

'Isn't Gareth coming tonight?'

It is beginning to make sense to me now. Of course Olivia is plotting to kill Matilda with some kind of poison. Had she already killed her first child? But why would she do such an awful thing? Was it to be free to run off with Gareth? I feel like I am in the middle of some kind of horror movie. Could it really be the case? How could she want to kill her own child? But it was possible. There were people who did such things. I had read about them in the papers – that terrible sick couple in England who buried their daughter in the garden. I remember the story of Medea in Greek mythology who killed her two little boys out of revenge for love, mad crazy love. Maybe Olivia and Gareth were pure evil.

There is no such thing as evil in this world. Just damaged people, Barbara, damaging other people.

But I push my mother's words to the back of my mind. I have to help Matilda. I am sure she is in danger, and I have to tell John Finch what his demonic wife is up to as soon as I can. I might have been unable to save Mattie, but I would make up for it now. If I were able to do this one brave thing, if I was able to save Matilda Finch's life, then maybe I would be forgiven.

Eleven

Mattie was a mammy's boy, but I was never a daddy's girl. My father was a predominantly absent one. When I was very little he would arrive like a sudden shower of sunshine on a grey Sligo day, a rainbow of colour and life, arching over our boring world. I loved the spectacle of Daddy, always returning with a tanned skin, a broad smile, lots of gifts and hugs, kisses. Mammy would treat him like the most honoured guest, pull up the best chair by the fire, and make him a hot whiskey, saying he must be feeling the cold after being abroad. That was when there were just the three of us, our perfect triangle of love.

Mammy would tell me to get up and show Daddy the new dance I had learnt in Irish dancing. And while she sang the reel in a strong, clear voice, I hopped from foot to foot, doing my best for my father, my hands straight down by my side, feeling like the pogo stick I had got for Christmas. I didn't like the dancing, and I don't think Daddy cared too much for it either. I was trying to please her.

Then Mammy would interrogate Daddy, ask him about all the foreign places he had been to, savouring each detail, of which there weren't many for my father was not the descriptive sort.

'Have you found it?' she would ask him hungrily. 'Have you found our nirvana?'

'Yes, Daddy,' I joined in, 'did you find it?'

Every time Daddy came home, Mammy would ask him this question. This hope was what kept her going, the promise of a new life,
somewhere else, somewhere warm and Mediterranean, away from
Ireland, poverty and the rain. Everyone else was leaving, so why
shouldn't we?

But Daddy would always put her off. Not yet, no, although he
had heard of a place in the South of France or northern Spain or in
Tuscany and so it would go on. Next time he might find it, next
time he would come and take us with him.

At night when Mammy tucked me into bed, on the nights Daddy
was there, she would tell me that soon we would be moving, and
I would learn to speak another language, and so would she.

'Of course we will always live by the sea because we have to,'
she said. 'But it will be hot, Barbara. It will be so hot we won't have
to wear shoes. And we'll be able to grow lots of different fruit and
vegetables like lemons and olives and oranges . . .'

'Oranges?'

'Yes, we'll have orange trees.'

The idea of this delighted me. An orange tree seemed something
completely fantastical. I wondered if they were big shaggy trees or
small, neat, bushy trees and how many oranges you might get in
one tree.

After she left the room I would close my eyes and dream of our
happy little nirvana. I imagined it like a paradise island with palm
trees, and parrots. There were dancing people waving their arms
and legs, all jiggly and free, unlike the torturous Irish dancing I had
to do. And all the while I could hear my parents making love for
the walls between our loft bedrooms were paper-thin. I loved the
sound of it. It was a lullaby to me. The rise and fall of their sighs,
the whispered caresses, the waves of love rolling through the
house, bringing us out to sea and across the ocean to nirvana.

Mammy kept believing for a long time. When I was little she adored my father, poured all her love into him, and all her hope rested in him. He was her adventurer. He was a man who valued her love as paramount for hadn't he been willing to leave his wife, and turn his back on his own family all for my mother? My parents were never married, for they couldn't be, my father already being married. They were outcasts. And I was the outcasts' child.

Of course I didn't know this when I was little, but everyone else did. Both my parents were from Sligo, so when the scandal was out that he, a married and older man, was seeing my mother and she was with child, all hell broke loose. This is why I never knew my grandparents, on either side; why we moved out of Sligo town to Culleenamore; and why I remember the parish priest singling me out at school and making sure I got the wooden spoon more than all the others, no matter how good I tried to be. And this is why my mother was desperate to leave for a new life with Daddy, somewhere foreign where nobody knew who we were or what they had done. But I suppose there were other people involved all along: Daddy's wife and Daddy's other children. And although they were never spoken about, and I never knew they existed until I was much older, Daddy must have spent half his time with them, probably more, for we only saw him every couple of months.

Mammy was different. So what did she do? She made herself even more different, with her cure, and her readings, and her gypsy clothes. She had to make her own living, and through her psychic work she was able to get by but she stuck out like a sore thumb in our community. She refused to be ashamed. Even when she was pregnant with Mattie, she strode about Strandhill, head held high, ignoring the gossip.

After Mattie was born, things changed at home. Mammy stopped talking about nirvana. She stopped asking my father if he had found it when he came visiting, which was more and more infrequent. And now when he walked through the door she no longer rushed into his arms, or made him a hot whiskey.

'There's tea in the pot,' she would say, sitting by the fire, nursing Mattie, and barely looking up.

I would try to make it up to my father.

'Look, do you want to see my pictures I did in school?' I asked. 'I learnt this song, can I sing it for you?'

I tried my best, but all the time I felt an ache in my chest when I saw my father and sometimes I wished he wouldn't come back at all because it hurt too much every time he did. As soon as he arrived I would be wondering when he would leave. Sometimes it would be suddenly, sometimes it would be without even saying goodbye.

Instead of hearing their love in the night, now I could hear its disintegration – my mother's voice strangely bitter and shrill, my father getting angry and shouting back, and then Mattie crying in the middle of it all. And I would hug my pillow, wish it were a person, or a dog or cat, something with a heart I could feel, to beat against my chest and comfort me.

That is why Mammy always loved Mattie more than me. She couldn't help it. All the love and passion she had felt for my father she transferred to my brother, and he lapped it up, like a grateful puppy, and that is how Mattie became a mammy's boy, and no matter how much I tried to compete with him, he always won her first.

There was the time we went to Lough Key. Mammy had just got her first car. It was a rackety old Ford Cortina, but we thought we were royalty, as we trundled along the byways of County Sligo in our poster-red automobile. She had never passed her test, but had a provisional licence and a big red L stuck on the back window, and as far as Mammy was concerned that was enough.

'There are no such things as accidents,' Mammy announced. 'If we are going to crash then it is going to happen anyway,' she said as she confidently let out the clutch and the gears crunched.

It was just six months before the fire and we were as carefree as three naughty children on a summer escapade. Of course Daddy was away, but that didn't stop Mammy packing up a picnic and taking us for a family outing to Lough Key. She was used to being a single mother now. She was used to doing everything on her own.

We parked the car near the lake, and taking our picnic out of the boot we immediately devoured our egg sandwiches and Kimberley biscuits, sitting on picnic benches, and looking out at the island with the castle in the middle of the lake. We watched people in rowing boats being rowed out to the island by teenage boys, and posh people in their big cruising boats, docking and getting out, in their white shorts and boating hats, and walking up the lawns to the restaurant for their lunch.

'I want to go in a boat,' Mattie said, dropping his sandwich on the ground. I picked it up, dusted bits of grass off and gave it to Solomon, who chomped it hungrily.

'We can't, darling,' said Mammy.

'Why not? I want to go to the island.'

'We can't, Mattie,' I repeated in my grown-up voice, knowing why we couldn't. It must cost too much. A lot of things we couldn't do or have cost too much.

Mammy stood up and dusted the crumbs off her dress. It was a long gypsy-type dress, purple with gold paisley patterns. She wore at least six bangles on her wrist which jangled as she cleared up the picnic things. She was still a beautiful young woman, a head-turner, but she was not interested in men any more. Men could not be relied upon. For Mammy her life was her children.

First of all Mammy took us to the wishing chair. It was a big roughly hewn stone throne. We took it in turns to get up and make a wish, while Mammy took photos of us. Mammy said we had to keep our wishes secret, otherwise they wouldn't come true, so I wished mine in my head. I wished to be able to fly. To be able to jump off the roof of our house and sail through the sky. A silly wish, but in a strangely awful way it did sort of come true.

We walked along the trails inside the woods. Solomon charged ahead, sniffing in the undergrowth, hopeful for rabbits, and Mattie ran after him. I walked with my mother in the silence of her thoughts, honoured by her company, looking up at her magnificent presence, the miracle of who she was. We passed through an avenue of huge red cedar trees, which Mammy told us were brought to Lough Key from America. Mattie and I climbed on their sinuous branches, which were like giants' limbs, and I asked Mammy if everything was larger in America.

'It's a very big country,' she told me. 'You could fit Ireland into it dozens of times over. They have big skies and huge plains which go on for miles and miles without a tree in sight.'

We crossed the fairy bridge and as we skipped through the wood I imagined I could hear all the sprites and tree elves calling to us. Hello, Hello I sang back in my head. We were fairies too, little skinny Mattie, and tall red-haired Mammy and me with my thick red curls. We were wood folk and that was why we were always alone, the three of us, because we didn't belong with the other humans. We were earth angels. We were special. The wood enchanted me, and I wanted to stay in its green cloak forever, safe and belonging.

I chased Mattie through the bog garden, jumping from one tree stump to the other across the black bog, but then he got scared he might fall in so Mammy had to carry him.

'Look, silly,' I said, 'Solomon is running on it, you can't sink in.'

We climbed the ugly concrete tower, which had been built to replace the old house, burnt down during the time of the Land

League, my mother said, because the Lord who had owned it had been cruel to his servants.

'See all of these tunnels,' she said, pointing at several openings in the moat wall. 'They were built by him so he wouldn't have to look at his servants approaching the castle.'

I ran into one tunnel, Mattie ahead of me. Suddenly we were in the pitch black, and it was damp and echoing. I turned around and Mammy was no longer behind us. Mattie whimpered in the dark.

'I'm scared,' he said.

'Mammy is just coming,' I told him.

'Boo!'

We both jumped in unison and Mammy appeared with a big grin on her face.

Mattie got cross and teary but I laughed.

Back outside we found a soft grassy mound on the far side of the tower and Mammy lay down in the grass.

'Mammy, can we play hide and seek?' Mattie asked.

'In a while,' she replied. 'I just want a little rest before I have to drive home.'

She closed her eyes and sighed. I looked at her chest moving up and down, and the softness of her belly, which I longed to touch and cuddle.

'You can play here for a minute, can't you?'

'Can we go for a walk?' I asked.

'Just a little one to the edge of the woods, but don't go far, and bring Solomon.'

We threw sticks for Solomon, and he was brilliant at catching them, but wouldn't fetch them back, instead tossing them in the air and chewing at them as if they were bones.

'Can Solomon swim?' Mattie asked.

'Of course, he can,' I said, pulling a stick out of Solomon's mouth and throwing it into the trees.

'No, he can't.'

'He can, silly. Come on, I'll show you.'

And without thinking I took Mattie's hand and led him down the path into the woods away from Mammy and towards the lake. Solomon bounded in front of us.

It must have been ages later when I grew tired of throwing sticks into the water, and Solomon was wet and panting on the grass.

'We had better go back,' I said.

But Mattie didn't reply. Mattie was gone. I looked around in panic. Wasn't he there just a minute ago? I tried to remember, but I had been so busy having fun with Solomon I couldn't recall when Mattie had disappeared. I ran back down the path with Solomon at my heels, panic engulfing me, knowing this was bad, very bad.

'Mattie,' I shouted into the trees. 'Mattie!'

I prayed to the tree elves and wood fairies to give him back for I was sure he had been taken. The next moment I chided myself for surely he had gone back before me and he was with Mammy, tugging at her skirts and asking for an ice cream? But when I turned the corner I saw Mammy on the path in front of me, running towards me. She was pale and worried-looking, and Mattie wasn't with her.

'There you are! Jesus, where were you? Where's Mattie?' She spun around, beginning to shout, 'Where's Mattie?'

She grabbed my arms, pinching the flesh with her fingers.

'Where is he?'

'I don't know,' I whimpered. 'He was here a minute ago, I don't know where he is.'

It was beginning to get dark, which, being June, meant it was very late in the day. All the other visitors were heading back towards the car park, but we were going further and further into the forest. Mammy stopped each group of people. Had they seen a little boy in a red t-shirt and blue shorts?

'Where did you go?' she asked me, her voice urgent and panicked.

I gulped.

'We went to the lake to throw sticks for Solomon.'

'Oh Christ,' she muttered.

I felt sick because even though I was only nine I knew the lake was dangerous and my little brother might have fallen in.

We hunted along the shoreline. We yelled until our voices were hoarse. Mammy kept looking into the water, which made me even more frightened. Solomon sensed our fear, and he ran along beside us, but was unable to tell us where my little brother was. Please, I silently called to the spirits of the wood, please give me back my brother. Finally Mammy said we should go back to the restaurant and ask them to ring the Gardai. She was tearless, white as a sheet, like a ghost in the fading light. I tried to take her hand

'I'm sorry,' I whispered, but she pulled her hand away and talked to me as if I were an adult.

'Just don't,' she said harshly. 'Just don't touch me, Barbara.'

It was dark now, and I couldn't stop thinking of Mattie on his own in the forest, frightened, lost and crying, or maybe he fell in the lake. Maybe he had drowned.

'I knew it,' she kept whispering as she ran along the trail. We came out of the woods and ran down the grassy bank towards the restaurant, past the tower and the tunnels and the fancy boats. Suddenly Mammy skidded to a halt for there he was – a small blond-haired boy, in a red t-shirt and blue shorts, sitting on a picnic bench, waiting.

'Oh my God, Mattie!' Mammy yelled, almost tripping over as she dashed across the grass, picked him up and swung him into her arms.

My mother's emotion scared Mattie and he started to cry.

'I lost Baa baa,' he kept repeating. 'I lost Baa baa.'

'It's all right now. We found you,' Mammy cried with relief. But she didn't look at me, and I knew she was still angry with me. She put Mattie into the car, but she never told him off, not once, for going off on his own without telling me. He was the one who went into the woods by himself, not me. I told him to stay by my side. I had. But to my mother Mattie had done nothing wrong. It was all my fault he got lost.

She tucked a blanket around his feet and then she turned round and stared at me frostily. She said nothing to me, just got into the driver's seat and turned on the ignition. I got into the back, next to Mattie, and pulled the door shut. I was trembling. As we drove out the park through the trees and back onto the main road my eyes began to water. I pressed the backs of my hands over them to stop the tears. I was determined not to cry for that was the moment I thought for sure Mammy loved Mattie more than me.

Twelve

She is guilty. There is no doubt in my mind as I hastily iron John Finch's shirts. I want to make sure I have all the laundry done and can go with the Finches to Aigues-Mortes because there I might have the opportunity to tell John what his wife is doing to Matilda.

I have heard of such a thing, where a mother might make her child sick on purpose to gain attention. How could you actually want your child to suffer? The idea revolts me, makes me hate the woman even more than I already do. She should be locked up forever. I have a mental picture of Olivia Finch in a prison cell, repenting her evil deeds, confessing to poisoning Matilda with little red pills and to what she did to the little baby Marcus. She is a monster, not a human being. I am almost frightened of her myself. But I have to be brave and tell John Finch the truth, for Matilda's sake. I try to push Pascal to the back of my mind. What would he make of it all? Would he be angry with me for exposing his sister as a murderess? But how could he be? No, he would be sad, devastated but ultimately grateful. He would love me for my courage.

By the time we are leaving for Aigues-Mortes the sky has clouded over although it is still incredibly humid.

'I think we might be in for a storm,' John comments looking up at the sky.

'Did you finish the laundry, Barbara?' Olivia quizzes me. Her eyes are hidden behind dark glasses, but I can see them in my head: black and hollow and cruel as the dark Queen Maeve herself.

'Yes,' I reply surlily.

'OK, you can come.' She smiles falsely, ignoring my tone.

'I'll just get my jacket in case it rains.'

I run back upstairs, and then climb up into the attic. It has been so hot that I haven't worn my new denim jacket since we arrived. It is under a pile of clothes thrown out of my suitcase on the floor of the attic. Initially I am reluctant to put it on, because she gave it to me, but then I like it. So what if she did, it's not as if it is contaminated.

Of course she is guilty, I reassure myself as I put the jacket on, for why hadn't she confronted me about not giving Matilda the pills? Why hadn't she told her husband? Because the truth would come out, that is why. It is then I remember the piece of paper in the pocket of my jacket. I pull it out. It's not a receipt but a folded piece of paper, ripped out of a shorthand pad. I unfold it, and it is as I suspected (do I have my mother's sixth sense as well?), something secret, something Olivia wanted to hide from her family.

My love, I have to tell you this, you are my only true love. Every time I look at you I regret how I let you go before. It hurts me to see you suffer every day. I know things are complicated for you, but don't you think we deserve some happiness at last? I am right here. I have never left you and I can never leave you.

So they really were lovers. I suspected Gareth but somehow couldn't believe it.

The car beeps outside and I stick my head out the window. The Finches are waiting for me. I don't know what to do, so I shove the note back into the pocket of the jacket. More evidence, although I decide not to mention it to John, not quite yet.

'It's a shame Pascal can't come with us,' says John as we drive down the narrow lane away from the house. 'But your father and he were busy out on the horses. Never mind, maybe he can come with us another day.'

He winks at me through the rear-view mirror. He looks quite jolly for once, probably relieved Matilda is well enough to come with us, and happy Olivia has agreed to come. I feel sick in the pit of my stomach at what I have to tell him, my insides flutter and I feel alternately hot and cold. Matilda and I sit in the back of the spacious old Merc. She keeps grabbing my hands and knotting our fingers together.

'You two seem to have bonded,' Olivia says, turning round and looking at me, her big black shades hiding her expression.

'Yes,' I say defensively. 'We have.'

I stare back fiercely at the woman, and she is taken aback, retreating, and turning round to face the front again. I catch her glancing at me in the wing mirror a couple of times, but apart from that she is silent for the rest of the journey.

We approach Aigues-Mortes through the flat plains of the salt marshes. The sky is overcast, leaden with humidity, and the road is like a straight white ribbon cutting through the dark reed beds. The wind is blowing the leaves of the willow trees at the edge of the ditches, and they turn from green to silver. Swallows dart in front of the car. We pass cypress trees, all standing in a line, and a copse of dark green trees, with thick foliage, which look like they have overgrown umbrellas on the top of them.

'What kind of trees are those?' I ask.

'Parasol pines,' John tells me. 'There are loads of them here.'

We pass another lone parasol pine, at the side of the road, bent to one side like a crippled old man. It is testament to the fierce mistral winds which blow across the landscape in the winter.

We drive through the outskirts of the town, over a little bridge crossing a canal, and then we are facing the medieval walls of Aigues-Mortes, place of the dead waters.

'It is quite dramatic if you approach Aigues-Mortes from the direction of the salt works,' John tells me. 'It rises out of the watery plains as if it is a mirage from another age.'

He parks outside the walls and we wander under a stone arch-way into the town. It is crowded with tourists bumping into each other on the narrow cobbled streets.

'I'm hungry,' Matilda announces. 'I want an ice cream.'

'We've just had lunch, Matilda,' John protests.

'Oh come on, it's our holidays,' says Olivia, oddly upbeat. 'Let's go sit down in a café and have an ice cream or a coffee.'

'I tell you what, why don't you two get something in that Salon de Thé over there, and we will join you in a while. I want to show Barbara the ramparts.'

Olivia puts her hands on her hips. She looks smart and sophisti-cated in her dark glasses, tiny silk camisole and linen trousers.

'The ramparts?'

'I want to go too,' Matilda chimes in, tugging at her father's long legs.

'No, darling, it's too far for you to walk. You're not well enough,' John replies.

'But I want to, Daddy,' Matilda wails.

John looks at Olivia.

'Go on, get her an ice cream,' he says quite sharply. It is the first time I have seen him forceful with his wife, and it gives me hope.

'OK, go look at your stupid ramparts,' Olivia grumbles, but complies. 'Come on, baby, I'll get you two scoops.'

To my surprise Matilda doesn't complain and even takes her mother's hand.

They walk off down the bustling street. Now's my chance, I think.

'This fortress town was built by King Louis in the Middle Ages, as the departure point for one of the crusades. It is one of the best-preserved thirteenth-century fortified constructions in Europe,' John is saying as he leads me around the ramparts.

It really does feel as if we are in a fortress, an outpost on the edge of a mystic world. The water below us is dusky pink (from an algae which is the only organism able to survive its high salt content, John explains) and the sky is so dark now (John's prediction of a thunder storm imminent) that it reflects onto the water, turning it an even deeper shade of pink, almost purple. I can see mountains of salt, which look like pure white peaks of snow or a marble quarry. They are the only breaks in the flat horizon. Their dazzling white mineral ridges contrast against the extreme colours of the landscape: bright green, blue, pink, red and purple. Fuchsia flamingos take off and fly in a curvy line across the sky. The whole scene has a psychedelic quality, reminding me of the one time I took magic mushrooms, up near Maeve's cairn, and how I felt the landscape pulsing within my body, and watched my hands turn green, the colour of the grass.

The view from the fortress walls is a place I might dream of, a fairy castle in the middle of a magical land, water the colour of candy, and puppet birds in the sky. I imagine St Louis making this the last ethereal point of his kingdom before turning his back on the sanctity and safety of these sturdy thick fortress walls, the spiritually heightened landscape, a place where angels might dwell, and setting sail for something foreign and dangerous, deserts and the violence of the very devil himself.

'My God, look at those storm clouds gathering,' John is saying. 'I think we're going to have a big one tonight.'

I put my hands onto the stone wall, let the lumps and bumps of its rough surface scratch my palms. I take a deep breath and I tell him. I tell John Finch about Matilda's angel tale, hand it to him, and let him read it. I am nervous, but I know I am right. He has to see it, the truth staring him in the face. Surely the love for his daughter is greater than that for his wife? I decide not to mention Gareth, or the note, for hasn't the man suffered enough? Anyway I am far too embarrassed to mention his wife's infidelity.

He finishes reading the story, his right hand drops to his side, his fingers gripping the piece of paper fluttering in the breeze, like a small white flag of surrender. He is looking down at the rocky ledge we are standing on.

'Why are you showing this to me, Barbara?' he eventually asks.

'Because . . .' I stutter. 'Because I don't think Matilda is really sick,' I manage to get out.

He looks up at me. I can see he is disappointed in me and he shakes his head.

'I thought you had more sense than the others.'

'The others?'

'Matilda does this with all of her au pairs. That's why none of them have stayed very long. She tries to convince them we are trying to . . .'

His voice breaks off.

'No, no,' I say hastily, 'I don't think *you* are . . . I just . . .'

'You think Olivia is trying to hurt her own daughter?' He flares up angrily.

Then, just as suddenly, his anger subsides and he is shaking his head again.

'It's my fault, I should have warned you about Matilda and her vivid imagination. And I should have told you about Marcus.'

I say nothing for I am so confused I cannot speak.

'We had another child,' John says very quietly. 'A little boy. He was only a few months old when he died. He was a sickly baby, very weak but he was getting better, and then one day I went into the nursery to pick him up and feed him and he had turned blue.'

John's voice breaks. I look away. I cannot bear the expression on his face.

'Cot death or sudden infant death. It is a terrible thing, Barbara, to lose a child, but even worse when you don't know why. Olivia thinks I blame her because she was smoking a lot at the time. But I don't. That's not true.' He pauses. 'I think she blames herself though, and her way of dealing with that is to be angry with me. Ever since then, ever since Marcus died, Matilda imagines things. She says she sees angels flying in her room and talks to them. Every time she meets someone new like an au pair she says the pills are making her sick, and her mother and I are making her take them. But Barbara' – John suddenly reaches forward and grabs my arm, digging his fingers into my flesh, making me feel the vehemence of his pain – 'if you saw what happens to her when she doesn't take them.'

I look at him and his eyes are flashing, the pale blue of his irises flecked with white. He drops my arm suddenly and sighs deeply.

'Maybe it is a made-up illness, but the only person making it up is Matilda herself. No one can explain why she goes into these sudden fits. It's not epilepsy, she's been tested for that. That's why I, myself, have taken her to every specialist I can think of, and finally I found someone who seemed to know what they were doing. And since she has been taking the new medication she has been much better, Barbara, a little nausea as a side effect but overall much, much better.'

He begins to walk away along the parapet, his back to me.

'I thought things were going to work out. It's evident Matilda has grown to like you, which is unusual. However, in the light of what you have just accused my wife of, indirectly, but I know what you are thinking, it would be best when we return to London if you find a new position. We will give you an excellent reference, of course.'

I feel like crying I am so ashamed, but part of me knows he is wrong and I am right. I have to make him believe me. He stops, turns to look at me, shoving his hand through his hair as he speaks.

'Maybe if you had lost someone close yourself you might understand how it can make your world turn upside down, and cause you to behave in ways you never thought you would.'

'My brother died,' I whisper, without thinking.

John raises his eyebrows.

'Pardon?'

I look at him, into his watery blue eyes.

'My brother died in a fire when I was a little girl.'

I begin to cry. I cannot help it.

'I was nine and he was four.'

'That's terrible, Barbara,' John says, walking back towards me, and puts his hand on my arm. He really does look concerned.

I burst into loud sobs, and before I can stop myself I have plunged my head into his shirt. He steps back, and then tentatively puts his arms around me.

'It was all my fault,' I mumble into his chest. 'It was all my fault.'

John Finch holds me kindly, and how I wish he had been my father when I was a little girl. A father who could hold me and let me cry, a father who might understand.

I tell him everything. I cannot stop myself. It is as if I am purging myself. I tell John Finch what I did, and how I killed my brother. He strokes my hair gently and assures me it wasn't my fault. He keeps saying again and again, 'But, Barbara, you were only a little girl.'

And when I have finished telling him, and I have dried my eyes on the handkerchief he gives me, I feel different. Lighter. Something connects John Finch and I, our shared grief and sorrow. I know he has forgiven me for my accusations of his wife.

He puts his arm around me and hugs me tight.

'A parent always wants the best for their child, Barbara. No matter how it seems. Remember I said that.'

I look up at him, his eyes are creased against the light, and he smiles kindly. I feel safe.

'Thank you,' I sniff.

He lets me go.

'Not at all. What you have to do is forget about the past, and move on. You're a bright young woman, with everything to look forward to in life.'

We have walked along all of the ramparts and are back where we started. He pauses at the top of the staircase.

'Considering what you have just told me I can see now why you are over protective of Matilda. If this situation is too much for you, then really we should try to find you a new position, don't you think?'

'Yes, maybe . . .'

'Good girl.' He pats my shoulder. 'Well, let's go and have a cup of tea. I could do with one now, couldn't you?'

We climb down the stone steps, and back out onto the cobbled streets. I walk behind him as he strides through the crowds, back towards the Salon de Thé where we left Matilda and her mother only an hour ago. But everything is different now. Something invisible connects myself and John Finch, something like trust. I will not let him down, for although he doesn't believe me, I know I am right. I know Olivia Finch is slowly killing his daughter.

Thirteen

The line of my life is turning back on itself. I was a kite buffeted by the wind in a sun-stippled sky, falling down, lifting up, fluttering here and there, but with no fixed direction. About me were tatters of clouds loaded with memories; and the ground far below, like a green sea, waves of grass carrying me across its shifting surface. I never stayed still.

One summer, when Liam was a little boy, we went nearly every day to Hampstead Heath and flew his kite. It was a dragon kite I had bought him in Chinatown for his birthday. How it fascinated us to watch this inanimate object take on life, somersaulting in the sky, twisting and turning, its bulging dragon eyes intimidating us from above, its tail undulating across the sky like a row of pink flamingos flying across the panorama of my memory. We thought we controlled the kite, but really it was the wind, who decided where our kite would fly and how high.

My husband held me on a tight rein, but we let the line to our kite go slack, so that our dragon could soar as high as possible. It was a risk. For one particularly windy day we lost our kite, as a powerful gust pulled the end of its string out of Liam's hand. Chasing it across Hampstead Heath we finally had to give in and watch our dragon fly away. Liam sat on the grass and cried for a while. But when I told him the dragon had probably gone back to China to find its dragon family and breathe fire again, he was almost pleased.

'It's good we set the dragon free,' he announced as we got on the tube on our way home. That's my Liam for you. An old sage in a boy's body. He steadies me.

It was grown-up Liam's idea I should go home. My son, with his Irish name and Irish parentage, who has never set foot in Ireland yet still calls it home.

'You've land, Mum. You've money in the bank from the sale of your mum's house. Why don't you build on it? Why don't you start a new life? What do you want to stick around here for?'

I could tell he was worried when he watched me drift around the house every weekend in my dressing gown, drinking endless cups of coffee, hardly eating, not sleeping at night. I was holding him back. I will not do to him what my husband did to me. If you really love someone you can let them go. And that is why I am in Dublin airport sitting on a plastic chair, drinking a cup of coffee and eating a soggy cheese sandwich. I am waiting for my old best friend, Fiona, to pick me up.

Since I have been a single mother we have been talking again. At first I sent a Christmas card, and signed it just Barbara and Liam. She rang immediately, as if it were only the day before when she had told me to get a life and stop being so weak.

'Barbara, what's happened?'

'He's gone.'

'For good?'

'Yes.'

'Oh Barbara, how are you?'

And then it all came tumbling out. My sorry little tale of marital infidelity, finding out my husband no longer desired me, and having to leave our home of fifteen years.

'You've got to get a good solicitor,' she kept repeating.

It was thanks to Fiona I got what I was due, and I now have enough money to start a new life. I had been stalling for three years, in my rented house, due to be demolished year in year out. I always had an excuse: I'm not divorced yet, Liam's doing his A levels, Liam needs somewhere to live while he's at college, I can't let my boss down in Odette's, my father lives only five tube stops away.

Then within the space of a few weeks everything started happening. Like Mammy always said, if you didn't change things yourself, change would be forced upon you. We finally had to leave the house. Liam wanted to move in with some friends closer to his college. Julie, my manageress, practically pushed me out the boutique door saying I wasn't suited to shop work and not to take offence because it was a compliment.

'Go home,' she said, pursing her red painted lips and wagging her finger at me. 'Go home and find a new man.'

And then she shoved a load of risqué lingerie into a carrier bag, by way of a leaving present, and sent me on my way.

As for my father, well, I knew I was fooling myself to imagine I would ever go and see him again, and there was no chance he would come to visit us. I didn't want to know him. I had given up. I even avoided travelling through his tube stop in case we might meet. Every time I was on the tube I would stare at the London Underground map, drawn to the brown Bakerloo line: Kensal Rise, Kensal Rise, Kensal Rise, home of my disappeared father.

Once I went there. Mammy had just died. I suppose that must have been why I went. Maybe I thought he would like to see me, considering I had just lost my mother. I was on my own, with Liam, the grandson he had never met. My husband didn't come.

He was nice to us. It wasn't that. And he seemed genuinely sad when I told him Mammy had died. He went quiet and pale, and looked down at the ground. But he wouldn't say her name. He kept saying 'your mother' and that annoyed me.

'I remember your mother was a very special person,' he said, as if he was talking about someone he knew a long time ago, only vaguely. 'She was such a sweet-natured gentle soul.'

I stared at him, my mouth as wide open as a fish's. I let go of Liam's hand, and my three-year-old son started pulling ornaments off the sideboard and shaking them. Who was my father talking about? Had he forgotten her completely?

'I don't think anyone would have described her as sweet-natured,' I said sharply. 'You make her sound like an old granny. She was a young woman, Daddy, she died young.'

My voice shook and the guilt rose in me again. We had both abandoned her. We had left her behind in Sligo, with Mattie.

My father looked uncomfortable, coughed and took out a packet of cigarettes. He offered me one and I shook my head. He lit his cigarette. We looked at each other and I was shocked to see he was dry-eyed.

'Your mother bewitched me,' he said quietly, almost under his breath.

'What?'

He took a drag of his cigarette, and then with the fag between his two fingers he indicated a framed photograph of a blonde woman and two children, a girl with black hair like him and a boy who looked like his mother.

'Noreen is the only woman for me,' he said bluntly.

'But you loved Mammy,' I protested.

He shook his head.

'No love, I'm telling you this so you'll understand why it is I can't see you and the little fella there. I have my own family, and I can only look after them. I'm not a superman.'

I felt my cheeks burning.

'I'm not asking for anything off you. I never have. I just thought you'd want to know about Mammy, that's all.'

'Yes, sure, it's sad.' He nodded, putting his cigarette out. 'But Babs your Ma had powers, and she enchanted me so she did. What else makes a man walk away from his wife and two small children?'

'You promised her!' I exclaimed, standing up suddenly and giving Liam such a fright he dropped the ornament he was holding, a prancing horse with a tiny soldier on its back.

'Christ, Noreen will go mad, that was her Da's.'

But I was furious and I didn't care.

'She loved you and you promised her you'd find nirvana. We were going there, the three of us, and we were going to be happy.'

My father looked at me and frowned. It was obvious he didn't know what I was talking about. He had forgotten.

'Your mam cast a spell on me, Babs. Sure you know she was a witch. They all said it.'

I looked into his eyes and for the first time since Mammy had died I felt her presence with me, as if she was standing behind me, her hand pressed into the small of my back. If Mammy was a witch, what did that make me? All my life I had not wanted to be like her. Yet I was. I knew it in my heart.

'Say what you want.' I gathered up my bag, and Liam's coat. 'You know that's not true.'

I looked at my father and it was as if he was from another planet. I could read his mind. The fear. He was terrified of me, and my son, and all I reminded him of. When he had met Mammy he had been brave and listened to his heart. But then he got frightened and ran back to his old life. He would never change. That was when I gave up, like Mammy had given up.

I took Liam's hand and dragged him out into the hall. My father followed us to the door. He tried to put a hand on my shoulder but I shook him off.

'I'm sorry, Babs,' he said. 'But you know how it is?'

I looked at him. His eyes darted from me to the door and, as I opened it, I saw his wife walking briskly up the garden path. She stopped when she saw me and stared as if she had seen a ghost. She let out a tiny squeal, like a small kitten.

'What's *she* doing here?' she hissed.

'No, it's not her, love, it's her daughter.' My father pushed past me and went towards his wife.

She stared at me again and her eyes narrowed. She didn't need to say anything as I walked past her. She hated my mother. She hated me.

So what else held me in London? The sanctity of anonymity, something my mother had always craved. And then there were the days I would go back to Winchester Gardens, walk up and down that road, well-heeled professionals running in and out of the houses, rows of smart cars lined up outside. I would stand at No. 5 and look up, and sometimes imagine I saw Matilda looking out at me. Of course, the Finches no longer lived there, but still I would imagine running into them, and what I would say to Olivia. It was hard to let go of that possibility.

'Barbara! Oh my God, Barbara!'

Fiona swoops down on me, hugging me tightly. She stops, stands back and just stares at me. There are tears in her eyes.

'I can't believe it,' she exclaims, hand to her forehead. 'After all this time, you've finally come back. Christ, you look great.'

She is even taller than I remember. Her hair is still blonde, but no longer long, and is cut into a short bob. She has lost a little weight on her face, which accentuates her coffee-brown eyes. Her skin is still flawless and glows healthily. She is beautiful, and she is pregnant.

'Fiona, why didn't you tell me!'

'I know,' she grins impishly, a flash of the confident little girl I once knew. 'I wanted to tell you in person. But you took so long about getting yourself over here I was worried the baby was going to be born before you arrived.'

She links my arm and I pick up my suitcase.

'Come on, let's get going, it's a long enough drive home and we can talk on the way.'

'You shouldn't have come to get me. I could have caught the train.'

'Don't be cracked,' she laughs. 'I *had* to come and get you. I was way too excited to wait for you at home.'

She squeezes me tight, and it is then I remember how good Fiona was when I first had Liam. She came to stay with me in London the week I was due, taking time off college and missing some exams so she had to repeat a year. Of course Liam was nearly two weeks late, but Fiona did her best to preoccupy me. She took me for little walks in the park, and tea and cake in the café round the corner. She helped me buy things for my hospital bag – Babygros, nappies, cream and giant knickers for me. She was even there when he was born.

We walk out into the car park, and sunlight blinds me, spilling out from behind dark rain clouds. The sky is so Irish – one moment sun, next rain. I look for a rainbow. My heart is fluttering inside my chest. I am nervous and at the same time finally relaxed. At last I am at home, and with someone who understands me.

'Fiona, I've missed you so much!' I declare, and to my shock I burst into tears. It starts to rain, but we don't care. We are two forty-year-old women embracing in a downpour, clinging to each other like shipwrecked sailors on a raft. Fiona pulls back and wipes her eyes, and then she looks at me and starts giggling, pointing at my shirt. I look down and realise that the rain has made it completely see-through. I am wearing one of Julie's goodbye gifts – a red and black lacy number made by La Perla. It is revealing to say the least.

'Still as saucy as ever, Delaney!' she teases me, and I burst out laughing as well. It is as if a dam has burst, as our laughter and tears merge into sisterly euphoria.

'When are you due?' I ask, as we spin down the motorway.

'Four weeks,' she says, glancing over at me, her eyes sparkling. 'I can't believe it Barbara, I'm finally going to have a child.'

Things never turn out the way you expect. Fiona married young, not to Murtagh, but in fact to his elder brother, Desmond. They planned a large family. Yet they never had children. In the end Fiona discovered Desmond was having an affair with his accountant, and she threw him out. They had been married thirteen years. Since then as far as I knew she had been single, focusing on her career as a teacher, and was now the principal of the local national school. She had done very well for herself, even owned her own house, but she had never mentioned another man since the day Desmond left.

'Are you back with Des?' I ask.

She throws back her head and laughs loudly.

'You must be joking. Jesus, no. I have so changed, Barbara. I can't imagine what I saw in him. He's gone so fat. He hasn't looked after himself at all. Even that bitch of an accountant dumped him. No, he's pathetic. Thank God we didn't have children.'

She takes the exit for the Sligo road, negotiating heavy lines of traffic in the lashing rain. The sun has completely disappeared and the sky is flat grey. I wait for her to tell me. I look at her profile.

She looks so familiar yet we haven't seen each other in over ten years.

'There's someone else.' She smiles, glancing over at me, her brown eyes lit by a hidden light.

I feel a pang of jealousy. She looks so happy, and so buoyant with love. Then I feel immediately guilty, for I know how much Fiona wanted a baby, and how it broke her heart never to be granted one.

'He just had to look at me, and I got pregnant. I can't believe it,' she gushes. 'We haven't even been seeing each other that long. It's just happened so fast, but I guess when it's right you just know and you don't hang about.'

'That's great,' I say.

'He's called Jim, and he's a builder. In fact I have him lined up to do your house. Special rates. Things have been crazy though. The board have gone mental at the school because we're not married. It's not that we don't want to be, but bloody Des is dragging his heels about the divorce. It could take years. Murtagh's been sweet and is trying to get him to get a move on. You remember Murtagh?'

'Of course I remember Murtagh.'

'I certainly married the wrong brother. But then, I'd hate to have fallen out with Murtagh, the way Des and I have. You know he's married now, with three kids. To a Spanish girl, met her when he went to teach English in Barcelona years ago.'

Fiona chats on and my eyes drift shut. I am dreaming of pink flamingos again, and riding in the Camargue on a white horse when my heart was at its most open. In my dream our hands meet, mine and Pascal's, and his are so warm and safe, unlike any other man's hands I have touched. He uncurls my fingers and opens up my palms, and then fills them with little *telline* shells, as tiny as worries.

I wake up brimming with anxiety. What am I doing back in Ireland? The last time I was here I buried my mother, and it hurt me so much I thought I wouldn't be able to bear to step on home turf ever again. Yet here I am. It is twilight and we are driving up a narrow hilly road, the hedgerows dripping with cow parsley, and I can smell the earthy odour of home, the land rising up to meet me, ready to reclaim me once again.

'You're awake,' Fiona says, leaning over and patting my lap. 'I thought we should come here first, before I take you home.'

She pulls in off the road, turns off the engine and pulls up the handbrake. She switches off the headlamps. It is a field. Just a field. I get out of the car, and Fiona gets out as well, standing by the bonnet, waiting. I walk forwards, peering into the fading light. I cross the road. The gate is still there, fallen off its hinges and leaning up against the stone wall. I walk through its opening, knee-deep in thick grass, thistles and wild flowers. It is a warm May evening, the air buzzes with flies, and swallows swoop deliriously around us.

The cottage is even more of a ruin than I remember it. The roof is fallen in, the attic is completely gone, the staircase destroyed in the fire. Even some of the downstairs walls are gone now, the floors covered in verdant moss. The fireplace is still there, no stove of course, but it is like a black hole, a gaping open mouth. I shiver.

'Jim says you'll have to tear it all down and start again.' Fiona walks up behind me. 'It's too far gone.'

I nod, walking across what was once the back room. I kneel down. This was the spot where Mattie liked to sit, on a cushion, watching his cartoons. It is so long since I have thought about him properly. He is like a fairy-tale creature, the way I have described him to my son, and the way my son became him: a little Mattie to heal my heart.

'He really did exist? I did once have a little brother?' I ask Fiona. She looks at me kindly. 'Yes, I'll never forget Mattie.'

I kneel down and pick some bluebells. They are in Mattie's spot.

'It killed my mother,' I say softly. 'She couldn't give him up, so in the end she went to get him.'

Fiona nods. She puts her hand on my shoulder.

'Come on,' she whispers into my ear. 'Let's go back to my house. I've a bottle of wine we need to crack open.' She pats her belly. 'You'll have to drink most of it, though.'

I put my arm around her.

'I still can't believe you're pregnant,' I say as we waddle back through the shell of my old house and out to the car.

'I know, nor can I sometimes.' She giggles, just like she used to when we were fifteen.

Fiona reverses the car and then drives back onto the road. I see the bungalow we lived in after the house burnt down. I can see lights on behind closed curtains.

'A family from Dublin live there now. The Flynns. The children go to my school. They're very nice.'

'That's good,' I say. I don't care. I have no desire to revisit my family's place of exile. I couldn't get away from it fast enough when I was eighteen. I hope they are a happy family who live in it now, full of enough noise and laughter to drown out the ghosts.

We drive down the dusk-laden lanes back to Fiona's new house, and yet again I wonder what I am doing here, back in Sligo.

'Do you remember years ago you said I didn't belong here?' I suddenly ask my old friend.

She pauses, smiles, gripping the stirring wheel tightly.

'Yes I do. It was just before you went to London, wasn't it? We were eating ice creams by the river in Sligo. It was just after the Leaving Cert.'

She pauses, glancing over at me. 'It was the right thing to say then.'

'But not now?'

'No. You always have to come home sometime, Barbara, otherwise you can spend your whole life running away.'

It is when she says this I suddenly feel overwhelmed, so tired I could lie down on the road in front of us and just pass out. I have been running away, but not from a place, no, the place never actually mattered. It was from my memories. Fiona is right. It is time to come home.

Fourteen

By the time we return from Aigues-Mortes the sky is laden with murky storm clouds. As we drive into the yard I see Pascal leaning against the stable wall, smoking a cigarette. Two horses are saddled and ready to ride.

'It looks like someone's been waiting for you,' John teases.

I blush.

'I don't think they should go now. There's going to be a storm,' Olivia says. 'Besides, Barbara should stay here and help *Maman* with the dinner.'

'She has to have some time off, Olivia,' John says firmly, patting her arm.

She shrugs. 'Well they are stupid,' she says, getting out of the car. 'They will get wet, but I know there is no talking to my brother when he has got the heat of the hunt.'

And she looks at me and grimaces.

'That's not a very nice thing to say about your brother,' John admonishes her gently.

'But it is true.' She pushes her sunglasses up onto her head and regards me coldly. 'You watch yourself, young lady,' she warns me before going off into the house.

Matilda gets out of the car.

'Can I come with you? Can I ride a horse?'

'They're far too big for you darling.' John Finch picks her up and swings her in his arms. 'When you are better, we can take you to riding lessons in London.'

He puts her back down onto the ground. 'Go on, you go in to *Maman* Celeste. I'm sure she wants to give you a cuddle.' Matilda skips into the house. John puts his hands in his pockets. I look over at Pascal, who has gone back into the stables.

'Are you all right now?' John says quietly.

'Yes, thank you.'

'OK, well enjoy the ride.'

I walk over to the stables. My heart is thumping, all thoughts of Olivia and her evil-doing are suddenly secondary to my emotions. Pascal comes out of the stables with a rope in his hand, grinning broadly.

'*Bonsoir, Mademoiselle* Barbara. Would you like to go for a little trek before dinner?'

'Do you think we should? It's going to rain.'

He looks up at the sky.

'It will be OK for a while,' he says. 'There will be a storm later but not for a few hours. We have plenty of time.'

I pat Pedro and then Lilly.

'Go on,' he says. 'Get changed into your jeans and I will wait for you.'

Pascal gives me a *gardian* hat to protect my face, although the sun is hidden behind inky clouds. I clamber up onto Lilly, and I feel like I am in the Wild West, not the South of France. We start off along the road, and then he leads me through a gate, and we begin to amble slowly through the reed beds away from the cultivated land and towards the flat plains. The low-lying land has a whitish hue from the pervasive presence of salt, which I can taste on my lips. The heat has caused the land to crack up in places, yet other spots are fertile with small lagoons of seawater, home to clusters of pink flamingos. I see small groups of white horses too, their distinctive colour standing out against the reeds, which vary from dark green to silver, black, dark brown, red and mauve. Pascal points out a herd of black bulls in the distance.

'They look so different from the cattle at home,' I say to him. 'They look so wild.'

'Well, they are not strictly speaking wild,' Pascal says. 'All the bulls belong to someone. We have our own *manade* and our own brand. But you are right, they still enjoy more freedom than most cattle, roaming the wide expanses of our Camargue.'

He sweeps his arm wide to indicate the landscape.

I look at the lean black animals with white horns shaped like lyres.

'They have the head of a Minotaur,' I comment.

'Yes, they look like ancient bulls. Still we have the myths of the bulls, as an earthly force close to the gods and confronted by man in our traditional rituals.'

'The bull run,' I say.

'Yes, of course.' Pascal leans down and pats Pedro's neck. 'And we, the *gardians*, have allied ourselves with the horse to dominate the bull, a dark and primary force. We are the St Georges on our white horses vanquishing the dragon!'

He sits up and laughs, but there is an edge to his laughter, and it makes me remember what he spoke about in Nîmes and his reluctance to compete against the bull. 'Here in the Camargue everything is symbolic.'

He speeds up and begins to trot. 'Don't be worried,' he shouts, turning around. 'The horses can cross these marshes without hesitation, without stumbling on a stone or a stump, they know by instinct the best way.'

Lilly follows Pedro. I see tiny purple flowers, sea lavender Pascal tells me, another emblem for the *gardian*, in amongst the reeds, bright yellow bog irises, a blue mist of forget-me-nots, large daisies and bushes of small red flowers. In places the grass is glossy black and looks as if it has been burnt. It has the same look as some of our bogs. How strange to be in such a similar landscape, yet so far away. But the sky here is different. It is so wide, as if stretching away forever, and so full of light, even when there are rain clouds. There is a glare off it, which is almost blinding even when the sun isn't shining. It is pure exposure.

'I love this place,' Pascal says, as he slows down again. We tack through the sea meadows, Lilly and Pedro side by side.

'It's beautiful.'

'Nothing is ever the same here. It is a place of constant movement, where water rules.' He points over to the west. 'From there comes the Rhône, the great river, and it meets the sea. And so we have a coming together of river and sea worlds. Water, whether it is fresh or salt, is everywhere in the Camargue. And since we humans are mostly composed of water, it is a place that affects us deeply.'

He sighs. 'I love it, but I think La Camargue is a rather sad place. Like the land is weeping, and her tears are slowly washing her away, as she sheds little pieces of herself into the sea. One day I fear La Camargue may just flood completely, disappear under water and never resurface.'

'Do you paint the landscape?'

'No.' He laughs. 'It's odd, isn't it? You'd think I might. I am interested in people and situations as my subjects.'

'I liked the picture you showed me.'

'Thank you.' He nods, tipping his hat forward so it almost hides his eyes completely. 'I don't know why I paint, to be honest,' he suddenly says. 'It is foolish because it is not my life. My father keeps telling me this. My life is here, on the land, with the bulls and the horses, keeping our traditions alive. What place does a painter have here?'

'But isn't it what you love to do?' I ask shyly.

'Ah yes, but then maybe I am just indulging myself. My father let me study art in America so that I could learn English. He said it would be useful for tourism but he never thought I would get serious about painting.'

'You're lucky,' I say quietly.

He looks over at me, tips his hat back. His eyes are bright blue and astonished.

'How so, pretty Barbara?'

I blush deeply, but carry on.

'Because if I was as good at something as you are at painting, I would be so happy.'

'But of course you are good at something, everyone has a talent.'

I shake my head.

'You have just not discovered it yet. There must be something. I am assuming you don't want to be an au pair for the rest of your life. So, what would you like to do?'

I hate this question for I never know what to say in reply.

'I don't know.'

'Well, you have plenty of time to find out, you are very young.'

He lifts up the reins.

'And when you find out what it is, don't let anyone tell you what you should do. Follow your heart.' Then he winks at me and says, 'Thank you.'

'What for?' I ask, confused.

'For not telling me I am stupid to want to be an artist.'

'Why would I say that? You're so good.'

He laughs but his eyes are serious.

'Oh Barbara, you are a gem.'

I laugh as well, enjoying his pleasure in my remarks.

'Shall we have a canter? I think the horses would enjoy it,' he suggests.

Lilly and I chase Pascal and Pedro across the plains. I watch Pascal ahead of me, amazed at his understanding of Pedro – each shudder the horse makes, the movement of his ears, the pounding of his hooves, and his breath. Pascal senses it all. I can see why Hubert wouldn't understand his son's yearning to become an artist for even I can see that this land, these horses and even the bulls are in Pascal's blood. I have never seen such an assured horseman.

And for me, how wonderful it is to be back on a horse, to be in one movement with my animal, just me and her together streaking across the landscape. Freedom surges through me, and I feel empowered and positive. I shove thoughts of the Finches to the back of my mind.

The marshes turn to sand dunes and we come to a halt. Pascal jumps off Pedro and ties him to a wooden post at the end of a sandy path. He holds out his hands to me and I jump down, letting him put his hands round my waist and lower me to the ground, our eyes level for a moment. There is a current between us. It makes my lips dry and my hands shake.

'Shall I show you the sea?' he asks me, tying Lilly to the post.

'Oh yes.'

We walk through a little gateway and I look to either side of me, at swathes of dunes falling and rising, and little wooden stick fences lacing their contours. We walk up and down, slipping on the sand. Pascal takes my hand and helps me. We stand on top of a dune and then I see a ribbon of silver sea in the distance.

'It's so far away.'

'Yes, even though the tide is coming in, it is still a very big stretch of sand and a long walk to the sea,' Pascal says.

'Oh look.' He points up into the sky where a large bird is circling us. 'A buzzard,' he says, jumping down between two sand dunes and pulling me down with him. We are hidden from the sea and the horses and anyone who might be on the beach. Suddenly I hear a low raucous call, like the lowing of a cow, and it makes me jump into Pascal's arms.

'It's just some flamingos,' he whispers. 'They must be close by.' Without saying another word Pascal takes my head in his hands and begins to kiss me. The sand shifts beneath our feet as we move closer together. He stops, pulls back and takes my hands into his, looking earnestly into my face.

'I am falling for you,' he says, putting my hand against his beating chest. 'See, feel it.' He laughs wildly, lifts me up and spins me around. He then pulls me closer to him and kisses me, pushing his tongue inside my mouth. I kiss back eagerly, my breath is shallow and my mind is made up. I want to do this right now. In this very moment I want this man to make love to me.

We fall back onto the sand, giggling and excited. All my self-consciousness has dissipated. I trust him. It is insane, I know, for I have only known him a couple of days, and yet it is as if I recognise his taste, his smell. He takes my shirt off and undoes my bra, kissing my breasts.

'I am in love with you,' he whispers, cupping each breast with his hands. He pauses and we look at each other for an eternal moment. The feeling between us is so pure. I pull his shirt out of his jeans, kissing him all the time, a little shy still and not knowing quite what to do.

Pascal unbuttons my jeans and pushes his hand into my briefs, all the way down, until his fingers are touching me. I shiver.

'Barbara,' he moans, closing his eyes. My name sounds different, like the roll of a wave.

He fingers me, and the sensation this creates inside my head and my body is incredible. I have never felt like this before. I feel as weightless as a particle of sand, as hot as the centre of the sun, and as free and wild as the white horses on the salt plains of the Camargue. Eagerly, I begin to pull at his jeans. I want to see him. I want to touch him. But then he stops me, puts his hands around my waist.

'I want you so much Barbara,' he says huskily, 'but not here. I want it to be special.'

'It is special,' I whisper.

'I would like to take you somewhere nice. We can go to Arles for a meal and then maybe we could go to a hotel.'

A hotel! The idea is so romantic. I am completely taken by it.

'We could pretend the car has broken down and we have to stay the night.' He smiles, gently stroking my hair and pushing it behind my ears. 'But that is only if you want . . . I don't want to push you . . .' he stammers, his hands dropping down to the sand. 'I have never felt like this before. I fell in love with you at first sight, as they say. But you are so young, and you must have a boyfriend . . .' He looks away at the sea, unable to continue.

'I want to,' I reply, picking up his hand, and curling his palm around mine.

His face lights up. 'You're not such a shy little flower after all?' I colour and he laughs.

'I love it when your cheeks go the colour of pink roses,' he says. 'It is so sexy.' And then taking me in his arms again, he says, 'Tomorrow, I will organise it for tomorrow.'

'I don't have a boyfriend,' I tell him.

'You don't? Those Irish men must be blind.' He showers my lips with tiny kisses and then one long one. He pushes his hand back down my briefs and touches me until I am wet and throbbing. I am completely exposed but I don't care. I am in love and it is ecstasy. I let him pull my jeans off, and then my briefs, so that I am naked in the sand. He bends down and starts licking me and I cannot stop myself. I go over the edge.

Afterwards he surprises me. While I am still lying there, spinning in my bliss, he sits up on his knees and takes a small notebook and pencil out from his back pocket.

'Can I draw you?' His eyes are shining. I lie on my side, and bring my knees up to my chest, feeling suddenly shy again.

'Why?'

'*Parce que tu est très, très belle.* You are the most beautiful creature.'

Without asking me again he takes up his pencil and begins sketching. I lie in the hot sand, staring at the sky, watching the clouds darken. A spot of rain falls on my breast, then another and another.

Pascal puts his notebook away.

'Can I see it?' I ask, sitting up.

'It's not finished.' He puts my shirt back on, delicately buttoning me up.

'Tomorrow.'

Our eyes lock, and I feel my heart race again. Tomorrow. Yes, tomorrow I am going to lose my virginity in a hotel in Arles to a *gardian*, the first man I have ever loved.

'Come on, we better get back. I think the storm is about to start and it is dangerous to ride in a thunderstorm.'

'Why?'

'The horses' shoes. They are metal. We could get fried!'

He laughs boisterously and we run back through the dunes as the rain starts in earnest.

'Can you gallop?' Pascal asks me as he helps me get back onto Lilly. I nod. 'OK, then go Lilly, go!'

He slaps Lilly's rump and we take off like a silver arrow across the cracked earth which is already filling with water from the rain. We weave between marshy lagoons, under the threatening sky, and I can feel the horse thundering between my thighs, and the thunder beginning to roll in the air around me. The rain is so heavy now I can hardly see where we are going, but Lilly is on automatic pilot. I feel safe on her back.

We are just trotting into the yard when we see the first lightning bolt flash across the sky, and a moment later there's a boom of thunder. The horses side step and whinny in fright.

'*Vite*, quick, get down, Barbara. Let's get them in fast.'

We lead the two nervous horses into their stalls and unsaddle them. We are both drenched to the skin, our clothes sticking to us, our hair plastered on our heads, rain running down our cheeks. But we are giddy like two children, elated by our love.

Just before we go back into the house Pascal grabs me and we kiss again, deeply, passionately.

'Tomorrow,' he whispers as he traces my face with his fingers, giving me a final peck on my forehead before we go inside.

It is only when I go through the back door, out of the rain, and into the light of the kitchen to the group gathered around the table that I remember where I really am. The air is thick with cigarette smoke and pungent with the aroma of garlic. They are all staring at us as we drip onto the tiled floor: *Madame et Monsieur*, John and Olivia Finch, Matilda and Gareth.

I look at Gareth in shock. I had forgotten he was coming. He is leaning back in his chair, glass of wine in his hand, and laughing at us conspiratorially with Olivia. A flare of anger shoots up inside of me. Tomorrow I will tell Pascal everything and he will convince

John I am right. I will tell him what Olivia and Gareth are doing to Matilda, even if Olivia is his own sister, for it is the siblings who are the only ones who know each other best. We know which of us is good, and which is bad.

Fifteen

Three weeks into the summer holidays and still my father hadn't come. It was wet and windy, no difference from winter except the days were a little milder and a lot longer. More time to be bored. What made it even worse was Fiona and her family had gone to England for the whole summer to stay with their cousins in Yorkshire. Without the company of my best – in fact only – friend, the summer stretched ahead endlessly.

Mammy was in bad form. She had been in a foul mood since the priest called around ordering her to stop reading the cards, telling her it was the work of the devil. His shrill voice vibrated through the cottage and I put my hands over Mattie's ears so he wouldn't hear Father Doyle calling Mammy all sorts of bad things – charlatan, witch, black magic woman.

'I'm only helping people, Father,' Mammy tried to explain. 'It's harmless fun, that's all it is. I need to make a living.'

But the priest wouldn't listen to her. He tore into Mammy, saying what kind of example was she setting for her two poor illegitimate children, and if her father weren't a pillar of the community, he'd get the social services on to her. But he couldn't bear to shame the poor man.

That made Mammy mad and she lost her temper, telling him to

fuck off back to his sorry little hypocritical life and mind his own business. Father Doyle was shaking with rage. I could see him from upstairs, wagging his finger at Mammy, his face the colour of beet-root.

'Are you cursing me, Mrs?' He asked furiously. 'Has the power of the black Queen Maeve turned your head?'

'Just get out of my house,' Mammy said, opening the door wide and shooing him out. 'You are about as close to the spirit of Jesus as Queen Maeve herself.'

I took my hands off Mattie's ears and the two of us looked out of our bedroom window at the black figure of our parish priest scurrying away, half angry, half afraid. I wondered who exactly my mother's father was. And what it meant if the social services came. And I wondered what a curse was and what it had to do with Queen Maeve buried on the hill behind us.

The summer dragged on. We stopped going to church, and Father Doyle didn't come back, yet still the women came to get their fortunes told. We waited for Daddy but he never came.

In the second week of August a new family arrived in Culleen-amore. There was great excitement because they were from America. The father, Gerry, was a carpenter, originally from Sligo, and had always wanted to come home, but his wife, Sandra, and their three children – Blake, Ryan and Cindy – had spent their whole lives in New York. They came from a place which to most of us was the promised land, modern and full of action like on the television. For them Sligo and its slow pace was a shock.

Sandra was slim and athletic, with bright red hair, cut into a shiny angular bob.

'She's not a real redhead, out of a tin,' Mammy told me scathingly, but I was delighted for here was a good-looking American woman championing red hair.

The other mothers were wary of Sandra and she couldn't

understand them. 'They're slaves,' she told Mammy. 'Always cooking and cleaning and running after their damn husbands. And then they're asking if I know this cousin of theirs or some long-lost uncle in New York as if it's some kind of village. They drive me crazy.'

She liked Mammy, said her own mom had been a single mother, raising her and her four brothers on her own.

'Us redheads have to stick together,' she'd say, winking at me and sipping yet another mug of instant coffee in Mammy's kitchen. She stared out of the window, at the rain.

'Does the sun ever come out in this godforsaken place?' she'd exclaim, shaking her head.

Blake and Ryan were sixteen and fourteen, and spent most of their time learning to surf down at Strandhill or helping their father out at his workshop. Sandra would drop them off at the beach and then come up to our house with Cindy, who was just one year older than me.

'Cindy and Barbie!' Sandra would always say. 'You guys belong together, like the dolls.'

I hated it when she said that because I hated dolls, particularly Barbie. Sean Kelly had once called me 'Barbie' in school and asked me where my blonde hair was. I had given him such a smart punch on the face his nose had bled. I had been sent home for that, but no one had ever dared call me Barbie again.

Cindy had blonde hair like Fiona, but she was less of a tomboy. She brought dolls with her and wanted us to play with them. Often I would leave her and Mattie together playing families with his teddies and her dolls. Mattie loved Cindy because she always had sweets in her pockets, and he called her Candy instead of Cindy because that was what she called the sweets.

But there were two things that made me like Cindy. First, she liked Solomon, and always brought him doggie treats when they came to visit.

'You're so lucky,' she'd say. 'I want a dog so bad but my mom says we might go back to the States and what would we do with it then?'

'I'd look after it for you.'

'You would!' she said gratefully, patting Solomon on the head. 'I have to tell my mom. I want a puppy just like Solomon.'

Solomon lay down on the ground and offered her his belly. We both rubbed him furiously, until he was wriggling and licking us frantically in doggie delight.

The second thing that made me like Cindy was she was the reason I learnt how to ride. Now they were living in the country, Sandra said, Cindy should have riding lessons. But Cindy was nervous of going on her own and didn't know any of the other girls. Sandra asked Mammy if I could go as well. Mammy was hesitant, and I knew it was because of the money, but then Sandra said could she not pay for me, and Mammy could pay her back with a reading once a week? Mammy agreed and I was giddy with excitement. Suddenly the summer picked up.

Every morning I would walk down the lane and meet Cindy at the stables. We'd often get there so early they'd let us muck out and groom the ponies. Then the other children would arrive and we would start with a lesson in the arena. As we improved, they began to take us out into the fields and for longer treks. We both took to it like ducks to water. Cindy's favourite pony was a cheeky bay called the Fonz, like in the programme *Happy Days*. I think she liked him best because he had an American name like her. My pony was a dappled grey mare. She was called Saoirse, an Irish name meaning freedom, which she was to me.

We rode all morning, and at dinnertime we would reluctantly bring our ponies in and sponge them down lovingly. Then we'd head back to my house for dinner, all the time talking about ponies. After Mammy fed us, usually fish fingers, potato waffles and baked beans, we would hang out in my bedroom, reading and swapping *Jill* books – *Jill's Gymkhana*, *Jill's Pony Trek*, *Jill and the Perfect Pony*, *A Stable for Jill* – until Sandra arrived to collect Cindy.

So the summer had improved for me, but not for Mattie. Mattie had lost Cindy as his playmate, and now that we were both out all day riding he was left on his own playing with his toy cars. By the time we arrived back he was demanding and whingeing, which made us even more reluctant to play with him. Mammy thought we included him, but often we made him sit in the corner on his own, which resulted in crying. We told him he was bad to make such a fuss. In reality we were the bad ones for being so mean.

I was living every eight-year-old girl's dream, riding ponies every day with a pretty friend who said she wished she had red hair too. I was a little better than her at everything, and she wanted what I had – a dog, a little baby brother and a magical mother. I was saving up for a pony and Cindy thought that was great. She had lots of ideas for how I could make money – washing cars, collecting messages for our mothers, cleaning windows. I promised Cindy that when I got my pony I would let her ride it too. I said that when my daddy came he might buy me one for my birthday.

But in the end I never got a pony. Mammy just laughed when I asked for one for my birthday.

'Don't be daft, Barbara,' she said. 'Where would we put it? And besides, I'd end up looking after it. It's hard work you know, minding a horse. It's bad enough having a dog about the place, needing to be walked.'

Sandra and Cindy were there, having tea with us.

'Never mind poppet,' Sandra said, winking at me. 'If Cindy gets a pony when we go back to the States, you can come and stay with us and help look after it during the holidays.'

'Are you going back?' Mammy asked, handing her a mug of coffee.

'I keep on hoping!' Sandra exclaimed, rolling her eyes.

Cindy looked more disappointed than me about my dashed dream of a pony.

'What about her daddy?' Cindy asked. 'Won't he get her one for her birthday?'

'She'll be lucky to get a card off her father, so she will,' Mammy snapped back sarcastically, and then my mother blushed because she knew she had said something cruel. It had just spilled out of her mouth in frustration. All I knew was, I looked silly in front of Sandra and Cindy.

Sandra patted my arm and smiled at me kindly. 'Why don't you two girls go up and play with Mattie?' she suggested.

My mother looked at me and her eyes were watery, green like seawater.

'Sorry, Barbara,' she said.

Maybe it was guilt because of what she'd said about Daddy forgetting my birthday but Mammy got me the best birthday present she could afford: a pair of brand-new riding boots. They were long and black and made me feel like a proper horsewoman. Sandra and Cindy got me a pair of cream jodhpurs and now I looked as smart as Cindy when we went riding.

Those boots did something to me. When I was wearing them I felt a little bit of my heart harden. I would strut up and down the loft stairs in them like a soldier. I was proud and strong and so grown up now I didn't need a birthday card from my father. Those boots made me mean. That's what I like to think, because how else can I explain the way I treated Mattie.

He annoyed me so much that summer. Every afternoon he wouldn't give Cindy and me any peace, on and on he wanted to play families with us, or doctors, or schools like Fiona did.

'Go away, Mattie,' I'd tell him, and the little fellow would go into the corner and cry, looking at me through his tears.

'Baa baa,' he would plead. 'Baa baa, play with me.'

Cindy often took pity on him and gave him more sweets, but they were never enough because he wanted us to play with him more than he wanted candy.

'Oh just leave us alone, Mattie,' I would snap back at him.

And then one day I did something terrible. Cindy and I were lying on my bed, reading out loud to each other, and Mattie was pestering us yet again to play with him. He pulled at my elbows and I ignored him, and he pulled at my legs and I still ignored him. He sat down on the floor at the bottom of my bed and cried, and then he pulled the blanket hard so that all the books fell onto the floor. And without thinking, I kicked. In my smart new black riding boots, I kicked my little brother Mattie in the chest. It was such a forceful kick that he fell back on the floor and lay quite still. Cindy jumped up and looked at me in horror, and then she ran over to Mattie and picked him up. He was white in the face and quiet. He had stopped crying. She cuddled him.

'Are you OK, Mattie?'

I lay on the bed, not moving, my legs stretched out like stiff poles, my feet throbbing inside my boots.

Cindy looked at me again, and although we were only little girls of eight, she knew I shouldn't have done what I did.

'That was bad, Barbara,' she said.

I sat up on the bed.

'He was annoying me,' I countered defensively.

'He's only little.'

From then on, Cindy insisted we play with Mattie every afternoon and, churlishly, I agreed. But before school started again and I could show off my new friend to Fiona and all the others, Sandra announced they were going back to New York. She couldn't bear the rain any longer; and besides, Gerry couldn't get enough work here.

'You should come out,' she told Mammy. 'You know you're welcome any time.'

Mammy thanked her, said she might, but I knew we never would. If we couldn't afford a pony, how could we afford to go to America?

Cindy never told our mothers about the time I kicked Mattie in my riding boots. Maybe she should have. I could have hurt him badly. But she wasn't a telltale.

When Cindy went back to America she was the only one who knew how bad I could be; and how good Mattie was. For only five minutes after I had kicked him in the chest, he had sat on my lap, kissed my cheek and told me he loved Baa baa.

'He's such a lamb,' Cindy said. 'Look, isn't he cute, like a little angel?'

And Mattie smiled at her sweetly, his blond locks tumbling over his forehead, and I tried to swallow my jealousy really hard.

Sixteen

We have a very fishy dinner, starting with huge prawns, *les gambas*, and pale green salad leaves, or what the French call *endive*. I have never been a fan of shellfish. I find it a little too graphic. The little heads and black beady eyes of the prawns turn my stomach. But tonight I eat with gusto, watching Pascal, and copying him as he breaks their heads and tails off and gobbles their fat bodies up.

Celeste follows this hors d'oeuvre with another regional dish: *rouille*, layers of potato and octopus in a rich creamy garlic sauce. I have never eaten octopus in my life but it is not as bad as I thought, although rather chewy. The garlic sauce is divine. I am ravenous after our ride.

'Did you enjoy yourself?' John asks, filling my glass with red wine.

'Yes, it was fantastic.'

I feel like I am glowing. My hair is now dry in the humid house, and curling like mad, but I don't care. I have changed back into my grass-green dress, for although it is pouring with rain outside we are not cold. Every now and again white light flashes across the room, and we hear a deep growl of thunder. Matilda makes a little scream and cuddles closer to her daddy, and poor Rafi burrows further under the table between our feet.

Everyone is washing dinner down with copious amounts of wine. The conversation is lively and in a mixture of French and English for Gareth's benefit. No one else seems to notice how close he is sitting to Olivia, how much they talk to each other on the side and how she looks at him. They are subtle, but I am looking for it, and I can see Olivia's infidelity as clear as day.

Maybe Olivia notices me watching them for while the others begin to move to the sitting room to drink coffee she asks me to take Matilda up to bed.

'You can go on to bed yourself,' she adds dismissively.

Everyone else is too preoccupied in chatter to notice what she has said. I try to catch Pascal's eye but he is in close conversation with John.

Matilda and I reluctantly trail up the stairs.

'Do you want to go and see the Black Virgin?' she asks me, as I tuck her into bed.

'Who's the Black Virgin?'

'She's a saint, and she lives in a cave full of red candles. Mama said she'd take me tomorrow. Do you want to come with us?'

'OK.'

I wonder who the Black Virgin really is. It reminds me of Maeve, sleeping eternally in the cairn on top of Knocknarea at home, our own Black Queen, though certainly not a virgin.

I turn on the nightlight and switch off the main light. Suddenly there is a crash of thunder and the room is lit up by a shaft of lightning. I look through Matilda's closed window. The sky is white for an instant, then navy, and I can see forked lightning in the distance.

Matilda scrambles out of bed. She takes my hand.

'I'm scared. Will you stay with me?'

'Sure, Matilda. But you have to try to go to sleep.'

'It's hard because of the storm.'

I make her get back into bed, pull the covers up and stroke her forehead.

'Why don't you dream about some of your angels? Think about cloudland.'

'OK.' She closes her eyes and then opens them again, looking at me like Mattie used to.

'Barbara.'

'Yes.'

'I took the pills.'

'You did?'

'Yes. Daddy told me to.'

I sigh. Why couldn't I get John Finch to believe me?

'Don't worry about it. Soon you'll be better, I promise.'

'You do?'

Matilda smiles weakly, and I lean down and kiss her forehead. She is a different girl to me now. No longer an inconvenience. She is mine to protect; all mine.

'Yes, Matilda, I promise I will help you get better. Now close your eyes and go to sleep.'

I must have fallen asleep myself because the next thing I know I am woken by a loud bang, and the room is lit up by a blinding white light. At first I think there is a fire, and I sit up with a start, my hand to my throat in terror. But then I remember where I am, lying on the end of Matilda's bed, listening to a thunderstorm. There is no fire here.

I look at Matilda. She is fast asleep undisturbed by the thunder. I get up and walk over to the window, look out at the raging storm. I cannot believe it is still going on. I see prongs of lightning dancing across the flat plains, lighting up random areas, like electric fingers prodding the earth. I yawn and look at my watch. Two-twenty in the morning. I tiptoe across the room. It is odd neither

John nor Olivia came to check on Matilda, or maybe they did and just left me sleeping on the end of her bed. Like her pet dog.

The salty dinner has made me thirsty so I creep down the dark staircase to get a glass of water. It is on my way back upstairs I hear noises, and without thinking, maybe because I am still half asleep, I go to explore. There is a light on under the sitting-room door, where Gareth is sleeping tonight. I don't know why I do this, but I look through the keyhole, expecting to see nothing. To my surprise I have a clear view of Olivia sitting on the couch. She is talking to Gareth. I cannot hear what she is saying, but I can see the expression on her face. She is crying. It takes me by surprise for I have never seen Olivia look like this. Her face has dissolved and is vulnerable. It strikes me how like a little girl she looks. Gareth has his back to me, but he leans forward and puts his arms around Olivia.

How could they? Olivia's husband and child are in the same house, and her parents. How could they be so blatant? To see Olivia sobbing her eyes out in the arms of her husband's best friend is a revelation. She doesn't give a damn. It is as if she wants to be found out. Why, I think to myself as I creep back upstairs, trying not to splash water out of my glass. Why?

I am on my way up to the attic when a light flicks on below me. I look down from my hatch, and I see John coming out of his bedroom. I begin to panic for I am sure he is going to go downstairs and discover his wife and his best friend together. I hesitate. Should I go down and warn him? But instead of going downstairs he walks across the landing, opens Matilda's door and peers in as if he is checking something. He pauses and then he goes into her room. I sigh with relief.

I fall into my bed with exhaustion, my head spinning with so many images from the day: angels and babies, Mattie's eyes, Pascal's eyes and his lips, the feel of Lilly between my thighs, pounding across the Camargue, flashes of lightning in a dark shadow-filled house, and Olivia's tear-stained face, its openness as she talked to Gareth, an expression I had not seen her share with anyone else. Her eyes follow me all the way to sleep and my scattered dreams.

I wake suddenly and still the storm rages on. The rain hammers on the roof of the attic, lightning illuminates the room, blinding me for an instant, and the thunder bangs down upon my head; but there is another noise too, like the sound of an animal screaming in pain. I jump out of bed. Maybe Rafi got caught outside in the storm and is hurt. I open my hatch and clamber down the stairs. But on the landing I realise it isn't Rafi, for the noise is coming from Matilda's room.

I open the door and see Matilda shuddering on the floor. I run towards her, but John is there, and he puts out his arm to stop me, hold me back.

'It's all right, Barbara,' he whispers. 'She'll be all right, she's just having a seizure.'

I look at my little six-year-old charge in horror, as she thrashes around, her pupils dilated, her chubby arms swinging out, her tongue lolling out of her head, her chin wet with drool.

'The best thing is to put her on her side, on the floor,' John says. 'She'll be OK in a minute.'

Lightning flashes across the room so that it looks as if Matilda is dancing to a strobe light, her body twisting backwards and forwards, her face contorting. I look for her inside her little tormented body. I search for the little girl who is well, and then I see a glimmer, a tiny hint of recognition in her eyes, as she slowly comes into focus and sees me. And when she does, it stops. When Matilda Finch sees her guardian angel she is well again. And her guardian angel is me.

Seventeen

I am a tourist in my own hometown. Nearly everything has changed, apart from the mountains and the sea. Sligo is bustling, and busy, with cosmopolitan cafés serving cappuccinos, and shopping centres full of trendy high street stores, swanky hotels and swish restaurants. There is even a fancy lingerie boutique, where I toy with the idea of applying for a job, and decide against in the end. I have already spent too many years measuring strange women's breasts and doing window displays of g-strings, bras and panties.

Fiona enthuses about how the town is booming and the new road to Dublin.

'There's no need to be going up to Dublin anyway,' she declares, 'for everything you need is here, right here in Sligo.'

But I am sad to see some of the changes, such as Hargadon Brothers closed down. It was our haunt: Fiona, Murtagh and I. It seems such a short time ago, the three of us would sit in one of the snugs sharing two pints of Guinness between us, we were so broke.

I cling to the past for I feel lost in the present, listless and anxious. The first week Fiona is still at work, and I shuffle around her house, drinking coffee, and staring out the window, enchanted by the changing colours of the sea and the clouds casting shadows on the mountains.

They are so close, I think, so close to heaven.

Then the telephone rings and I feel my pulse quicken. It is Fiona, reminding me what to eat for lunch, and to relax. It makes me worry. I think back to the conversation I had with Pascal when we went riding in the Camargue, and how certain he was that he wanted to be an artist. I envied him his vision.

Always I remember my conversations with Pascal – so few as they were. They have marked me more than fifteen years with my husband.

I am forty years old, and I still don't know what I want to do. It's hard to explain this to someone who has a dream. Fiona has always wanted to be a teacher.

'You must want to do something,' she says, filling my glass with wine and smiling at me generously. 'It's just you don't believe you can do it. Come on, tell me, what is it?'

But I shake my head, and she thinks I am too shy. But the truth is, I don't know what I am going to do. Now I no longer have a little boy to raise and protect, I have no purpose.

I meet Jim. He is older than Fiona, with a thick head of curly hair, a jolly smile and kind hazel eyes. He is full of ideas for me. His friend needs a secretary. Can I type? Another friend needs a salesperson, great perks. Can I drive? What about catering. There's an opportunity to take over someone's thriving business. Can I cook? I am useless. But still this doesn't put Jim off. Both he and Fiona are sure they can help me, and when I mention that maybe I should go back to London, they tell me to shush and have patience. I can stay with them as long as it takes for my house to be built because I have come home, and I am meant to stay.

'You can't go, Barbara,' Fiona coaxes me. 'You haven't given it a chance yet. Besides, you're going to be a godmother soon.' And she pats her belly proudly.

'I don't deserve it.'

'Of course you do, you're my best pal.'

And then she gives me a present – a deck of oracle cards called 'Healing with Angels', which she says might help me decide – smiling benignly at me, patting my hand so full of love and patience I wonder how I have coped without her all these years.

I have to walk. I go for long, lonely strolls along the beach, letting the wind rip into me and pull at my hair, and I walk up the lane past our bungalow where the Dublin family live, and to our old ruin, which is swiftly becoming my new house. I should be excited to stand and look at my site, the architect's plans in my mind's eye, envisaging my new home to be. But instead I fret. Is this such a good idea? Will it just make me depressed to live in the spot where my family died? I cannot stop thinking of Mammy.

I climb Knocknarea, clamber on to the top of Maeve's cairn and squat on its roof, fingering the rocks about me. I am filled with regret. I wish so hard my mother was with me, and the feeling of loss is more powerful than it ever was. Mammy has been dead for close to twenty years and yet it is now, when I am nearly her age, I start to grieve. I had shoved the event of her death into a back room of my mind in London, and I had been too afraid to open the door. Now I cry, all alone on top of the Black Queen's cairn. Now I miss her and ask for her help.

There are so many things I wished I had told her, and now of course it is far, far too late. I close my eyes and smell the air, and know I am home. How different it is from anywhere else, the way it tastes so fresh and sweet in my mouth and nostrils. I can hear Mammy telling me the story of the 'Tain' and the way she described Queen Maeve's obsession with the bull and how she was prepared to kill men to get it. 'The red hatred and the black woman wailing,' she kept repeating.

I open my eyes and look out at Culleenamore Strand, hypnotised by swathes of silver sea running through the red sand edged with black seaweed. I look further out at blue Ben Bulben, and west to the Atlantic. I hear a voice.

I am right here. I have never left you and I can never leave you.

I know I have heard it before but I cannot think when, although I know what it means.

I put my hand into my pocket and feel the hard edge of the box of Angel Cards Fiona gave me. I take it out, open it and put the cards into my hands. I shuffle them and one falls out. I flip it over and see a picture of a woman sitting on her own in a ruined house, a big hat hides her face and her head is in her hands. She is crying. Through the glassless windows behind her are the blue sea and green and brown mountains. And beside her is a transparent angel, reaching out. The card is called Guardian Angel. I read: 'You are not alone. You drew this card as a love letter from your guardian angels who want you to know: *We are right here. We have never left you and can never leave you.*'

My guardian angels take me by each hand and they lead me down the mountain, and each step I take I say goodbye to my mother; and she tells me, 'Stay, Barbara, stay in Culleenamore for me.'

The next day Fiona takes me to the seaweed baths in Strandhill. It is a beautiful sunny day and the landscape has never looked more stunning.

'Jesus, when the sun shines, you just can't beat it here, can you?' Fiona says, as we sit on the sea wall drinking smoothies from the new juice bar on the front. I look at the sparkling sea and the surfers coasting along the rip currents, and I agree with her. Fiona glances at her watch.

'OK, in you go.'

'Can't you come as well?' I ask, finishing my juice.

'No, I can't, not this pregnant. Go on, I'll meet you in the pub in fifty minutes.'

I lie in a tub full of seaweed, the colour of my eyes, and melt into the brown salty water. I wrap seaweed around my thighs, my belly, my chest and my hair, and sink, sink, sink. The water is hot and the seaweed is warm and slimy, but soothing. Its long flat leaves cling to my perspiring skin, compressing me into a cocoon of healing green energy. And when I have let go of my body, my mind finally relaxes, and it is then, in one instant, I know what I must do. I see a picture. It is Celeste, of all people, with her heart-shaped face, cupid lips and childlike eyes – her sun-creased face the only trace of her age. She is smiling at me, and is handing me a bunch of lavender.

'*Pour toi, petite Barbara,*' she says. '*Lavandula latifolia, l'aspic de Provence pour le médécin. Tu es une guérisseuse, ma fille.*'

Now I remember this moment. I remember she called me her daughter.

Fifty minutes later I emerge from my seaweed bath into a different world. I stride with purpose across the sunny car park, past the hot glaring cars, past the golf course and the sound of golf clubs whipping through the air. I can feel the power of my body as I move. I know what I want to do. I am getting stronger day by day. I am a woman with intention, like my mother.

Eighteen

I am standing on the roof tiles, and the heat from the fire is burning the soles of my feet.

'Jump!' they shout.

I see them in a ring below me – Fiona's mother and father, the Reillys, Dr Flynn and Solomon barking and barking.

'Jump!'

But I shake my head, tears from the heat streaming down my face. I can't jump, because I have to go back. I have forgotten Mattie.

I kneel down and look through the window. Black smoke puffs into the room under the door frame and fills the space. It is hazy and suffocating in there, oxygen being squeezed out by the smoke. The fire rages on the other side of the door. I can hear wood splitting, the house cracking up. Where's Mammy?

I push my head back inside the room, coughing and choking, trying to breathe, trying to speak.

Mattie sits up in his bed. He sees me. But there is someone between us, a creature, half woman, half beast, dancing. She twists and turns writhing with the smoke in a terrible *danse macabre*. She looks at me and her eyes are red burning coals, red hatred. She wails piteously. Her skin is charred, peeling off her face, her arms and bare legs revealing more black skin underneath. She is a dark being from the other world, and although I am only nine I know she must be an angel of death. She is black Queen Maeve back from the grave.

I sit up suddenly. My breath comes in short rasps. I feel as if someone has punched me in the stomach. The storm is over, but it is still raining. I hear it on the roof of my attic room and smell the dampness in the air. I shiver and get up, putting on a jumper. Then I sit cross-legged on the bed, and stare into space. Mammy would explain all this to me: why it is I am looking after a little girl with eyes like my brother's; and why it is I have to save her. I have no choice.

I go downstairs. There is no one in the kitchen. I put a pan of water on the stove to boil and hunt inside the cupboards for a tea bag. The room is still shuttered but it suits me to move around in the half-light. I'm not ready to face the light of the day. I hear the hall door slam, then footsteps.

Pascal comes in. His hair is wet from the rain, flattened against his head, and his skin shines with moisture. His eyes look even bluer in the gloomy room.

'Good morning, Barbara.'

He walks over and puts his arm around my waist so naturally, so easily, as if we have known each other all our lives. He kisses me on the forehead. I blush, my hand shakily taking the boiling water off the stove.

'Careful,' he says, moving out of my way.

'Do you know where I can find some tea?' I ask him.

'Sure.'

He opens a cupboard and takes out a round tin, opens it.

'Breakfast tea?'

'Yes, thanks.'

He looks at me, his head to one side.

'Are you all right?'

I pour the water over the tea bag in the cup. I am still half in the disturbed world of my dreams and the nightmare vision of last night: Matilda writhing on the floor. And the look she gave me. I cannot forget that look.

Pascal puts his hand on my shoulder.

'Barbara, what's wrong?' he asks me gently.

I can trust him. I know I can. I burst into tears. He puts his arms around me and lets me cry into his neck. He smells of hay, and lavender, and it soothes me.

'Are you missing your family? Do you want to go home?'

I shake my head, pulling back, wiping my eyes with the back of my hands.

'What is it then? What's wrong? Has my dreadful sister upset you?'

I feel so out of my depth. I need someone to help me.

'It's Matilda,' I whisper.

'What about Matilda?'

'She had a seizure last night.'

'Ah . . .' He nods, switching on the coffee machine. 'Yes, that is very upsetting. The poor little thing. It is hard to remember a time when my niece wasn't sick. My sister is desperate with worry over it. You may not think so, but she is. We're all worried. It seems the doctors cannot tell us what is wrong. They can only contain the symptoms. They can't cure her.'

I sit down at the kitchen table, my head is pounding and my hands are trembling.

'I think something terrible is happening.'

My voice emerges cracked and hoarse.

Pascal sits down opposite me. He picks up my hand, plays with my fingers.

'Tell me.'

I take a deep breath and look into his eyes. Just looking at him makes my stomach flutter, and there is a part of me which wishes I could forget all about Matilda, and concentrate on just him, on being in love with him.

'I think Matilda isn't really sick.'

Pascal looks confused.

'What do you mean? She's been sick for over two years now. Olivia and John are constantly taking her to hospital.'

'She told me the pills make her sick.'

'Matilda is a little girl, Barbara. Of course she is going to say something like that. No child likes to take medicine.'

Pascal lets go of my hand and shakes his head. Still I plough on.

'I think there must be some kind of drug in them which makes her have the seizures, because when she stopped taking them she was all right.'

'What do you mean when she stopped taking them?'

I colour, uncomfortable by my confession, but I can't stop now. I have to tell him everything. He is my only hope, the only person who can help me.

'I stopped giving them to her the day before yesterday and she was fine. She felt better. She didn't have a fit until after Olivia gave her the pills again.'

'What is it you are saying, Barbara?'

I look at Pascal. His expression has gone from relaxed bewilderment to fierce concentration.

'Someone is making her sick on purpose.'

'Who exactly would want to do that?'

I can't say it, possibly because I can't quite believe it. Her name is on the tip of my tongue. Olivia, your evil sister, but it is too hard to do it.

'One of her parents,' I whisper.

Pascal says nothing for a moment. He pours himself a small dark expresso and then drinks it in one gulp. He takes out his cigarettes and offers me one. I shake my head. He lights his cigarette, and only then after he has exhaled for the first time does he speak.

'Barbara, I know you find it hard to like my sister, but she would never do anything to harm her own child. I know this. I grew up with her. She has suffered a great deal recently and this is why she is difficult, and this is why she has not been well herself. And as for John, well it is quite clear he is devoted to Matilda. A sick child is every parent's nightmare; why on earth would my sister and her husband actually want to make their own child sick?'

'I don't know.' I shake my head tearfully, feeling ashamed and confused, for now I have lost Pascal. Surely he must hate me for making such accusations?

'You are shocked by what you saw last night, and you look exhausted.'

'I don't want Matilda to die.'

My voice trembles and I can feel tears pricking my eyes again.

'Barbara, you are being dramatic.' Pascal leans across, squeezes my hand reassuringly and then says with conviction, 'Matilda is not going to die. She will get well again, she will.'

He picks up my hand, brings it to his lips and kisses it.

'I know you are not speaking out of meanness or being vindictive, but you are wrong, Barbara. No one is trying to kill Matilda.' He laughs suddenly. I can see he is trying to lighten the mood. 'Although she can be a little brat sometimes!'

And he brings his hand up to my face and wipes my tears away. He leans over and kisses me on the lips. I melt into the safety of his touch, but I am torn. Why can he not believe me?

'I have to go to Montpellier today and I might not be back until late. So would you like to go to a restaurant in Arles tomorrow night? Would you still like to go out to dinner?'

I look at him hazily. I imagine him touching me.

'Yes,' I reply shyly.

I crave him now. I am aching with desire.

'Good.' He gets up and ruffles my hair.

'Maybe you should go back to bed this morning, get some more rest, you look tired.'

'What about Matilda?'

'If she had a fit last night, I should think she'll be in bed most of the morning.'

He pauses by the door. 'Try not to think about it all too much Barbara. You are tired and emotional. It is hard to look after a sick, demanding child.'

He walks back towards me. 'Here,' he says, pulling a chain out from inside his shirt. A small pendant hangs on the end of it. He takes it off and shows it to me.

'This is *la croix de la Camargue*,' he says. 'See, a cross of the Camargue for the brave, piercing through the centre of a heart, and resting in an anchor of safety: *foi, charité et espérance* – faith, charity and hope.'

He puts the necklace on over my head.

'Have faith, hope and be kind to yourself.'

I finger the ends of the cross. Each point ends in three short prongs.

Pascal touches my finger with his. 'The ends of the cross represent the pole we use when we herd the bulls. You see everything here is a symbol.'

He kisses the top of my head and then he leaves.

I sit at the table, holding the cross in my hands, feeling its warmth from where it has been lying against his skin. I cling on to it. I try to have faith.

Celeste comes into the kitchen and starts gabbling to me in French.

'*Pardon, pardon.*' She slaps her forehead with her hand. '*J'ai oublié que tu ne parles pas français.*'

She opens the shutters and the windows, but the room is still dim. She shakes her head, looking at the rain, shrugs her shoulders and smiles at me. I smile back, all the time holding the cross in my hand. Celeste bustles around the room preparing the breakfast but I hardly notice what she is doing for I am hypnotised by my love for her son.

Matilda sleeps half the morning. I lie on my bed listening to Kate Bush on my Walkman. The hounds of love are pulsing through my head, reminding me of Solomon, and every song I listen to is a message. There are big skies with clouds shaped like Ireland, witches being hunted, ghosts watching me, which I can't see or hear, and mothers standing for love. The lyrics seem to be written for my ears alone. I close my eyes and let the music lift me up.

I am flying around my room like one of Matilda's imaginary angels. I perch on the pile of boxes in the corner of the attic, and my wings close behind me. I look down at the floor and sun spills through the small window casting a shadow in front of me. I look like a large bird of prey, watching and waiting. One of my feathers flutters down onto the floorboards. It is white and soft down, like a swan's feather. I pick it up and tickle my chin. I spread my wings and take off again. In one easy leap I am through the window and out in the rain, which sweeps across my face. The land is obscured below me, flooded and fertile, abandoned by man and beast. Only the birds remain. My angel self flies me across the reed beds and the salt plains, my winged shadow gliding across the pink water, until we reach the sea. Up we go. High in the sky, and until all I can see in every direction is the ocean. I look down at the choppy waves, and with my eagle's eye I can see a boat bobbing up and down. It has no rudder, no oars and no sails. It is directionless. In the boat are four women. They look up at the sky in a plea. They kneel down, and they pray, to me.

When Matilda wakes she is cranky and demanding, insisting she go with her mother and Gareth to Saintes-Maries-de-la-Mer on an outing to see the Black Virgin.

'Barbara has to come with me,' she whines.

'Of course she doesn't,' Olivia replies, irritated.

'Have you been to Les Saintes?' Gareth asks me.

'No.'

'Well, we should take her then, Olivia.' Gareth pats her arm. 'Barbara should see the church, and Black Sarah.'

Olivia sulks, pulling another cigarette out of Gareth's packet and lighting up. I look over at John, who is eating a piece of cheese, saying nothing.

'Are you coming, Finch?' Gareth asks loudly.

John looks at him oddly.

'No thanks. That place gives me the creeps. No, I think I'll stay here and rest. I didn't get much sleep last night.'

I catch his eyes and look away quickly. They pierce me. I wonder what he might be thinking. Is he remembering what I told him in Aigues-Mortes? Maybe he is a little suspicious of his wife and Gareth, for the next moment he says, 'But you should go, Barbara. You can look after Matilda.'

The rain hasn't let up. Gareth drives us in his smart hire car. We speed down the wet roads, across water-logged marshes. Now it is raining, the landscape appears similar to an Irish bog but even darker. The reeds have turned black, and look as if they are burnt. I can see yellow irises, michaelmas daisies and red poppies, all illuminations of colour in the dark grasses. The odd white Camargue horse stands out against the murky landscape, trying to shelter under a tree.

'The poor horse,' Olivia comments. 'Someone should bring him in.'

The grey clouds have turned the sky indigo and although there is so much space here, such a big sky and such a vast flat expanse of land, it is oddly claustrophobic. I wonder why. And then the answer occurs to me. It is impossible to see a way out.

We drive into Saintes-Maries-de-la-Mer. The rain is still cascading from the sky as we drive through the streets, past squat sun-bleached buildings, towards the old stone church rising above the terracotta rooftops dominating the small town. It looks like a fortress rather than a church. We park and run across the square, our jackets over our heads to protect us from the rain, and Gareth carrying Matilda in his arms.

Don't touch her, I want to growl. But I am powerless. I am only the au pair.

We enter the church through a small door in the side of the nave. There are clusters of tourists around the entrance, and we walk around them, heading straight for the crypt glowing with candle-light. Hanging above the low round arch at its entrance is a black medallion with an image of the Saintes Maries in a boat. Gareth pauses, standing next to me.

'The story goes that when Mary Magdalene was exiled from Egypt, after Jesus died, she ran away with two other Marys: Mary Salome and Mary Jacobe (the mother of James) and her old Egyptian maidservant, Sarah. All of them at the mercy of the sea in a boat without oars or sails were said to have miraculously come ashore in this part of the delta. Mary Magdalene moved on to spread the gospel but the two Marys and Sarah were too old to travel further and stayed here. It is said they lived in a little cabin, which was built out of branches, reeds and earth, in the Camargue style.'

He points up to a large arch in the choir of the church. I see a big wooden painted box.

'They are the shrines of the two Marys. Inside are supposed to be their bones. Twice a year the shrines are lowered down and brought to the sea along with the statue of Sarah. It is a coming together of the fishermen from the village, the local herdsmen and the gypsies. The settled people venerate the Marys, who are supposed to be able to cure the sick; and the travellers worship the gypsy saint, Sarah. It is a fascinating festival, a load of hogwash, but interesting all the same.'

The heat from all the candles is fierce as we walk down into the crypt. I see Black Sarah in the corner, surrounded by votive offerings and candles. She looks like a toy doll, dressed up in a resplendent gown with crosses hanging off it, a crown and jewels. Her little doll's head is tiny within her huge garments. She looks ridiculous, not at all precious or regal.

'She is the Black Virgin, a combination of the pagan Sarah, and the whore priestess Magdalene,' Olivia speaks. I feel her standing close to me. She smells of expensive perfume, exotic and musky. 'She is good and she is bad.'

I look at her, and Olivia holds my gaze. Her brown eyes harden, flecks of clove black darkening the irises.

'Unlike the Virgin Mary, Sarah is a woman who represents the power of women. Her heart is black, not white. For it is like charcoal, a life which has been lived, full of burnt promise.'

Olivia's voice trails off and she walks away. Gareth follows her. He puts his arm around her waist and she leans into him, like the parasol pine swaying into the wind. I wonder how they can be so obvious as if Matilda and I are blind. And yet there is a fragility to Olivia, beneath her hard, outer shell, which intrigues me.

Matilda slips her hand into mine. We stare at the Black Sarah doll.

'Do you think she is real?' Matilda asks me.

'No, of course she's not real. It's just a statue.'

'But do you think Sarah really existed?'

'Maybe, I don't know.'

'I want to light a candle.' Matilda tugs at my arm, pulling me towards the rows of little red votive candles on either side of Black Sarah. I put five francs into the box and then light one of them.

'Shall we say a prayer?' Matilda asks me.

'OK.'

I watch her close her eyes and whisper something silently. I look at the flickering red lights in front of me and feel the heat of fear in my heart for Olivia Finch. I close my eyes for a moment and pray to God to help me save Matilda, for apart from divine intervention I am on my own. Pascal and John don't believe me and there is no way I could get either of Olivia's parents to understand me.

Back out in the nave of the church we find ourselves looking at a wall of paintings. They are behind glass and there are lots of different sizes and styles but they are all about the same thing: sick children. Dozens of little oil votive paintings of sick children in bed, with their parents praying on their knees and the two Saintes Maries in their boat in the sky, on fluffy clouds like magic carpets.

Ex-voto, Eugene Priad, âge de trois ans, se trouvant gravement malade a été sauvé par les Saintes Maries . . . Ex-voto de Marie Bariavel, guérie miraculeusement le 25 Mai 1860 . . . ex-voto Marie Trophinette, guérie 1867 . . . ex-voto Marthe Marie Elisabet Benet, guérie le 18 Mai 1850 . . .

What is the same about the pictures is all the children get better, not one of them dies. They are lots of little miracles.

Matilda and I stare at the miniature paintings for ages. Neither of us speaks. I finger my *croix de la Camargue* necklace. Faith, charity and hope. The words spin around and around in my head. Which is the most important, I wonder.

Saintes-Maries-de-la-Mer has a strange atmosphere to it, which is not helped by the pouring rain. Apart from the old church, which is quite beautiful, the rest of the buildings are low, squat and dour. They cluster around the church and create a warren of slippery cobbled streets, a mixture of restaurants, souvenir shops and places selling riding boots and cowboy hats. There are hordes of tourists knocking into us in the narrow streets, their umbrellas poking us. Gareth and Olivia have linked arms and are hurrying down the street. We move as fast as we can behind them, the rain cascading down upon us. They turn suddenly into a patisserie, waving for us to hurry up.

'Jesus,' Gareth says, shaking his hair and spraying us with water.

'Watch it.' Olivia playfully swipes at him.

'Let's get hot chocolates and crêpes,' Gareth announces.

'Yummy!' Matilda clasps her wet hands.

Olivia orders in French, and we sit around a table. Olivia is facing Matilda, and Gareth is opposite me.

'Are you OK, Matilda?' Olivia asks her. 'You're not cold?'

'No, Mama. I'm not cold.'

I stiffen. The woman is unbelievable. How dare she pretend to care? I am not convinced by her concern.

'So, how do you like France?' Gareth asks me.

'It's lovely,' I reply tersely.

He looks at me with a puzzled expression on his face and then smiles at Matilda, sticking his tongue out at her in fun.

Our crêpes arrive. They are steaming hot, melted chocolate drips out of them onto the plates.

'It is so unusual for it to rain like this in the summer,' Olivia says. 'In the winter it can be terrible here. The wind, it's awful, can blow your head off. But in the summer it is hot, all the time.'

'I think it will stop raining soon,' Gareth says. 'By the time I get to St-Tropez the sun will be back out.'

Olivia frowns.

'What time are you going?'

'Not till later.'

There is an uncomfortable silence. I see Olivia push her hand under the table, and I know what she is doing. She is touching him.

'Maybe I can stay one more night,' Gareth speaks up.

Olivia brightens. I look away, embarrassed by her lack of subtlety.

'Where's Pascal today? He could have come with us,' Gareth suddenly says, gulping down his hot chocolate.

'He has gone to Montpellier to see Violette.' Olivia smiles slyly, looking over at me. Then she notices it, my pendant. Olivia sees the symbol her brother has adorned me with. She is surprised, I can tell.

'Who's Violette?' Matilda asks, her mouth full with crêpe.

'Violette, Violette . . .' Olivia holds my gaze, smiling cruelly. 'Why, Violette is my dear brother Pascal's true love.'

My crêpe sticks in my throat, nearly choking me.

'Are you all right Barbara?' Gareth asks me, passing me a glass of water. Olivia ignores my discomfort. She carries right on.

'Violette is going to be my new sister-in-law, when my brother finally gets his act together and marries her.'

'And then will they have children?' Matilda asks excitedly. 'Will I have cousins?'

I get up, falling over my chair as I stumble to the toilet. I try to hold my tears back, but I am devastated.

'You're a stupid little fool,' I hiss to myself, sitting on the toilet seat, crying like a baby. I get up and look in the smudged mirror. My eyes are rimmed red, my skin blotchy. How could I possibly imagine someone like Pascal would be interested in me? I still look like a schoolgirl. Pascal is a man in his twenties. He is self-assured, experienced. Why on earth would he want to fall in love with me?

Besides we have only known each other a couple of days. All he wanted was a bit of fun. He didn't actually mean what he said. For God's sake why am I so upset? And yet, despite this shocking revelation, despite the knowledge of Violette, I still want Pascal to make love to me. It makes me feel sick inside.

We walk back to the car. The rain has died down and spots us now and again, but we can see blue sky pushing the clouds away. We pass the sea, grey and foaming, not so unlike my Atlantic. Rocky fingers of coastline reach out into the Mediterranean.

By the time we have returned to the *mas* the rain has stopped completely and there is not one cloud left. The heat has returned. The sky is a blank bright canvas of blue and the sun blasts down.

'I'm hot,' Matilda moans, as we pull up outside the house.

'Well, get into your costume and you can go for a swim,' her mother says.

'Are you going to join us?' Gareth asks me.

Olivia looks cross but she says nothing.

I only have Fiona's old bikini with me. A last-minute gift from my best friend when she discovered I had no swimming gear.

'You never know, they might take you on holidays,' she said, stuffing it into my case, the night before I left.

What would she think now if I were to tell her everything? Would she believe me? Of course she would. Best friends never doubt each other.

Fiona is smaller than me, and I am spilling out of the yellow and blue top. I button up a cardigan over the bikini, suddenly self-conscious. I am still shocked by the revelation about Violette. Part of me is relieved Pascal has not returned from Montpellier. At least I don't have to face him tonight. Yet there is another part of me which is dying to see him. Maybe he was going to Montpellier to break it off with Violette because of me? The idea is silly, I know, but I cling to it for I want everything to carry on, no matter what.

I want to go to a hotel in Arles and I want to lose my virginity to a *gardian*.

Everyone is by the pool apart from Celeste. I walk over to the only free sunlounger, next to John.

'Did you enjoy Saintes-Maries-de-la-Mer?' he asks me, his eyes hidden by dark glasses.

'It's an odd place,' I reply.

'It's a bit spooky, isn't it?'

He takes off his glasses and stares at me intently. His eyes are penetrating me. They are icy blue and make me shiver in spite of the heat. I clutch my book in my hands and take off my cardigan. I can feel John's eyes upon me, so I look at Matilda in the pool. I get up to swim and Gareth wolf-whistles. Olivia is furious.

'Barbara, can you go inside and help *Maman* with the dinner.'

I stop in my tracks, my bare feet on the edge of the pool. She is behind me, and I am tempted to dive right in and splash her with water. I want to drown the bitch.

I turn around and she regards me haughtily. She is dressed impeccably in a tiny, polka-dot bikini, big white glasses, and a white turban on her head. She looks like a Hollywood starlet in the thirties.

'Aw come on Livie, don't be such a spoilsport,' Gareth calls from the pool.

Olivia ignores him. 'Go on, you had the day off as it is. My mother needs you in the kitchen.'

I turn on my heel and go back to the sunlounger, bending down to pick up my cardigan. John looks at me, but he says nothing. I bend down further, knowing I am giving him a splendid view of my breasts, but I don't care. If I can annoy Olivia by flaunting myself in front of her husband then I will do my best. I strut back into the house. Gareth and Matilda are splashing in the pool but I know both the Finches are looking at my body: its youth, its firmness, how ripe it is. I hope I have made Olivia jealous. I hope she sees her husband looking at me and wishes she were young again.

I put on jeans and a khaki shirt I bought in an army surplus shop in London. It is way too big for me, but I like the colour of it. As I approach the kitchen I can smell a mixture of garlic, herbs and roasting meat. It makes my mouth water. Celeste is singing in French. Her voice is as light and clear as a bell. When I walk into the kitchen she stops suddenly, looking shy and slightly embarrassed.

'Barbara? Have you come to help me?' she asks in French. I nod, and she smiles at me.

'You understand a little French then?' she asks.

I nod again.

'Come, come.'

I go over to the table, which is covered in chopping boards, stacks of knives, bowls, bunches of herbs and other ingredients. She puts some garlic into a mortar and indicates that she wants me to grind it.

We work well together, although we hardly speak. I find I am enjoying myself. Mammy and I have never cooked together. In fact Mammy never really cooks. It is always a chore to her. Food is functionally flung together so that we don't starve. For Celeste cooking is an art. What I learnt in one hour in a kitchen with a Frenchwoman was more than I had learnt my whole life, and it was to be the basis of all my culinary skills from that time forwards.

First we make aïoli to go with potatoes. After pulping my garlic with the pestle and mortar, Celeste adds a pinch of salt and pepper and an egg yolk. Then she shows me how to add a little olive oil at a time, so that we end up with a thick mush. Finally we squeeze half a lemon, and stir it into the mixture. I taste a little on my finger and it is divine.

'It's good, yes?' Celeste asks me in English.

'*Oui*,' I reply. '*Très bon*.'

Then she shows me how to make a lemon tart for dessert. I have never baked a cake, or a pie, or any kind of pudding my whole life but Celeste is a patient teacher. The lemon tart is in three layers. First we make the base, a kind of paste of flour, butter, sugar and milk. Then the filling is made. Celeste gets me to whip the egg yolks, sugar, lemon juice and lemon peel. We add fresh cream and then pour it onto the chilled base. At this stage Celeste puts the tart in the oven while we make the topping. Again she gets me to whisk the egg whites and sugar until my arms are practically hanging off. She takes the tart out of the oven, coats it with this meringue and then puts it back into the oven to brown.

I can see the meat in the oven is nearly ready. Celeste indicates the herbs she has used with the meat: rosemary and thyme. The aroma of all the food curls around the room making my stomach groan. Celeste pats me on the back.

'You are a keen little cook,' she says in French, 'unlike my daughter. She is good, but so lazy.'

I wonder if she knows I can understand her. I don't react, embarrassed she might say more. Celeste takes two wine glasses out of the cabinet and uncorks an open bottle of red wine. She pours us both a glass, and then raises it in the air.

'*Salut!*' she says.

'*Salut!*' I reply, sipping the wine and enjoying its plummy flavours.

We have nearly drunk two glasses of wine by the time we prepare the *tellines*. I am feeling a little light-headed, but relaxed. It is a nice sensation as if I am going with the flow. Celeste shows me where she has steeped the tiny shellfish in salted water.

'*Pour quatre heures*.' She holds up four fingers. She hands me a sieve and indicates I should sieve the shellfish, thoroughly picking out any small stones or alien crustaceans. Meanwhile she melts a large lump of butter and some oil in a frying pan. We pile the *tellines* into the big steaming pan and she puts a large lid on it.

'*Quinze minutes*,' she says, pointing at her watch and picking up her wine again. Then she points at a large bunch of parsley and a knife. I begin to chop away, little pieces of green herb sticking to my fingers.

Hubert comes into the kitchen and sniffs the air. He pats his stomach with anticipation, smiles kindly at me and, talking to his wife, he speaks in French.

'Is the little au pair helping you cook, my dear? She is very sweet, is she not? I think Matilda likes her.'

'Yes,' Celeste replies, chopping garlic for the *tellines*. 'She is different from all those other girls. And she is learning fast.'

I continue chopping parsley, pretending I don't understand, but my mind begins to race. I could tell Hubert and Celeste about Matilda. Maybe they would believe me? But how? I try to think of the French words to explain what is happening but my head is fogged by wine, and I can't think how I would express myself.

It is too late. Everyone else comes into the kitchen, drawn by the smell. Matilda is given napkins and I am given cutlery, and we are sent outside to lay the table.

In front of the house the sky is exploding. A few grey clouds have returned for the night. Bursting out from behind them, deep shades of orange, pink and gold illuminate the shadowy landscape. Matilda and I pause. We are hypnotised by the drama of the setting sun.

'It looks like a fire at the end of the world,' Matilda says.

The wine combined with the rich food makes me sleepy. I feel so tired from worrying about Matilda I cannot think any more. Pascal is missing from the dinner table. I try not to think why. I hardly notice Olivia and Gareth, sitting side by side, and their subtle flirtations; or the way Celeste and Hubert try to talk to me in broken English. I don't even notice John, how silent he is, slowly chewing his food and staring, not at his wife, but at me.

All I want to do is go to bed, and in the morning I hope things will be different.

Maybe John and Pascal are right, maybe my dislike of Olivia is blinding me and I am imagining things. For what woman would want to make her own child sick? But despite this reasoning, I feel a cold prickle down my spine and my instincts tell me different.

Your intuition is always right.

I see my mother's face, with hair like mine, and her long elegant fingers, sparkling with rings, shuffling the cards. She smiles and says, *Believe in yourself, Barbara.*

My intuition tells me not to leave Matilda alone. So instead of going up to my attic bedroom I lie down on Matilda's floor, like Solomon lay on mine, year in, year out, when I needed watching over. It is so warm I need no covers. I curl up on my side, not caring what the Finches might think if they come in.

I sleep, my knees up to my chest under Daddy's white dinner shirt. I dream of angels in aeroplanes, and Mattie and I flying outside, above the clouds and free, waving at the angels inside the aeroplanes, with faces all the same, the face of Matilda Finch. They are saying something to us, all of them in celestial unison, two words in high-pitched demand. 'Help me.' And in this dream I have another dream that I wake up and I am lying on the floor of Matilda's room. John Finch is standing over me, looking down. Is he looking at me, or Matilda? He is as silent and solemn as a statue. He is watching over us.

Nineteen

I am back in the hospital, running down the empty corridors. My heart is throbbing in my chest and I am falling over myself in fear. Where's Mammy? Her bed is empty. The sheets pulled back, the drip hanging limp by the metal bars of the bed. Where has she gone? Did black Queen Maeve take my mother as well?

I cry out in terror, but nobody hears me. All the nurses are gone. It is the middle of the night, and the hospital is deserted, as silent as a morgue. I keep running, sliding on the shiny floor, the magnolia walls of the corridor flashing by.

My heart jerks for I see her. Just ahead of me. Her long white gown trails behind her like a ghost, her feet are bare, and her hair is a red flag for me to follow.

'Mammy!' I call, but she doesn't hear me.

She disappears into a room. When I get there I look through the open doorway and see a crowd of people around the bed. Father Doyle, his stern face even more serious, and clutching his rosary beads, and I see Fiona's mother, a doctor with grey hair and several nurses fluttering around. My mother pushes through them all.

'Where is he? Where's my baby?' she screams.

My mother is like a being from another world. With super-human strength she pushes the nurses away as they try to calm her, and shoves the doctor back against the wall.

'Mattie!' she cries out. The sound is piercing and makes every-one in the room flinch as if scalded by the heat of her pain. She bends over her little four-year-old son. But his soul has gone. She knows this, only his body remains, his little burnt shell.

My mother bends over Mattie and starts licking him frantically. The doctor looks puzzled, the nurses are shocked and step back, the priest shakes his head. Only Fiona's mother is brave enough to try to stop her.

She puts her hand on Mammy's shoulder.

'It's too late, darling. It's too late, the poor lamb is gone. He's with baby Jesus now.'

My mammy groans but she cannot stop what she is doing. She continues to lick my brother. His head and his chest, his arms. She cannot stop and no matter how much they try to stop her, she pushes them away. I stand at the door and no one sees me. I look at Mammy and she reminds me of Solomon's mother when I watched her lick her new-born puppy clean. Solomon had just been born; and my brother had just died.

Twenty

Pascal is back from Montpellier. I hear him in the water, helping Matilda to swim. I can't look at him. I don't know what to think any more. I have missed breakfast, waking long after everyone, stiff and disorientated on Matilda's bedroom floor. I wonder who saw me there. Was it just Matilda? She says nothing now, too distracted by the fun she is having in the pool with her uncle.

I am back in Fiona's bikini. My head is sore from the wine last night, and I feel depressed from my terrible nightmares. All I want to do is get into the swimming pool and float. All I want is for everyone to leave me alone.

'Barbara, did you finish the ironing?' Olivia asks me.

'What ironing?' I reply churlishly.

'I left you a pile in the hall.'

'I never saw it.'

'Well, can you please finish it? You're not on holiday you know.'

'Don't be such a witch, Livie,' Gareth drawls, reclining next to her on a lounger.

'We're all enjoying the view, aren't we guys?' And he winks at me. I scowl back. Wasn't he supposed to have left for St-Tropez by now?

Pascal laughs and calls me, splashing water in my direction. I ignore him and look away. I catch John's eye. He has taken his sunglasses off and is staring at me.

'Come on, jump in!' Pascal calls.

I head towards the pool. Olivia gets up and stands in front of me. She is half my size, in her tiny polka-dot bikini. She hands me a towel.

'Please, do your job. When you are finished you can come back and swim.'

I drop the towel down on a chair.

'I don't need this. I'm not wet.'

She screws her eyes up at me. She is angry but controls herself. She doesn't want to show herself up in front of Gareth. I walk slowly back towards the house, in a long circuit around the pool. All the men are looking at me. I ignore Pascal who calls out to me from the pool again, and Gareth who wolf-whistles, but I look at John Finch and I try to speak to him silently.

Now, do you see? I am trying to communicate. Can you see how horrible your wife is? Don't you think she might be capable of what I am suggesting?

I know he understands me because his pale eyes bore into me. He cannot pull them away from my face.

I go into the kitchen. Celeste is nowhere to be seen. I find the ironing board, pull it out of the pantry and plug in the iron. I iron a couple of shirts and then go back in the hall to the downstairs bathroom. I hear the hall door open and look over my shoulder to see John Finch storming towards me as if propelled by another force, as if he is a charging bull. I am holding the handle, and he comes up behind me. Before I can react he has pushed me inside and shut the bathroom door behind him.

The bathroom is a large room. The floor is made of big old flagstones, and the sink is a huge porcelain object with big brass taps. There is a tall oak wardrobe in the corner of the room, full of linen and towels. There is just one tiny window in the room, with a grille on the outside. The room is cavernous, like an underground cell.

I look at John Finch in confusion, and then my heart begins to skip in fear for his eyes are pure red hatred.

'How dare you!'

John Finch's face is seething with white anger. I am frightened. I go towards the door but he locks it, stands in front of it.

'You are a nosy little so and so, and I've just about had enough.'

'John, Mr Finch, I . . .'

But our intimacy from the day in Aigues-Mortes has completely vanished.

'How dare you insinuate either Olivia or myself would wish to harm our own daughter? Do you know what could happen if you carry on saying things like that? If someone actually believed you, they might take Matilda off us . . . We could lose her.'

He slaps me sharply on the face. I put my hand to it in stunned slow motion. I am speechless, unable to talk. All I know is, Pascal must have betrayed my confidence. He must have told John what I said to him yesterday morning.

'You have no idea how much I have suffered.' John is practically screaming. 'I have to watch my wife cavorting with my best friend, right in front of my nose, and put up with it, all for Matilda, all so I won't lose Olivia. I have to keep us together, as a family.'

He trails off. And then he steps forward and grabs my hand. He is talking so fast he is spitting in my face. I am terrified.

'And you thinking you know it all, only because you are so screwed up by your own past. Just because you are responsible for your own brother's death it doesn't mean we are harming Matilda. You're a stupid little bitch.'

He hisses at me.

'Throwing yourself at me like a little tart, showing off in front of me. I saw you trying to egg me on.'

He shoves his face into mine, and then he starts kissing me. I try to close my lips, but his teeth bite them.

'Stop,' I try to say. 'Stop.'

'I know you want it,' he growls.

He pushes me back against the wall. The rough stone grinds into my back. He is fast, and harsh. He pulls down my bikini bottoms.

'Parading yourself in front of my family like a fucking whore . . .' He whispers into my ear, 'I've had enough, if Olivia can, so can I.'

I am trembling, begging him to stop, but John Finch has been possessed by a dark hatred. He is like one of the bulls out in the wild Camargue, full of primal rage, and this is a battle. He wants to hurt someone, and I am his target. He pulls down his shorts, presses himself against me. I try to clamp my legs shut, but he pulls them apart and then, before I can do anything about it, he is in me. It hurts. He pushes against me gasping and groaning, and then his body springs back, as if a torrent inside him has been released. He steps back and pulls his shorts up. I crumple onto the floor.

I hear the tap dripping in the sink, and the noise of John Finch ripping off some toilet paper.

'Barbara,' he says weakly. 'Are you all right?'

I can say nothing. I am frozen in shock, staring at the floor.

'Barbara, I'm sorry. But you wanted to, didn't you? The way you looked at me when you came out in the bikini last night. And then this morning when you turned and winked at me before you went back into the house to do the ironing. You wanted me to follow you, didn't you?'

I look up at him incredulously. He is wiping the sweat off his face with the toilet paper. He steps back nervously.

'I'll let you gather yourself together. We'll talk later. I won't mention what you said about Olivia and Matilda if you say nothing about this. Things are difficult enough without her accusing me of adultery.'

He unlocks the door and slips out. I am kneeling on the cold tiles, my bikini bottoms in my hands, as still as death.

Just one moment passes, and then she is there: Matilda. I don't see her come into the bathroom but she just appears, sitting down on the hard floor in front of me.

'Baa baa,' she says, her little fingers lightly touching my arm. 'Baa baa, don't cry.'

Mattie called me Baa baa.

'It's Daddy,' she says.

I look into her eyes, at first not comprehending what she is saying. They are as grey as thunderclouds, full of foreboding.

'It's Daddy who makes me sick.'

I stare at my little six-year-old charge and I know we are not alone. An angel is flying above us, protecting our heads with its wide white wings. I can hear them flapping behind my head, like the whir of the bathroom fan. The shadow of the angel covers our shoulders like a cloak, and our two heads fall together. I breathe in the sweet innocent breath of Matilda Finch, and all of a sudden everything is clear. I know exactly what I have to do.

Twenty-One

After the fire they built us a new bungalow. The whole community clubbed together. Everyone felt sorry for us. The pity hung like blossom on the trees, bright pink cherry blossom, tactless, gaudy and hard to miss. That spring as I walked down the lane to school, I faced the kind nods of the adults as I went through the school gates; and the looks of the other children, afraid to play with me in case they might upset me, something their parents warned them never to do. The only person who treated me the same was Fiona, maybe because she had been with me on the night of the fire, or maybe because she had loved Mattie too.

Before he died, Mattie used to love playing schools with Fiona. Every time she called round, he would chant, 'Skools, skools.' She was delighted for she had a willing victim for her game. Mattie hadn't started proper school yet. I am sure if he had he wouldn't have been so keen. But Fiona and Mattie adored playing with each other. He amused her, making her laugh with his silly noises like a monkey. Sometimes it used to annoy me, and I would imagine she was more interested in playing with Mattie than me.

Even after he was dead, Fiona insisted we play schools, and always made a space for Mattie and pretended he was there. Sometimes it irritated me but she was different from Mammy, she knew when to shut up about him. As we got older she mentioned him less and less, as if she sensed I wanted to forget.

Mammy, Solomon and I lived in our little bungalow, Knocknarea at our backs, overlooking Culleenamore Strand. I'd try to train my eyes to look only in the distance at the blue mountains and rolling fields behind the inlet of water, for if I looked around me I could see the field to our left, and the burnt-out shell of our old cottage.

That's where Mattie died, a voice would whisper in my head. That's where you let him die.

Several times that first year, I would suddenly rush out onto the road, no matter what the weather, sometimes in my bare feet on the icy tarmac and boggy grass and run into the derelict cottage looking for him. I wanted time to go back. I wanted to bring him out of the fire. After a while I tried to stop remembering. Every time thoughts of Mattie came into my head I would push them back and do something, wash the dishes, sweep the floor, polish the windows. Our house was the cleanest one for miles.

This was when I learnt to be lonely. This was the apprenticeship for my life to come: a loveless marriage in London. I have always had to stay in the shadows. When I was a child my mother was the main event. People still called to our bungalow constantly. At first it was to comfort her, and then gradually to gain comfort themselves. But it was to see Mammy, never me.

Eventually she was persuaded to take out the cards again. As a teenager I lay on my bed, Solomon stretched out beside me, listening to my three records – Steely Dan's 'The Royal Scam', Supertramp's 'Breakfast in America' and Kate Bush's 'The Kick Inside' – trying to ignore the noises from the room next door. The women's hushed whispers, the scent of incense as it wafted under the door, the occasional embarrassed laugh, if my mother said something unexpected. I would sing along to my records, trying to drown it all out.

My mother and I lived side by side and she was not a depressing woman. Quite the contrary. In fact her optimism annoyed me. When Mattie died she wept for three whole months, and banished everyone from around her: especially my father, and even me. Then one day she got up, washed her face and never cried again. Instead she started talking, on and on, but she wasn't talking to me, or even to herself, she was talking to Mattie. She told him little things about her day and she asked him questions. How was he feeling today? Did he know how much his Mammy loved him?

At first I was frightened. I thought she had gone mad. But then Fiona's mother explained it to me.

'Don't be scared, Barbara,' she said, kindly patting my shoulder. 'It's just your mother's way of coping.'

But she went on and on. She couldn't give it up. She couldn't let Mattie go. Her conversations with her dead son finally drove my father away. Things were never the same anyway after Mattie was gone. Every time my father visited he looked stung when he walked through the door and remembered someone was missing. It was easier for him to stay away and forget we had ever existed.

Once, when I was fifteen, I challenged Mammy.

'You've got to stop,' I snapped, slamming down the bread knife and whipping around.

Mammy looked at me, entranced. She had been sitting at the table, shelling peas and talking to Mattie, telling him what a lovely pea soup she was going to make and didn't he just love pea soup.

'What is it, Barbara? What's the matter?'

'Stop talking to Mattie.'

It was hard to get his name out. It stuck in my throat for it had been so long since I said his name.

'But why should I do that?'

'Because he's dead, Mammy, dead, dead, dead!'

I was furious, hopping mad, but Mammy stayed calm. She walked over to the other side of the kitchen and put her hand on my back.

'He's here with us, Barbara. He's here all the time. He says you've to stop feeling guilty.'

I spun around, my eyes stinging with tears, and slapped her face. She stepped back, stunned, but said nothing. She just looked at me sadly. I ran out of the kitchen, ashamed I had hit my own mother, yet angry still. I felt trapped in the past and it was suffocating me.

When I had Liam I remembered how my mother was about Mattie. I began to feel a new compassion for her, which I had never felt before. But I was in London then, and she was in Ireland. She never even got to see her grandson before she died. Maybe if she had, she would have lived.

Mammy warned me. She said she read it in the cards, the impending disaster of my relationship. She said my husband-to-be was the devil card, a manipulator, an angry man. I was furious with her. How could she say such things about someone she had never met? I wasn't going to let a deck of tarot cards rule my life.

I asked her to come to London to meet him, but she said she wouldn't come. It would only make things worse for me. And I was never able to persuade my husband to go to Ireland. He didn't like the Irish, even though he had married me. He was always ranting on about the IRA, and if a bomb went off somehow it was my fault, because of where I was from. I became ashamed of my homeland – a place of terrorists and rule breakers – and of what I was. It was my husband who kept reminding me he had saved me.

When I met him I had nothing and he helped me. There was something about him which reminded me of Pascal: his height, the dark hair and blue eyes. He laughed a lot. I was attracted to him. Once we slept together I was addicted. We had a dramatic physical relationship, arguing constantly, making up passionately. I lived for sex. As long as I had enough, I felt all right. I was afraid he would leave and no one else would want me. But the rows wore me out. I began to worry about Liam. What kind of home was my son growing up in?

One day I looked at my husband and realised he didn't resemble Pascal in the least. I had imagined their likeness, superimposed my old fantasy onto this man's face. I had slept with him for years, yet he looked like a stranger now. I no longer desired him. But I couldn't refuse to sleep with him because it was the only way we knew how to communicate. If there was no sex, what was left?

He never hit me. But when he was angry, his words were like fists hammering me in the chest. And I saw myself how I thought he saw me: ugly and unloved. By the time Liam started school he had stopped giving me presents or taking me out. When I look back on my marriage, I am astounded by what I put up with. How many times did I let him have sex with me against my will? It was as if I wanted to be punished.

Sometimes, on the evenings he was out with his mates, after I had put Liam to bed, I would take out the little pendant Pascal had given me, my *croix de la Camargue*, for I kept it still. I fingered it and remembered the moment Pascal gave it to me. It was the one truly romantic gesture of my life. I tried not to think about what happened afterwards. I just remembered the way Pascal looked at me in the kitchen the morning he gave it to me and told me to have faith, hope and charity. I remembered how that moment made me feel. Treasured.

They say revenge is a negative activity, but in some cases I believe it necessary, even positive. So it was with me. The day my husband threw my freedom at me, carelessly as if he were throwing a set of keys to me, as if it wasn't important, I caught it in both hands and

I celebrated. And how did I do this? In a very childish way, I suppose.

He told me over breakfast, as if he were telling me about something at work. He said he had met someone else, and she was pregnant with his child, so that was it. He had waited too long for me. I'd let myself go, anyway. I was boring. I was a moan, a nag. I said nothing. I can't say I was surprised. He waited for me to say something back, get angry, but I said not a word. It made him furious.

'Well, aren't you going to say something? Don't you bloody give a shit?'

He started yelling.

I buttered the bread for his sandwiches, and mixed some prawns up in mayonnaise. Still I said nothing.

'You're something else. Christ!' he exclaimed. 'I'm out of here. But I'll be back tonight and I want you out. Kelly's moving in.'

I froze.

'What about me and Liam?'

'This is *my* house, remember. *You* moved in, so *you* move out.'

'That was fifteen years ago!'

'So, it's still mine. I want you gone, I'm sick of seeing your bloody face.'

He went into the hall to get his jacket. I opened the medicine cabinet, took out a packet of laxatives. I put three in a small bowl, crushed them up, and mixed them into his prawn cocktail. I layered it thickly between the two slices of bread, stuck them together, cut them and wrapped them in foil.

My husband popped his head round the door.

'Well, that's it then, Barbara.'

He looked slightly abashed for a moment.

'Sorry, you know, but it hasn't been working for ages has it? You're better off without me.'

For once he was right.

'Here, your sandwiches,' I said, handing them to him.

He looked guilty, then cross, shoving them into his jacket pocket.

'Why the fuck do you do that? Try to make me feel bad.'

And then he was gone. Fifteen years wiped out in one morning. I stood motionless in the kitchen, watching a robin come up to the patio doors and rat-tat-tat on them. I slid them open, and it hopped into the kitchen, peering up at me with beady black eyes. I took a piece of bread, crumbled it and dropped it on the ground. The robin hopped forward, took a crumb in his beak and then turned and took off, flying away in an instant. I crouched down on the ground, hugging my knees. I smiled to myself.

Fifteen years. Maybe my husband would think about that when he was sitting on the toilet, his insides erupting. And as I went around the house that day, packing our suitcases, cutting all of his ties in half, writing *adulterer* in black marker all over his best designer shirts, and pouring runny honey into his Gucci shoes, I burst out laughing again and again. I knew he had an important meeting with a client that afternoon. I hoped he suffocated him with flatulence. Again I was off, beside myself with mirth. It had been a very long time since I had laughed so much. It felt wonderful, as if I had taken the lid off my tomb and come back to life.

Twenty-Two

Rafi follows us. Every time I turn around and ask him to go home, he stops in his tracks, looks at me dolefully, but doesn't move. When we start walking again, he follows us.

'Go home!' I stamp my foot, but Rafi doesn't move.

'What's the French for go home?' I ask Matilda. 'Maybe he doesn't understand me.'

'*Rentrez à la maison!*' she says.

'*Rentrez à la maison!*' I shout at Rafi, but he pays no attention. He has obviously decided he is coming with us, no matter what.

'I give up,' I sigh.

'Rafi!' Matilda calls. He trots up to her and licks her hand.

'I thought you didn't like dogs.' I stroke Rafi's head. He has a white mark under his chin just like Solomon did.

'Daddy doesn't like dogs. He says I have to be careful because a strange dog might bite me.'

I stiffen at the mention of John Finch. I try not to think about him, or what just happened under an hour ago in the downstairs bathroom. My mouth tastes of metal. I bite my lips, taste blood, and lick them. I don't want to think about the rest of my body. I walk along and I feel like a giant lumbering across the landscape. I am fat and ugly. Every girl needs a father to love her, and if neither of us has one, well we have to take care of each other. How could John Finch love his daughter if he was harming her?

I wasn't sure what drove me to leave the house in the Camargue. I was in such a hurry. I left everything behind, even my Walkman and Kate Bush tape, even my new denim jacket. All I had was my passport, money which my father had given me the day I met him for lunch – just enough to get us home – a change of clothes and towels in a beach bag slung over my shoulder.

We left because we had to get away from John Finch.

On the way up the drive we had passed Celeste carrying a large bunch of lavender in her hand. We had all stopped walking and she asked us where we were going.

'To the sea,' Matilda told her.

'It's a long way,' she said in French and looked at me curiously. 'Ask Barbara if everything is all right?' she said to her little grand-daughter.

'*Maman* says, is everything all right?'

I nod. My eyes feel tight with the strain of trying to look normal.

'*D'accord*,' Celeste says, and then she hands me the lavender, lifting it to my nose. I smell it and it engulfs me with sensuous calm. It reminds me of the scent of Pascal. I shudder and feel close to tears. Celeste touches my hand gently, her eyes are loving and caring and I wish I could confide in her.

'*Pour toi, petite Barbara*,' she says. '*Lavandula latifolia, l'aspic de Provence pour le médecin. Tu es une guérisseuse, ma fille.*'

We walk on. I try to remember what the word '*guérisseuse*' means but it evades me. My eyes focus on the horizon and the sliver of silver sea I can see sparkling in the midday sun.

'I'm thirsty,' Matilda complains.

I take a water bottle out of my bag and hand it to her. I wipe my forehead. We are about halfway across the marshes. The heat of the

morning has already drained all the moisture from the air and dried
up all the rain from the previous day. My skin is prickling with the
heat. My hands and fingers feel dry, and parched, like the cracked
earth beneath my flip-flops.

We eventually reach the edge of the *sansouire* and clamber up
through the sand dunes. Rafi runs ahead, barking at a couple of
seagulls, which take off swiftly and head out to sea. The tide is in.
We pause and look at the ocean, and its invitation to enter the
unknown. Matilda puts her hand in mine. I feel the weight of her
small hand in the cup of my palm. I turn and look at the silhouette
of her face against the sun. She is looking at me, but I cannot see
the expression on her face. She points ahead, and I follow her
fingertip, across the salt marshes, pointing west.

We start walking again, slipping and sliding on the sand dunes.
It is hard work. But we keep on moving. We are in an unearthly
land, halfway between heaven and hell. Water and heat are one hazy
sheen hovering above the flat plains. We are two tiny figments floating in this seaside mirage, two outcast angels swallowed by the
barren landscape and the heavy sky. We are each other's guardians.

My head pounds, for no one can help us. Matilda's grandparents
don't understand me; Olivia despises me, and I am sure wouldn't
believe me. Why should she when I have been so hostile? Nor
would Gareth or Pascal. To think about him pierces my heart.

We are standing looking at the sea when I see them; the four
women in the little rowing boat. They are bobbing up and down on
the water. Rafi sits down on his hind legs, watching, sniffing the air.
He pants, but he doesn't bark. One of the women, the tallest and
the darkest, jumps out into the foaming water and pulls the boat
by a rope up onto the shore. She is dressed strangely, in long robes.
The other women get out of the boat and come towards us. All of
them are in long dresses, biblical clothes. It is only when they are
practically upon us I realize who they are.

Sarah, the Black Virgin, silently takes my hand and she spins me, and in her eyes I see my thousand lifetimes, some full of joy and some dogged by sorrow. We are dancing in the desert, rings in our ears, bangles on our arms, sparkling in the firelight under a star-laden sky. We are sitting in a cave, praying, the cold stone kneading our flesh. We are giving birth in a deep wood, in a shower of leaves from the trees making a bed of silver and green for the baby. We are nursing our child on soft down pillows made from white angels' feathers. We are floating on the ocean, in a tiny boat with no oars and no sails, in the company of women.

'*Ex-voto*,' I say, turning to Mary Salome, Mary Jacobe and Mary Magdalene.

'*Ex-voto Matilda Finch, âge de six ans, se trouvant gravement malade a été sauvé par les Saintes Maries et la Vièrge Noire.*'

The three saints bless our heads, and Black Sarah kisses us both, one kiss on each cheek.

'*Comme le taureau*,' she whispers in my ear. 'Be brave, Barbara the Strong.'

They turn and walk back towards their boat.

'Can we come with you? Will you save us?' I call after them.

They shake their heads, and Sarah says, 'No, Barbara, you must find your own way.'

I watch them row out to sea, until they are tiny specks bobbing on the horizon. The sun goes behind a cloud for an instant and when it comes out again they are gone.

I shake my head, confused. Am I going mad? Rafi nuzzles me and licks my limp hand. Matilda is standing next to me. She is motionless, strands of her lank hair fall in straggles across her face. She turns and smiles at me. And it is the first time Matilda has looked well since I met her. There is colour in her cheeks, and her eyes look bright, the black shadows beneath them gone.

'I'm better,' she says, jumping up and down on the spot. 'I feel better.'

I jump with her. We bounce up and down and then roll down the sand in excitement. Rafi barks and leaps up at us. Then we take off our clothes, our swimsuits are still on underneath. We run into the sea, Rafi at our heels, and splash each other, like two little girls just having a laugh with their pet dog.

Afterwards we eat our picnic: bread, cheese and chocolate. Then we lie down on the sand and sleep next to each other, curled around Rafi's damp sandy fur. When we wake up we swim again. This is how we pass the afternoon, as if it is a holiday by the sea.

The sun is sinking in the sky by the time we have dried off for the second time. The sky bleeds orange and red, the landscape fills with purple shadows. We peel our swimsuits off and leave them in a wet pile in the sand. We dump our damp towels on top of them, along with our dirty shorts and tops from before. We put on clean clothes.

'I'm hungry,' says Matilda. 'Are we going back?'

I hunt around in the beach bag and hand her a bar of chocolate. It has melted slightly but she wolves it down.

'No, we're not.'

'Good,' she announces, not at all surprised, as if she is expecting me to say this.

'We're going on an adventure,' I say.

She grips her hands in excitement, her face breaking into a big chocolate smile. It is hard to imagine this is the same Matilda Finch I met nearly two weeks ago. But this is what I believe the Black Virgin has taught me. Everyone is a mixture of good and bad, and sometimes what might seem bad, is in fact good. I am stealing a child, and that looks bad, I know it. But my ultimate aim is good, for I am rescuing her. Besides, I feel I have no choice, my mind is made up. I know where we have to go and what we have to do.

'Where are we going?' Matilda asks me.

'We're going home, to Ireland,' I say, taking her hand and beginning to walk along the beach. 'Come on let's go, Mattie.'

She looks up at me.

'Why did you call me Mattie?'

'Because that's your name shortened. Matilda . . . Mat . . . Mattie . . .'

'Oh yes.' She gives a skip.

I make sure we walk close to the edge of the sea, looking back, from time to time, and checking our tracks are being washed away. Our little heap of clothes and towels gets smaller and smaller, and Rafi sits by them not moving. It's as if he understands he has to stay there, so that when the others come they will think we were washed away by a rogue wave. They will believe we have drowned. I don't feel guilty for an instant. They deserve to lose her because they didn't take care of her when they could.

'Good boy, Solomon,' I whisper under my breath, and for a second Rafi becomes Solomon, looking into my eyes, and my heart, and understanding who I am more than any human being ever could.

Twenty-Three

I am sitting on the grass in the garden, a blanket wrapped about my shoulders, coughing and spluttering, tears streaming down my face. Fiona's mother has her arms around me, and is talking into my ear.

'It's all right Barbara, you're all right.'

Solomon is licking my face furiously. He cannot stop.

'Go on, Solomon.' Fiona's mother tries to push him away. 'Stop that, there's a good boy.'

I can hear the sirens now from the fire engine, and the commotion as people start running. I have my back to the house but I can feel the heat, although I am way down the end of the garden. It is like a giant bonfire, I think hazily to myself, the biggest Halloween party of my life.

Someone picks me up and carries me. They are taking me to an ambulance, which is parked on the road, the blue light still spinning above it. The people touch me gently. They listen to my heart. They listen to my chest. I am alive. They sit me inside the ambulance, and they wait with me. I am alone.

'Solomon,' I whimper.

'What darling?' says the girl in the ambulance uniform, who is sitting with me.

'Solomon,' I rasp, my chest tight and unyielding.

'That's her dog,' says Fiona's mother. 'He's fine,' she says, leaning down and hugging me. 'He's with the Reillys.'

'I want Solomon,' I repeat like a dummy.

'He can't come with you, Barbara. You have to go to hospital. They have your mammy now. They're bringing her to you.'

I jerk upright.

Mammy.

I see her being carried across the lawn on a stretcher, an oxygen mask over her nose and mouth. They bring her into the ambulance and she is lying down next to me. Her eyes are streaming and red, but they are wide open. She looks at me and tries to reach out. She looks around me. I know what she is thinking. Where is he? She looks at me again. I see the panic in her eyes, the fear, the incomprehension. She begins to choke, and they have to take me away, put me in another car to take me to the hospital.

'It's better, just in case,' I hear one of the ambulance men tell Fiona's father.

They wrap me in more blankets and put me in the back of their car. Fiona is sitting in the back in her pyjamas. She holds my hand and squeezes it. We drive away from our burning house. I turn around and look at it, black smoke churning out, flames blazing into the sky. I close my eyes. I see my mother's face. I see what she was asking me, although she couldn't speak. Where's Mattie? I begin to shake and I cannot stop. Fiona, all skinny nine years of her, puts her arms around me and tries to keep me still.

'She's shaking, Mammy . . . she's shaking, Mammy,' she keeps repeating.

'It's the shock. Just try to hold her, darling. We're nearly there.'

But it's not just the shock. It is a picture in my head, and I will never forget it. It is the moment I gave up, the moment I let Mattie die.

Twenty-Four

We start to hitch once we reach the road. Matilda is exhausted. We hobble along in our flip-flops, our feet black from sand and dust.

'Ow!' Matilda begins to hop. 'My flip-flop broke.'

The front piece of her blue plastic flip-flop has snapped. I can't believe I have been so stupid as not to bring any other shoes with us.

'What are we going to do, Baa baa?' Matilda asks me wide-eyed and trusting.

I shake my head, wondering if I can carry her, when at that exact moment a truck pulls up beside us. The driver is a small old man, swarthy and wrinkled from the sun. He is going all the way to Marseilles. I am too tired, and too desperate, to worry about whether we should go with him or not. The two of us clamber into the cabin at the front of the truck. As we set off I see the blue flip-flop stranded in the ditch at the side of the road, among the yellow irises and the green reeds. It is too late to get out and pick it up, so I leave it, the final symbol of our departure.

We are driving out of the Camargue and away from the flat plains, the confluence of sea and river, which have haunted my soul since I first laid eyes on them. We are leaving the place where I first fell in love and where my heart was first broken. And I am running away from the worst thing that has ever happened to me in my whole life. Although I am still sore and throbbing between my legs, I snap closed my heart and my mind and promise myself never to think about what John Finch did to me ever again. The wild Camargue with its primal landscape and awning sky has broken me. I hope never to return.

By the time we arrive in Marseilles it is dark. I give Matilda my flip-flops and she flaps along like a duck. I walk barefoot and we look like a couple of tramps but I don't care. I go into the first hotel I find and book a room. We are so tired we fall asleep in our clothes on top of the double bed. For once I have no dreams. My nightscape is blemish-free, and for the first time in my life I feel a weight has been lifted off my shoulders. Finally I am making amends.

In the morning Matilda is excited. She asks me lots of questions about Ireland. Are there fairies there? Have I ever seen a leprechaun? I tease her by telling her that they are as common as muck. There are cheeky leprechauns on practically every street corner, hugging their pots of gold.

'Oh, they tease you so, Matilda, with their tricks and their riddles. And they wouldn't give you a penny of their treasure.'

I have no idea really how to get home, but I reckon the best and cheapest way is by train, and then ferry, so after our breakfast we get directions for the station and head off, stopping only once to buy Matilda a pair of cheap runners. I try not to think about the others and what is happening in the Camargue.

Having called off the search last night when they found our things on the beach, everyone is now out in boats, looking for our bodies, looking for two dead girls floating in the sea. Olivia is hysterical, tanked up with valium and clinging on to Gareth. Her parents are trying to stay calm. Hubert is in the boats with the other men, and Celeste is making endless pots of coffee. John Finch is back in the house. He has shut himself in his room and he refuses to come out. No one has the time and the patience to coax him out, or to wonder why. Only Pascal.

It is my Camargue cowboy who notices his brother-in-law's strange reaction when we first go missing. There is something nagging him at the back of his mind, something John said to him yesterday morning when he came back out to the pool, just after I had gone in to do the ironing. He had said it to him in English.

You're not the only lady's man around here.

That's what John had said, and Pascal hadn't thought much of it then, but when he saw me and Matilda heading out of the yard with our swimming things he had had a bad feeling. He had called to me, but I had refused to go back, turning where I stood, trying not to catch his eye.

'Where are you going?' he asked me.

'Matilda wants to go for a swim in the sea. And then we're going to have a picnic.'

'Is Matilda able to go for such a long walk?'

'If she feels sick, we'll turn back,' I said defensively.

He looked at his little niece. She took my hand and squeezed it.

'Should we tell him, Baa baa?'

'Tell me what?' Pascal's eyes narrowed.

'Nothing. No.'

'What about Arles?' he called after me.

'We'll be back,' I said, still not looking him in the eye.

But he knew I had no intention of going to Arles with him, although he didn't know why.

Everyone thought we had drowned in the sea. But Pascal believed otherwise. It had been a calm afternoon, no surf to speak of, and the water in the place we had been was safe and shallow. So that night Pascal saddled up Pedro and rode like a *gardian* across the flat plains. And when he had no luck searching the salt marshes of his childhood, which he knew like the back of his hand, he got up early the next morning, got into his green 2CV and started driving. For some reason he felt responsible. Not just for Matilda but for me.

It is surprising how little time it takes us to get back to Ireland. Maybe it is because my body is functioning more efficiently now I have shut down my mind and am working on instinct. I am on autopilot. I negotiate our way around Paris, my schoolgirl French finally being of some use and amazing Matilda.

'You can speak French!' she exclaims as we board the boat train just in time.

'Well, a little.'

'You could have talked French to my mama, and *Papa* and *Maman*.'

By the time we travel across England, and take the ferry to Dun Laoghaire just one more night and two days have passed. No one, apart from Pascal, is looking for us, not yet. They still believe we are at the bottom of the sea. It will be the following day when the blue flip-flop is found and the search is widened throughout the whole of France. Sightings will be reported by several people: the concierge in the hotel in Marseilles, the shopkeeper in the shoe shop, a ticket seller in the Gare du Nord, a young English woman travelling on the Calais–Dover ferry, who watches us while we play snap.

I am not worried about being recognised because soon everyone will know the truth, and I will be congratulated for saving the life of Matilda Finch. This is what I believe. All I want to do is go home to Mammy because once I am there she will know what to do.

We sleep stretched out on the seats of the night ferry from Holyhead to Dun Laoghaire and pull into the harbour shortly after the sun has risen. The air is colder than I have been used to, but the day

is bright. It feels good to be on familiar territory. We catch the Dart
and make it to Connolly Station just in time for the morning train
to Sligo. We are grubby and tired, but both of us are in good
humour. We are having one big adventure.

The last stage of our journey is tortuously slow. The train chugs
through the landscape, and now all I want is to be home. I bought
Matilda a drawing pad and crayons in the station, and she is drawing away furiously while I stare out of the window. I just want to
arrive. I feel listless and edgy. I look at my reflection in the window
as we pass through the countryside. It is an average summer's day
in Ireland – blustery sunshine one minute, squally showers the
next. I look at myself. My hair is a mess, half in, half out of my
ponytail. I look different. Older. The pupils of my eyes are dilated,
pitch black, as if I have seen more in the last week than I had in my
whole life, and maybe I have. I notice something glinting against
the skin of my chest in the reflection. I put my hand up and feel it
– my *croix de la Camargue*. I look down at it, holding each side of
the cross with two fingers, the little prongs pricking me. I examine the heart part of it. The vertical of the cross drives straight into
the centre of it, cradled by the little anchor below. I sob once,
quietly, muffled. I am heavy and cold. My heart is sore. It confuses
me how quickly you can fall in love and how easily your heart can
be broken. And how you can be so wrong about people, like I was
about Pascal, and about John Finch.

We pull into Sligo station at around midday. I am so anxious to
be home that I get into a taxi. I have just enough money to cover
it. We drive towards Strandhill, passing houses, and people
strolling along the pavement. It looks like an average day but to me
everything is anything but normal. We take the turn for Culleenamore and climb up the narrow road, Knocknarea rearing to our
left, low cloud hiding its summit. Our views of the sea are hidden
by hedgerows one minute, and sparkling beneath us the next. The

distant blue bulk of Ben Bulben is shrouded in mist. It begins to rain. I have only been gone two weeks and yet everything looks different to me now. The land comforts me. Its soft green contours, its little dips and valleys soothe me and make me feel safe. The sea is silver. It seems to hold a more unearthly quality to it and I think of our vision of the three Marys, and Black Sarah, somewhere out on the oceans of time, bobbing up and down, on the seas of all the lost girls and exiled women.

We are rising up and up and it feels good to be on high land again. The low wetlands of the Camargue had been oppressive, the big sky like a weight hanging over my head. It is a relief to be cool again, even a little cold. The heat and humidity of France and the constant attention from the mosquitoes had irritated me continually. Now I am calm. We turn a corner and I am home.

Matilda and I stand on the road outside our bungalow as the taxi drives away. It is still raining softly on our heads, covering our hair in a glistening down, and then the sun comes out. Matilda points, and we look at the sparkling rainbow, which arches over our house. I am reminded of the first day I arrived at No. 5 Winchester Gardens, and the rainbow I saw then, and how I believed it was a sign. The door opens and Mammy is standing there, a tea cloth still in her hand, her face wide open with surprise. She stands in a dark blue dress, her red hair now cut at the nape of her neck, but still startling in the wet sunshine.

'Barbara!'

I take Matilda's hand and we walk up the path together.

'Barbara,' Mammy repeats, and I can see her face wan with shock.

Then she reaches forward and puts her arms around both of us. 'Thank God you're all right.'

We go into the house and I see a suitcase on the couch, open, clothes hastily thrown in.

'Where are you going?' I ask.

'What do you mean, where am I going?' my mother asks me incredulously. 'France of course! Everyone is looking for you and the little girl.'

Matilda sits down on a chair. She is shy and out of place. My mother looks at her.

'Do you want a drink, sweetheart? What's your name again?'

'Matilda. But Baa baa calls me Mattie.'

My mother steps back, as if hit.

'Mattie?' she croaks.

'Look at Matilda's eyes, Mammy,' I say, standing behind her. 'Look, aren't they just the same?'

My mother stares at Matilda, and Matilda stares back. Mammy reaches out and touches her face, as if it is a mirage about to disappear.

'Yes, you do look very like Mattie,' she says to Matilda.

'Who is Mattie?'

'He was my son, Barbara's brother. He died.'

'My brother died too,' Matilda says, looking about the room more confidently. 'Your house is very small,' she announces. 'I'm hungry.'

'Did you have any lunch?' my mother asks.

We shake our heads.

'Or breakfast even?' She puts her hands on her hips.

We look at each other.

'I bought a couple of currant buns for the journey,' I offer guiltily.

'It wasn't much,' Matilda pipes up. 'I have such a pain in my tummy. I think I'm past hunger.'

'Well, come and sit at the kitchen table. Let's get you both fed. Do you like baked beans?'

'Yes, I love beans.' Matilda trots into the kitchen behind my mother.

'Great, beans on toast it is.'

My mother goes to the fridge and gets out the orange juice. She pours us both a glass. She looks at me sternly.

'What on earth were you thinking of, Barbara?' she says under her breath. 'The little girl's mother is frantic with worry. I was only just talking to her on the phone half an hour ago.'

'You were talking to Olivia?'

I find it astonishing that my mother and Olivia would be talking to each other, discussing their missing daughters.

'Yes, she is practically hysterical. She was convinced you had drowned in the sea, but I kept telling her you were a good swimmer. I knew you weren't dead,' Mammy says matter-of-factly, taking a tin opener out of the drawer and opening the can of beans. 'I had better ring her immediately and tell her you're both here.'

I start to panic.

'Mammy, please don't ring her just yet. I need to talk to you.'

'It's all right, Barbara. You're not going to get into trouble.'

She is looking at me strangely.

'I'll tell you later,' she whispers, glancing over at Matilda.

Mammy toasts some bread and heats up the beans. While Matilda and I gobble up the food like two hungry dogs, she goes into her bedroom to ring Olivia. A few moments later she comes back out again.

'Well, they were on their way anyway. You were seen in Connolly Station this morning. They're in Dublin now, hiring a car. They'll be here this evening.'

I stiffen at the thought of John Finch arriving in my house. I don't think I can bare to set eyes on him again.

'Barbara, what's wrong?'

I feel sick.

'I think I ate too fast.' I put a hand on my belly and burp which makes Matilda laugh. Suddenly I jump up, rush out of the kitchen and into the bathroom. I lean over the toilet and throw up. My mother follows me.

'Are you all right?'

'I'm OK. I just ate too quickly.'

I get up and wash my mouth out. I look in the mirror. My mother is standing behind me, looking at me. We are so alike physically, as if we are sisters, not mother and daughter. I catch her eye in the mirror.

'Mammy, we can't give Matilda back.'

'Don't be ridiculous, Barbara.'

'We can't. They don't love her.'

My mother steps forward and puts her hand on my shoulder.

'I know why you did what you did, darling. Everyone does. But things will be different for Matilda now. It's all over.'

I don't understand what she is telling me.

She looks behind her, and then quietly clicks the door shut. She stands over me, while I sit on the edge of the bath and look up, waiting.

'They know her father was making her sick all the time.' My mother's voice is low and serious.

'They do?' I intone like a zombie.

'Yes, Matilda's uncle told them.'

'Pascal?' I whisper.

'Yes, I believe that is his name.' She stops, looks at me curiously as I colour.

'Mr Finch tried to insinuate you had kidnapped Matilda because of what had happened with Mattie. Apparently you told him all about the fire.'

My mother pauses. I look down at the bathroom floor. The linoleum is cracked and in need of a good clean.

'But Pascal told them everything you had discovered. About the pills and what they did to Matilda. It appears Mr Finch was afraid of losing his wife and child. He lied about her fits. He had all of the doctors fooled. Without realising it, they were giving Matilda medication, that was making her have more seizures and giving her nausea. He did the same thing to Olivia, pushing her to take anti-depressants he had got himself so that she constantly felt sick and dependent. She never had the strength to leave him. They even think he might have had something to do with the baby's death, Matilda's little brother, although they can't prove it. He denied everything of course.'

I gasp, horrified. I never would have believed it, until I saw the red hatred in John Finch's eyes, and what it could make him do.

'How do you know all this?' I ask my mother shakily.

'Olivia. She's told me everything, Barbara.'

Not quite, I think.

'But if they are coming to get Matilda, why is John Finch coming here? Why hasn't someone arrested him?'

'No, no, it's Olivia who is coming, on her own, with her friend Gareth. I believe you know him.'

'Yes.' I pause. 'They are having an affair,' I announce dramatically.

My mother doesn't flinch.

'Thank goodness for something,' Mammy says with warmth in her voice. 'That poor woman has suffered enough. At least she has someone in her life who will comfort her.'

I am astounded. *That poor woman.* I cannot apply the phrase to Olivia, even though she isn't guilty of harming Matilda as I thought.

My mother smiles slowly.

'You don't like her?'

'No, she was horrible to me,' I spit out.

My mother crosses her arms.

'Well, sometimes you have to look below the surface, Barbara. Sometimes people are not what they seem.'

It is one of her little sayings.

'So, is Mr Finch in prison?'

My mother looks away. She pauses takes a breath and whispers again.

'No. It would have been hard to prove anything anyway.'

'Would?'

My mother looks at me with her emerald eyes.

'Mr Finch is dead.'

I flinch as if hit. I put my hand to my mouth to suppress the scream.

'Did Pascal kill him?'

'Pascal? Oh God no, Barbara, goodness no. Mr Finch was a wretched soul. He killed himself, Barbara. He took all the pills he had got for Olivia and all the pills for Matilda, and then he drank two bottles of vodka. He had a massive heart attack. They're not sure whether he was drowning his sorrows, or intending to end it all.'

Mammy comes and sits beside me on the edge of the bath. She puts her arm around my shoulders. I am shaking uncontrollably, my teeth chattering.

'Barbara,' Mammy whispers, kissing my cheek. 'They said you had drowned, but I knew you were still alive. I asked the cards and they told me you were coming. That's why I stayed here, waiting for you. I only decided this morning to go to France.'

She kisses the crown of my head and speaks above it. I feel her breath on the strands of my hair, like a soft breeze.

'I knew you were coming and I knew you would bring Matilda. Mattie told me a little girl child was coming to the house. So I kept telling Olivia you were both safe.'

There is a knock on the bathroom door.

'Baa baa!'

I get up and open the door. Matilda stands in the hallway, looking very small and slightly unsure. Tomato sauce rings her mouth and she licks her buttery fingers. But she looks well. She is healthy.

'I have to wash my hands,' she says.

I show Matilda my old bedroom. I am touched to see Mammy has tidied it – washed and folded all of my old clothes in a pile, stacked my records and tapes, and made the bed with fresh sheets. There is a bunch of yellow freesias in a small vase on the bedside locker, filling the room with their sweet odour. It's true, she was expecting us. Matilda is excited by all of my things. I let her look at all my books and my photographs. She looks at the pictures of Solomon on the wall, fingering them and saying he is just like Rafi. I show her a photo of Mattie and she stares at it for ages.

'He is the boy in my dreams,' she says simply.

We look at each other, and I feel the deep connection between us. A sisterhood.

Matilda yawns.

'Why don't you get into my bed and have a snooze,' I suggest. 'Your mammy is coming to get you tonight, and you might have to stay up late.'

'OK.' She yawns again.

I tuck her in and put a cuddly toy in next to her. It is a little floppy dog, with black and white spots.

'What's his name?' she asks sleepily.

'Let's call him Solomon.'

Mammy is in the kitchen clearing up the lunch things.

'The water's hot,' she says, 'if you want a bath.'

I look at my mother's back. She is tall and straight as a poker. Her dark blue dress clings to her figure, her full breasts, her slim waist and undulating hips. Her hair shines deep red against the grey sky behind her. The rain is coming down in fat heavy drops, lashing against the glass.

'Thanks, Mammy.'

I bring the beach bag, now scuffed and tattered, into the bathroom, and rummage inside it for my toothbrush. My hands come across the bunch of lavender Celeste gave me. I pull it out. The stems of the lavender are broken, and some of the small purple heads have fallen off inside the bag. I bring what remains up to my nose and inhale. The scent of lavender is at once uplifting and soothing. And yet it takes me back to the moment I walked away from the Camargue and from Pascal. I break up the lavender and sprinkle it in my steaming bath. I get in, and lie in lavender, imagine its purple light filling my pores and easing my distress.

I look at my body. I look just the same as I did yesterday, but inside I am different. Inside I ache. I sink deeper into my purple ease, trying to forget what happened to me, when I suddenly remember what that word Celeste had called me, '*guérisseuse*', meant. Healer. Celeste had said I was a healer. I can't think what she could have meant by saying that. Yes, Matilda is better, but it was not I who made her well. Now, when I look back, I wonder if Celeste could see what had been done to me that day. Did she understand how damage can be a source of strength, and how the healer can turn it into something else, into miracles?

When I come out of the bathroom, Mammy's big red bathrobe wrapped about me, she has the fire lit. I walk into the kitchen, the linoleum chilling my warm feet. She is heating milk in a pan.

'Let's have hot chocolate,' she says, turning slightly towards me, and smiling. I think of all the times we drank hot chocolate together on cold winter nights, curled up under a blanket on the couch, watching old black-and-white movies on the TV.

I go back into the sitting room and sit down by the fire, stare at the crackling wood and smoking turf. I have never felt the same about a naked flame since the night of the 'accident'. For what is most beautiful is often most dangerous – a lightning bolt across a black sky, a naked man, even a candle you have forgotten to blow out.

It is while I am sitting, looking at the glowing peat, I sense his presence. I can hear the patter of his feet across the wooden floor, and his short puffs of childish breathing. He is here with me, in the corner of my eye. A flashing movement I can't quite get hold of, like a kite's tail or a passing figure at a window. He was with me in London, as he was in France. Mattie is by my side.

'Ah, you're back,' says my mother, bringing in the hot chocolate, but she is not talking to me, she is talking to Mattie.

For once I am not angry. I sit and I listen.

My mother hands me my mug, but she is distracted, listening for my brother's voice. I cradle my hot mug in my hands and take a sip.

Mammy sits down opposite me, and then she fixes me with her iridescent eyes.

'Mattie says it's time, Barbara.'

I think of all the parts of me which came from my mother: my hair, my eyes, my nose, chin and mouth, but not my soul, the one which can be black and also white. I am not pure like her.

'Mattie says to tell me what happened the night of the fire.'

I sit back on the couch, shaking my head.

'No,' I say through tight lips.

'He says that it is time to stop blaming yourself.'

'But it *was* my fault!' I wail.

Mammy is motionless. I close my eyes, and the image is there, the picture in my head, which I can never blank out. The moment I lost Mattie.

Twenty-Five

The angel of death dances between my brother and I. Black Queen Maeve rejoices at the thick plumes of smoke, which are pouring into the room and making Mattie cough. She wails joyously, swinging her hips from side to side, rolls her eyes and clicks her fingers, tiny red sparks flying off them in all directions.

'Mattie,' I call. 'Mattie, get out of bed.'

He looks so tiny in his big mountain of a bed. His sheets and blankets are piled up around him.

'Mattie!' I screech, thrusting the whole top half of my body into the room. 'Mattie!'

He gets out of bed and he walks unsteadily towards me. The she-monster gets in his way, but I jump down and I push her hard. I am only nine, and small for my age, but I put all my force into it and she falls flat on her face on the carpet. I grab Mattie's hand and begin to drag him towards the window, putting the other hand over my mouth. I can hardly breathe, and my limbs feel like lead. I just want to lie down and sleep. Mattie begins to pull away from me.

'No, Mattie,' I try to say. 'Come on, climb up to the window, come on.'

I clamber onto the chest of drawers and try to pull him up. He is as heavy as a stone. His blue eyes are the same colour as the smoke and they look right into me.

'I want Mammy,' he whimpers.

'Come with me,' I coax him. 'Climb up, Mattie, please.'

'No. I'm going to Mammy.'

And he pulls his hand out of mine.

'Mattie!' I scream, but can't stop coughing. I try to speak again, it comes out as a hoarse croak. 'Come here! I can save you. Mattie, Mattie!'

'I want Mammy!' he sobs and turns around. He begins to trot over towards the door.

This is the moment I go over and over again. How I wish I had behaved differently. Was it jealousy, even then; at that moment of crisis, did I let envy of my little brother get the better of me? Because instead of climbing off the chest of drawers, grabbing him and forcing him to climb out of the window with me, I let him go.

'Go on then, go to Mammy,' I scream at him. I watch Queen Maeve get up off the floor and take his little hand in her gnarled charred fingers. She laughs at me, her mouth a black cavern, and she leads him to the door. There is something on the other side, banging, banging, trying to get in.

Queen Maeve opens the door for Mattie. And when she does, the white bull with his red eyes of hatred comes charging in, flames shoot from his huge nostrils. Mattie is sucked out the door. The bull charges into the room and tosses me out the window. They say it was the blast created from the open door that pushed me out. But I saw the bull and I felt his horns pressed against my ribs. I slip down the slates, fly through the air and fall on the grass. It takes just a couple of seconds. Two seconds which anchor my heart with chains of guilt for that is how long it takes me to lose my brother, to extinguish his light.

Twenty-Six

The fire has burnt down in the grate, and the light is beginning to fade outside. My mother leans forward and takes my hands. They are wet with the tears I have tried to push back into my eyes, while I desperately told my mother the truth. I cannot look at her.

'Barbara, what is it you think you did?' she asks me gently.

'I killed my brother!' I cry out.

I am bad. I am bad. I am bad.

My mother comes and sits beside me, and then she turns me into her chest and embraces me.

'No, you didn't,' she says firmly. She kisses the top of my head and then pulls back, still holding me by the shoulders. We face each other, mother and daughter. How young she looks, I think, like a child. My mother's features appear even more elfin – her neat turned-up nose covered in freckles; and her green eyes, wet and bright, searching into my soul.

'If anyone was to blame, it was me,' she continues, and takes a deep breath. 'I forgot to blow out the candle.'

It occurs to me that we have never talked about this before. Over the last ten years we have never discussed what actually caused the fire.

'But, Barbara,' my mother speaks urgently, 'it doesn't matter what caused the fire for you know what I think.'

'There are no such things as accidents,' I intone flatly.

'And do you believe this as well?' She sits back against the couch, watching me.

I shake my head blindly. No, I want to scream. No! Sometimes things just happen to you, and there is no grand plan. It is life throwing its worst at you.

I get up and start walking around the room. My bare toes push into the thick rug in front of the fire. I stare at the hot embers and feel their orange heat enter my belly. I am angry for deep down I believe it as well. Nothing is random.

'I hate it!' I shout at the chimney-breast, my back to my mother, afraid to look at her. 'I hate it that you are always right and you know everything. I hate the cards and I hate you talking to Mattie.'

'But do you hate me, Barbara?'

My mother speaks softly behind me.

I whip around, my red bathrobe flying about me.

'No, I love you.'

'Well, then you must accept me. For the cards, and Mattie, are all a part of who I am.'

I say nothing. I want my mother to tell me that I am enough, just me on my own. But she doesn't, because she can't.

She stands up, takes my limp hands into hers and brushes the skin with her fingers.

'Mattie wasn't meant to be in this lifetime for very long.'

'So why don't you let him go then, why do you keep hanging on to him?' I ask brutally.

But she doesn't look hurt. She thinks for a moment.

'We were waiting for you to tell me what happened. He didn't want to leave you until he knew you were all right.'

'He's only a little boy.'

'But an old soul, my darling.'

My mother embraces me and I crumble within her arms.

'I'm sorry,' I whisper. 'I'm sorry.' And she shushes me and lets me cry. I feel safe inside my mother's hug, as if no one can touch me here and time can stand still. And around us there is light. It is warm and golden and forgiving. It belongs to my brother.

Eventually I stop crying and she hands me a clean handkerchief. I blow my nose.

'Why don't you get dressed?' she suggests. 'And I'll make some more hot chocolate.'

I tiptoe back into my room. Matilda is still fast asleep. I watch her breathing in and out. Her cheeks are rosy and her fair hair flops across the pillow as she hugs the little toy dog we called Solomon. I feel strong when I look at Matilda and sure I have done the right thing. Because now she is well, she is no longer the sick child.

When I come back into the sitting room my mother has put more turf on the fire. She has lit just one lamp. The sky is overcast outside, dark before it should be, and it feels like evening although it is only four in the afternoon. We sit side by side, looking into the fire, sipping our hot chocolate, and for the first time since Mattie died I experience peace and companionship in my mother's company.

Out of the blue, my mother laughs. It is a warm gurgling peal.

'What is it?'

She smiles at me and takes my hands.

'Mattie wants to tell you that Solomon is with him. They are having fun together, Barbara.'

I hug my sides.

'Mammy, I miss Solomon so much.'

'I know, darling.'

'Why did you have him put down? Couldn't we have saved him?'

'Did you not see the look in Solomon's eyes? He wanted to go.

He was in so much pain, Barbara, and he never would have walked again. He would have been living for you but not for himself. It wouldn't have been fair.'

'I want him back,' I whimper.

'And you will have him back, one day.'

She smiles at me and her eyes twinkle mischievously. 'Remember my darling, if you love someone you can let them go.'

She gets up and walks around the room, once, twice, her dark blue dress brushing against the coffee table. I wait, my pulse quickening, sensing what she is about to say.

'It's time to leave, Mattie.' My mother stops walking suddenly, smiles into space, through her tears.

And although nothing happens, no window bangs, no door opens, we know he has gone. The fire continues to crackle and we remain in silence as an angel passes over. I look around the room, at the dusty mantelpiece, the faded covers on the chairs, the painting of the fairy tree on the wall and the photos of Mattie and I everywhere. I remember how this bungalow always felt so full although we never had many things. Now it feels empty. My mother sits down next to me, takes my hand in hers, and I look at her fingers, how similar they are to mine, long and elegant with pale oval nails.

'Is there anything else you want to tell me, Barbara?'

And for a moment I think about what John Finch did to me and how it felt. But I cannot find the words to say it and for now I bury it deep inside me. I cannot tell her.

'No,' I say, bringing my knees up to my chin.

Twenty-Seven

Matilda and I are playing Snakes and Ladders when Olivia and Gareth finally arrive. It is strange to see them walking into my house. They look very tired, and suddenly old, particularly Olivia. The glamour I am used to is gone. Her hair is scrapped back with a black headband and she is wearing hardly any make-up. Matilda runs straight into her mother's arms.

'Baa baa and me had a big adventure,' she tells her. 'We went on three trains and two boats.'

Olivia can say nothing. Her face is flooded with tears as she clings on to her daughter. Suddenly I feel terrible. What did I do? I was so sure I was right, to run away with Matilda. I had to save her. I didn't think her mother loved her. Gareth puts his arms around Olivia and Matilda and the three of them hold each other for ages.

'Where's Daddy?' Matilda asks, looking around.

Olivia gives a little gasp.

'He's not with us, darling,' Gareth says levelly, squeezing Olivia's hand.

'Would you like a drink? Some tea, a brandy?' my mother asks, quickly changing the subject.

'Brandy, thank you,' Olivia says, and then she looks at me. Her dark eyes bore into me.

'What the hell do you think you were doing?' She storms over towards me, but Gareth puts his arm out to stop her.

'Don't, Olivia. Barbara only wanted to help Matilda.'

Olivia pauses. She takes a breath and, to my surprise, speaks almost politely to me.

'Why couldn't you have told me, Barbara?'

'I didn't think you would believe me.'

I look down at my feet, which are still bare and pink from my bath.

'Mammy,' Matilda says, tugging at her sleeve. 'Barbara's brother's an angel too.'

'I know,' she says, looking me in the eye. I can feel her cold anger still. I can't blame her for I did, after all, steal her child. She must have thought she had lost Matilda as well as her baby son.

'At first that was why we thought Barbara took you.'

'Baa baa didn't take me,' Matilda says crossly. 'We went on an adventure together.'

'And don't you look well for it,' Gareth says, attempting to deflate the tension. 'The picture of health.'

'I'm better,' Matilda declares. 'The Saint Marys and Black Sarah came in the boat and they made me better.'

The adults laugh, but I am looking at Matilda incredulously. I thought my vision by the seashore in France had been a dream. But not at all, if Matilda saw them they must have been real. How could that be? Surely it was impossible. My mother would believe it, but I find it hard to accept. It can't be true. I must have told Matilda what I saw and she has made it up as well. The idea of the three saints and Black Sarah actually appearing in the flesh makes me feel dizzy. I put out a hand against the wall to hold myself steady.

No one seems to notice. Olivia and Gareth sit on the couch, and my mother sits on the rocking chair, while Matilda scrambles onto the cushions on the floor. I go and get the drinks: brandy for the adults and red lemonade for Matilda and I.

'Would you like to stay the night. It's very late,' my mother offers.

'No, no,' Olivia replies hastily. 'We are booked into a hotel in Sligo.'

'Or dinner? Can I offer you something to eat?'

I cringe at the idea of my mother preparing food for Olivia. What on earth would she give her, hot dogs or burgers? Hardly what the Frenchwoman was used to.

'Thank you but no, we have just eaten.'

My mother nods and then goes into the kitchen. I can hear her rustling around with bags of nuts and bowls.

Olivia perches on the end of the couch as if it is contaminated. She sips her brandy and looks around her. I blush for I am embarrassed by our messy, dusty house. How small it is compared to her home. Yet Mammy doesn't seem to care what Olivia and Gareth might think of her.

'Your house is very sweet,' Olivia says to my mother as she comes back in with nibbles.

'Oh it's all right,' Mammy replies offhand. 'But it has never felt like home, not like our old cottage.'

'Where was that?' asks Gareth, conversationally.

'Next door. It was the house that burnt down.'

'Oh . . .' He looks uncomfortable.

Matilda is drawing again, using the pad and crayons I got her that morning. She is sitting on the rug in front of the fire, bending over her work, concentrating hard. She looks like any other normal six-year-old child.

Gareth gets up. 'I'm just going out for a cigarette.'

'You can smoke inside the house,' my mother offers.

'Not at all,' he says politely. 'It's stopped raining now. I could do with the air.'

My mother and Olivia talk. It appears they like each other. I see another side of Olivia. After a second glass of brandy she has relaxed completely. She laughs and chats away, every now and again bending down and stroking Matilda's head.

'I thought I had lost you, baby.' she keeps saying. But she doesn't look at me. We cannot bear to confront each other.

Before I know it, Mammy is getting her deck of tarot cards out.

'I'm going to give Olivia a little reading before she goes. It might help her.'

I get up off my cushion and go into the kitchen. I have no desire to hear what my mother has to say to Olivia. I slip on a pair of clogs and open the back door, breathe in the scent of my homeland. I stand there for a moment wondering what I am going to do. It is not quite dark. Knocknarea rears like a purple shadow in front of me, the clouds accumulate across the sky, for the sun is long gone. Twilight creeps across the landscape. Everything is so familiar, and yet I know I will not stay. This desire to carve out a new life is too strong within me. I remember Fiona's words, 'You don't belong here, Barbara.' And I know she is right. I need to be somewhere alien and try to forget what has happened to me. Maybe Fiona will come with me, I think hopefully, but in my heart I know she won't. I wonder where she is now. Is she out with Murtagh, walking along Strandhill beach, clasped in a romantic embrace, being in love and light-headed? I think of Pascal and I shiver. I was so sure he felt the same way about me.

I hear a cough. Gareth is leaning against the back wall of our house, puffing on his cigarette. He is staring up at Knocknarea as well.

'Hello, Barbara,' he says. 'How are you?'

I walk over towards him. 'I'm all right.'

We stand in silence for a moment. It is nearly dark now. A bat dives past us. Rainwater drips off the leaves of the trees and the air is humid and close.

'Why didn't you tell us, Barbara?' Gareth says, putting out his cigarette with his shoe.

He doesn't wait for me to reply and continues talking. 'It's because you thought Olivia and I were making Matilda sick, wasn't it?'

'I felt sorry for Mr Finch,' I whisper.

'John said you had stolen Matilda because you were obsessed with your dead brother and felt guilty about killing him.'

I stiffen with horror.

'Did you believe him?'

'No, not after Pascal spoke in your defence. He said you looked after Matilda like a guardian angel. He kept saying you thought you were protecting Matilda. And then we discovered the truth about John, poor bastard.'

'He was your friend,' I say, trailing my finger across the bumpy concrete on the outside of our house.

'Yes. We were school chums. But over the past couple of years he changed. I became Olivia's friend more than his. To be honest, Barbara, I suspected something wasn't quite right all along. Why else do you think I dropped by on my way to St-Tropez?'

'You knew all along?' I turn to look at him. Gareth returns my gaze. His expression is unusually serious, and for once I feel he is not sneering at me. In fact he is looking at me with respect.

'I had my suspicions.'

Gareth offers me a cigarette and I take it. He lights up another and then lights mine.

'It's all over now,' he says softly. 'Poor bastard Finch.'

'Why did he want Matilda to be sick?' I inhale, feeling the smoke curling inside me.

'I don't know.' Gareth shakes his head. 'Maybe he thought he could hang on to Olivia if he did. He was obsessed with family, probably because he never had much of one himself. His parents stuck him in boarding school when he was Matilda's age. He hardly knew them.'

Gareth shivers.

'But I didn't think he'd make his own child sick. I suppose it took an outsider to see what was going on. Well done, Barbara. I guess you're a hero.'

Again he looks at me hard, with appreciation. I blush and look down, kick some dirt off the path.

'Hardly,' I mutter. 'Just a bit mad.'

'Yeah, well that's a good thing, isn't it?' He laughs stoutly. 'We all need a little bit of madness to be brave, don't we? And good instincts. Good instincts are highly underrated.'

When we go back in, Mammy and Olivia have finished and the cards are packed away. Olivia looks happier, the worry lines have gone from her forehead and her brown eyes are warm and contented. She goes up to Gareth and hugs him in front of Matilda, but her daughter doesn't seem to notice.

Before they leave, Matilda gives me the drawing pad.

'I made you a storybook,' she says.

'Thank you, Matilda, that's so sweet.'

I bend down and we hug. I take one last look at Mattie's eyes.

'Thank you for stopping the police from arresting Barbara,' my mother is saying quietly to Olivia and Gareth.

'She'll have to be interviewed, tomorrow, but once we knew where they were, and that you were with them, it seemed pointless to have police turning up on your doorstep,' Gareth says. 'We thought it best to have as little commotion as possible.'

'For Matilda's sake,' Olivia adds.

Matilda holds my hands in hers and we spin for one last time.

She laughs and her hair flies about her face. I think again of Black Sarah spinning with me on the beach and the magic my little charge and I have shared. It unsettles me for I do not understand it.

'She really is better, isn't she?' Gareth comments, and my mother nods. Olivia watches Matilda and I as we spin our good-bye. Eventually we let go.

'Here,' I say, handing her the little toy dog. 'You keep Solomon, and he'll look after you.'

'See you soon,' she says sweetly, trotting down the path, Gareth holding her hand. '*À toute à l'heure!*' she giggles. But I know we will never see each other again.

Olivia pauses on the doorstep. She holds out her hand formally and I take it. She shakes my hand, but her fingers are limp and cold.

'I know you think I am a bad mother.' She looks at me fiercely. 'But you are wrong, young lady.'

I blush, squirming under her glare. She turns away and runs down the path after her lover and her child. Mammy waves good-bye, but I go back into the house. I cannot bear to see Matilda driven away. I am afraid I might cry and it shocks me how attached I have become to this little girl in just two weeks. I sit by the fire on the rug where Matilda had been, and I open her storybook.

'Once upon a time . . .' she has written at the top. Then on each page she has drawn a picture from our journey. It is a picture book of our 'adventure'. There we are walking across the dunes with Rafi, meeting the three Marys and Black Sarah as they float on a cloud in their little sailboat, playing in the sea with Rafi, sitting in a train – its tracks winding across green fields – on a boat waving goodbye to France, and in the taxi driving up a hill in Sligo.

The last picture is the best. Matilda and I sit at the table eating our beans on toast. She has yellow hair and mine is red; my mother is standing behind us with the same red hair. She has dressed us in the clothes we were wearing today, but she has added something else. Wings. We all have wings, shaped like butterflies' wings. And then, flying above us all, is a little boy angel, with white wings and yellow hair, and blue eyes. Underneath the figures she has written our names: Matilda, Baa baa, Baa baa's Mama and Mattie. I stare at the picture for ages, and then I hold it to my chest and breathe a sigh of relief.

Some little angels never grow up. They are special, like Mattie, like Matilda's little baby brother, Marcus. They come in this world for such a short time because they are testing the waters. Sometimes they decide to stay, and sometimes they fly away again, back to cloudland, back to bliss. It is always their choice, no one else's.

Matilda and I are meant to grow up. When I ran away with Matilda I thought I was saving her and it made up for letting Mattie die. I was wrong. It is true, I was saving a little girl, but the little girl was me. I was saving myself.

Twenty-Eight

Miracles can happen.

Mammy believed in magic. She said the world was full of it. The magic of nature and its constant regeneration no matter how much we abuse it. The magic of human compassion and our capacity to forgive. The magic of love and how it forces us out of the ordinary into the world of the extra-ordinary. The magical nature of healing: how the way we think and feel can affect our physical entity and how just through faith alone you can heal. She believed in the magical reality of another dimension, and the miracle was she could see it. This is how she spent her time after the fire, talking to her dead son, and sometimes she forgot about the living.

She lost my father, who came to see us less and less often and then purely out of duty. When I was sixteen he told me I was old enough to see him in London, and that was it for two whole years until I got the job as an au pair. But Mammy didn't seem to mind. She told me he had never really been hers to lose. She always knew in her heart of hearts he would never find our nirvana.

And this was how Mammy nurtured me. Never forget the dead. For their love lasts forever.

We are all energy, fires which can never be put out.

She was a positive woman, laughing, joyous even, filling my life with as much hope as she could, but always talking to Mattie. Her grief wasn't morose. It was active, alive, always with the promise of reunion. And she never blamed me.

'It was his time, Barbara,' she kept telling me. Even after I told her what happened the night of the fire, even after Mattie's spirit went away and she no longer had his company. It was his time. Just as it was hers, one wet November morning, as she was sweeping up fallen leaves. The heavy clouds multiplied, blocking out all light, all shadow, and the air around her grew still. And all she could hear was one note from the blackbird's song, before she dropped dead on the grass. She collapsed into the ground, like the last falling leaf, under the apple tree we had planted in memory of Mattie. No one understood why she had a heart attack so young – only forty-five, only five years older than I am now. But I knew what killed her wasn't heart disease; it was a broken heart. She wanted to be with Mattie, find nirvana at last.

I have been back in Ireland for over a year. It is summer again and my house is built. Liam is over to help decorate it. He loves it here, says he might move over to Ireland too. He says it feels like home, more than London ever did. He likes Jim, Fiona's new husband, and the two of them head down to the local most nights for a couple of pints while Fiona and I stay at home. We sit out on the new patio if it is fine, her little girl Roísín asleep in her arms. She is pregnant again, making up for lost time. Sometimes we stay outside for hours, looking at the stars, remembering. Fiona and I sit in silence as the angels pass over and we are spun inside their magical webs of memory, love, loss and joy.

I have tentatively started a new life. During the day, while Fiona is at school, I mind Roísín, and at night I study. I have begun a course in aromatherapy and reflexology. Fiona suggested it when she saw how interested I was in the herbs and flowers I planted in

my garden and all the uses I had for them. She said it was only natural I was a healer. She said it was in my blood. As yet I don't have
a cure for anything. Thank God, wild horses wouldn't convince me
to lick a stranger's burnt skin. Once or twice I have taken Mammy's
old tarot deck out and held it in my palm, but I go no further. There
is a part of me which always resents the cards, for they took my
mother away from me and made me share her with her clients. I
know I could read them if I want but I don't want to know what's
going to happen next. It didn't help Mammy to know so much.

Last time I fingered the deck, three cards fell out: Judgement,
the Page of Cups and the Knight of Cups. But I didn't think twice
about them. I shoved them back in the deck and I shuffled again.
Then I wrapped the cards in Mammy's silk scarf and put them back
in the box. I forgot about them.

Solomon has come back to me in the form of a small black mon-
grel – half Labrador, half something else – I found tied to a tree in
the woods one day. Despite putting notices up in the shops and calling the pound no one has claimed her. And so she has chosen me.
She is attentive to my moods, unwavering in her unconditional love
and devotion. And I in turn have made her mine. I bring her with
me everywhere and she is my constant companion. I call her Cleo,
after Queen Cleopatra. A regal name, like Solomon. She sits on the
passenger seat of my car as I drive the byways of County Sligo,
looking out the windscreen, confident this is where she belongs.

And yet, despite Liam, Fiona and Cleo, I am still searching. I have
never stopped looking for what I lost from the moment I left Ireland, standing on the ferry, gripping the wet railings and watching
Dun Laoghaire harbour getting smaller and smaller. I stood with
my face to the wind, shrinking the memory of my traumatic
summer in France and trying to throw it out like tissue paper,
hoping it would disintegrate, hoping I would forget. I wonder how
I survived that first winter on my own in London. It is hard to

remember the details for I have blacked them out. All I remember is the moment my husband found me and how I decided to hand my life over to him because it was easier.

Fiona and Jim have tried to reintroduce love into my life. They invite me for dinner with other single male friends. They take me with them to parties or to the races, where we meet up with jolly good-humoured male chums of Jim. They are usually recently separated and have children but are optimistic, generous, willing to share, wanting to have fun. It is I who am the problem. I find it hard to be casual and yet I am afraid to make a commitment. I am enjoying my solitude and self-sufficiency. In truth, I am still waiting for the mythical soulmate we all dream of.

The summer drifts by and I walk the laneways of my childhood. I have even started riding again. I let the horse take me along the country boreen and lead me back. A bend in the road, a certain bush or the shape of a cloud remind me of a moment spent with my mother, Mattie and Solomon, all of whom are dead but not gone. I am at peace. Each morning in my new house I savour the sensation of waking up in my bedroom without the sound of the city outside. It is a loft conversion, and three big skylights flood the room with summer sunshine. All I can hear are birds singing. Liam sleeps in late, and the house is silent, ticking over, breathing in and out.

And so the days wind into each other and, before I know it, it is nearly the end of the summer, the day before my forty-first birthday. It is like any other weekend. I get up late, let Cleo out for a run and make porridge. I sit outside on a chair, my bowl in my lap and a cup of tea perched on a stone. I have wrapped a cardigan about me to keep out the early morning chill. I watch the light wash over the green fields, and the glistening streaks of sea run through the wet sand. I might swim later if it gets warmer. I look at the sun valiantly trying to push more clouds out of the sky, and watch a small white butterfly with orange tips on the ends of its wings flutter, landing on a michaelmas daisy. Cleo lies down in the grass in front of me and closes her eyes. A moment later she sits up, sniffing the air, her ears pricked.

'What is it, Cleo?'

Liam appears. His hair is a mess, scruffy and endearing. He is wearing a pair of jeans and a t-shirt.

'Mum,' he says. 'Someone's at the door.'

It's too early for Fiona. I wonder who might visit me at this time on a Saturday morning. I hope it's not another one of my mother's old cronies looking for a reading, although most have given up by now.

I walk steadily down the hall, Cleo at my heels. I can see a figure standing on the other side of the frosted glass. Cleo starts barking, so it must be someone she doesn't know, yet there is something strangely familiar about the figure; something which makes my heart beat fast. I shut Cleo in the kitchen, and then I go back to open the door.

It is her. I recognise the face immediately. Matilda Finch. I step back in shock, bring a hand to my head, utter a little cry.

'Barbara Delaney?' she asks.

My chubby six-year-old duckling has turned into a beautiful swan. Her mousey hair is now a glorious shade of blonde, full of threads of honey, gold, silver and yellow. She is petite, like her mother, but pale-skinned. Her skin is perfect, like porcelain, with a faint blush on the cheeks. And her eyes, still those slate-blue eyes, which belonged to my Mattie. How could I forget her?

'Is that you?' I ask huskily, my voice suddenly without power. 'Is that you, Matilda Finch?'

'Yes,' replies the young woman, smiling.

I stare at her for a moment and then I catch myself.

'Come in, come in,' I stutter, and she follows me into the light-filled hall with its clean freshly painted walls still bare. We go into the kitchen. Cleo jumps up at her, wagging her tail. Liam is nowhere to be seen. My heart is pounding. I cannot believe Matilda Finch is here, in Ireland. I haven't seen her since the day she left with Olivia and Gareth, over twenty years ago. I lean against the counter, blood draining out of my face. Matilda blushes.

'I'm sorry, I've given you a big shock.'

'Yes,' I laugh nervously. I pull myself upright, gripping the Formica top with my hands.

'Would you like a tea or coffee?'

'Coffee, thank you,' she replies politely. She smoothes her hands down her front and fiddles with the rings on her fingers. She is neatly dressed in a tailored black suit but she looks far from composed.

'Please, sit down.'

My hands are shaking as I switch on the kettle. Matilda perches on top of a stool.

She continues to fidget. The clock ticks and the kettle boils. I lick my lips, suddenly dry. I don't know what to say to her.

'I have been looking for you for a while,' she speaks up.

'Why?' I ask hesitantly, pouring water into two mugs. She smiles wistfully, appears to relax a little.

'You are exactly as I remember you. My flame-haired guardian angel. Baa baa, my saviour.'

I shake my head.

'Matilda, you were a very brave little girl. It was you who gave me the courage to do what I did.'

I cannot be specific but we both know what I am referring to. I see the memory of it darken her pupils.

'Thank you,' she says simply, taking the coffee off me. 'Thank you so very much.'

She puts her mug down on the counter. We stare at each other. Again I am lost for words.

'I'm sorry to just turn up like this,' she begins.

'I never imagined I would ever see you again, not after all this time,' I say shakily.

'It's just . . .' She stutters, looks embarrassed. 'I needed to see you. The last couple of years I've been having these terrible dreams, and then I broke up with my boyfriend because I felt so angry with him all the time although he never did anything wrong. I knew the only way I could really forget what happened was if I remembered, and when I did I had to find you. I had to tell you everything.' She emphasises the word 'everything'. She holds my gaze, staring intently at me with her charcoal eyes.

'I lied to you,' she announces.

'What do you mean?'

'I'm not sure my father actually made me sick on purpose. I think I made it up. I loved my father like every other little girl.' Her voice cracks. 'But then I hated him . . .'

'But who made you sick, Matilda?'

'I did it to myself.'

I look down at the red tiles on my kitchen floor, their bright new shine. What could Matilda mean? Of course her father poisoned her because he was evil, the devil resident in my head all these years.

'In a way it was my father's fault,' she continues, her words running through me like a river of salt. 'I remember thinking that if I was sick he was happy. Because he would have to look after me and I knew he liked that. I liked it too. I pretended at the beginning. I used to imagine things in my head and start shouting and then my body just took over. I could make myself sick just like that. It has taken me years to change that habit.'

She sighs, smoothing down her trousers again. I look at my little Matilda all grown up and realise that it was never how I thought it was. Black is never the complete absence of light, and white is never wholly pure. What happened to me had nothing to do with Matilda. It was something else completely.

Over the years I have often wondered how it is a parent could willingly make their child sick. Just once I was given a tiny insight. Liam was seven at the time and recovering from a bad stomach bug. The two of us were curled up on the sofa watching a Batman movie, and he was cuddling me. My son was quiet, subdued and loving. He was a little boy needing his mum, and at that very moment I was the centre of the universe for him. All he wanted was me. It was our own little world, just the two of us, hiding from everyone else, and we were allowed to because Liam was ill. I was sitting there, my arm around him, looking at the flickering images on the television, and for a fleeting second I could understand what might motivate a parent to do such things. But I had got it wrong. It was not John who had wanted to create such exclusivity but his child.

Matilda looks worried. She licks her lips.

'And then, when I had a fit, my father got some of my mother's attention. As long as I kept having them, Daddy was happy. Who would have thought the mind of a six-year-old was so complex? I felt I had to be sick so Mama wouldn't leave. Poor Mama.'

I bristle at the mention of Olivia.

'She was very sorry about how she treated you. She told me to tell you, before she died.'

'Oh, I'm sorry.' I feel instantly guilty. 'When did that happen?'

'Three years ago. Cancer. But she had a good eighteen years with Gareth. They were very happy together. They talked about you from time to time, Barbara. They were very grateful to you. They think you saved me from my father. Everyone believed Daddy made me sick. I have never told anyone the truth, but you deserve to know.' She looks at me knowingly, and I wonder why she says this. She picks up her coffee and sips it.

I sweep my hand through my hair and look out the window at

Knocknarea, its verdant green lines and beckoning summit breaking through the clouds.

I feel a rush of relief. So John Finch wasn't trying to kill his daughter or even make her sick. Maybe I can pity him. Did he kill himself out of remorse for what he did to me, not Matilda? I remember my mother's words.

There is no such thing as evil. Just damaged people damaging others.

'Yes, you deserve to know,' Matilda repeats, placing her coffee mug down on the counter again and looking at me steadily, 'after what he did to you.'

I stiffen. The words hang in the air. They snake down my spine, chilling me to the bone.

'I remember,' Matilda says.

I look into her big grey-blue eyes, like two lakes, deep and full, and I see a memory reflected back. Me. On the flagstone floor of the bathroom in the house in the Camargue. I am on my knees. In my hands I am holding my bikini bottoms. There is blood on my thighs, mixed with John Finch's sperm. I am frozen in horror, unable to move or cry. And then I see something else, something I never remembered before. She was there. Matilda didn't come in through the door after it happened, not like I thought. Matilda came out of the large oak wardrobe in the corner of the bathroom. She had been there all along. Matilda had seen everything.

'I remember,' she repeats, her eyes shining like beacons of truth.

And then she stands up. She takes a step forward and she embraces me. She begins to cry. Her tears are in my hair, like drops from our shared memories, our shared pain and sorrow. She steps back, holding my shoulders, staring into my eyes. I cannot cry. All the years of trying to convince myself it never happened, that I had led John Finch on, that I had wanted to have sex, that it was my fault are lodged inside me, like a stone stuck in my throat making it hard to breathe.

'No.' I try to pull away. I am shaking, hot and cold all at the same time.

'Barbara,' Matilda whispers hoarsely. 'I saw what my father did to you.'

And finally it rips out of me. A scream so fierce it makes Matilda jump back and the dog bark in fright. I do not care if Liam hears me, I do not care if the whole world sees me wail, for I am naked in the centre of my awful memory and I am feeling the way I felt then all over again.

I rush out of the kitchen into the garden. I run to the end of it and hang on to the fence. I feel a surge of energy, like a fierce wind, a mistral of anger, sweep through me.

'No!'

I shout to the sky, to the clouds sweeping through its deep expanse of blue, to Knocknarea's peak shrouded in grey mist, to Queen Maeve's hidden cairn. My anger flies through me. It is like a banner flapping in the wind. See, it says, Barbara said no.

I close my eyes and last night's dream returns to me. Mattie running in the woods, Solomon at his side, and I am chasing him. It is a game. We burrow through the undergrowth, my brother, my dog and I, until I have caught him. He wriggles and squeals in my arms, but he loves me to tickle him. We are exhausted but happy, sitting opposite each other on the damp mossy ground. My brother looks at me, with the eyes of Matilda Finch, and he says 'I remember' in his sparkling little voice as clear as the day he died.

And like my mother knowing when things would happen, I knew this moment would come one day. The dream would keep repeating until Matilda came back. I open my eyes, let sunshine spill onto my face. Cleo has followed me. She jumps up on her hind legs and pushes her muzzle under my elbow. I look down at her and her black eyes are brimming with concern.

'It's all right Cleo,' I say, patting her. I squat on the ground next to her and stroke my dog until I feel calm again. I stand up and walk slowly back towards the house. Matilda waits on the patio, watching me, her hands shoved into her pockets.

'I'm sorry,' she says nervously. 'I shouldn't have . . .'

'No,' I interrupt her. 'It's OK.' And I smile at her. She relaxes, smiles weakly back. We bring our coffee into the garden and sit watching the bees buzzing around the bushes and the few small shrubs I have managed to plant.

Everything feels surreal. The grass is a brighter shade of green, and the sky looks picture-postcard blue, even the noise of the insects is amplified.

Matilda puts her coffee down on the patio stones and brings her knees up to her chest. I look at her curiously. She is so pretty, like a little doll, but I can see she is tough too, no shrinking violet.

We sit in silence for a while. The land hums around me and I breathe deeply. Cleo licks my hand and then lies down on the warmed patio stones at my feet. I am keenly aware of being alive. The blood pulses through my veins, the fresh mountain air fills my lungs and the scent of honeysuckle in the garden washes over me.

'It's beautiful here,' Matilda remarks. 'It's enchanting.'

'Yes,' I nod in agreement, watching her bask in the sunshine. She appears to be in the best of health. It is so odd seeing a part of my past sitting right before me in my new life. I wonder how she got here.

'Matilda, how did you know where I lived?'

'My uncle.'

'Pascal?'

My chest tightens. I am surprised by the reaction his name still has on me after all this time.

'Yes, of course. I only have one uncle.' She smiles at me. 'I have been living with him in Paris since Mama died. He could see things weren't going well for me so when I finally told him about why we ran away together he was appalled about what my father did to you. He helped me find you. It wasn't hard once you moved back to Ireland. Besides, he always knew where you were, he just didn't tell anyone else. He said he wanted to protect you.'

I am stunned. My world as I know it is spinning on its axis, very fast. I take a big gulp of coffee and try to steady myself.

'How did you get here?'

'Well, he brought me, of course. He's in the car, waiting.'

The colour rushes to my cheeks as of old. My throat goes dry.

'Pascal is outside my house?' I ask her, my voice trembling.

'Yes, he said he wouldn't come in because the sight of both of us might be too much of a shock for you. But he would like to see you again. Will you come out to the car?'

I look down at myself. How old must I look now? I haven't put any weight on since I was eighteen. In fact I have probably lost some, but what about my face, the dark shadows under my eyes, the wrinkles on my forehead and the grey strands in my red hair, how do they make me look?

'I don't know,' I say unsteadily.

'Please.' She stands up, offering me her hand. 'He has come a long way to see you.'

We are standing at the patio doors when Liam walks into the kitchen. The two of them start, stare at each other. The resemblance is uncanny. Long oval faces, light arched eyebrows, fair hair, narrow noses . . . and Mattie's eyes.

'Barbara!' Matilda exclaims, and swivels round to look at me. Her whole expression is a question. Liam looks over at me uncertainly. He is confused.

'Liam, this is Matilda,' I say calmly. My son looks at me and instantly understands. He turns to Matilda.

'You're Matilda?'

Liam looks excited.

'You've heard of me?' she asks incredulously.

'Of course I have. Mum told me I had a sister but we couldn't see her because of her dad. He wasn't married to my mum. I'm a secret.'

Matilda looks at Liam, astonished.

'An unbelievable secret!'

Liam starts asking her questions, and I slip out of the room. Mammy always told me never to tell lies, and I have tried to stay as close to the truth as I can. Liam has always known that my ex-husband wasn't his real dad. I told him I got pregnant when I was an au pair, to the father of my charge, little Matilda Finch. I told him his father was now dead, and that Matilda didn't know he existed. But I never told Liam I was raped. No. I always told him he was the best thing that ever happened to me my whole life.

I open the front door of my house, Cleo at my side, and there he is: Pascal, the *gardian* of the Camargue, my French cowboy, the artist of my heart. He leans against his shiny hire car, waiting for me. As he spots me, he straightens up and peers anxiously across the road. He waits for me to come to him. I cross, walking shakily, aware of my eighteen-year-old self still inside me, bashful and uncertain. I try to squash her. I try to be hard.

'Barbara,' he says softly, his French accent still as strong.

He takes off his glasses and he looks the same. Black hair flecked with grey, but the same lean body. He looks even better now than I remember. His face has aged well. It is still angular but with more character, as if he has lived a full life.

'Pascal, how are you?' I shake his hand warily. Cleo sniffs his feet, but she doesn't bark. He slips his glasses into his breast pocket, bends down and pats her.

'This must be a bit of a shock,' he says hesitantly.

I don't know what to say. Even after all these years a part of me is still angry at his betrayal.

'I'm sorry, Barbara.' He pauses. 'I'm so very sorry.' He moves towards me, but I step back. I look behind him at the hedgerow dripping with cow parsley, purple thistles and bright pink fuchsia.

'Let's go for a walk,' I suggest, and point at the sea beyond the hedges and the fields. I don't want to talk, not yet.

We cross the land silently, Cleo bounding ahead of us. He helps me over the stone walls, and his grip is firm, his hands as strong as I remember in my dreams. It is hard to think the man of my night-time fantasies (for how long? over twenty years) is right here beside me. I feel panic-stricken and horribly shy. How must I look to him? Am I a disappointment after all this time? I try to convince myself he is only here to say sorry for he must have a wife by now, surely he does, and a family.

We reach the grassy shoreline and walk down onto the beach. The tide is coming in. I take my shoes off and feel the soft sand pressing into the soles of my feet. He walks beside me, and still not a word is exchanged. I stop and sit down on a large boulder facing him. Cleo runs into the crashing white surf. I watch her pulling sticks and seaweed out of the water.

'How are you, Barbara?' Pascal asks me gently.

I cannot look at him. My eyes survey the horizon.

'I'm fine,' I reply tightly. 'And you? What are you up to?'

I try to speak lightly, but I know I sound forced.

'I'm OK,' he speaks warmly. 'You know, I took your advice. I decided to try to be an artist full-time. It was tough at the beginning but it has finally paid off. I am doing quite well.'

'That's great.' I nod, trying to remain distant.

'I moved to Paris not long after you left the Camargue, and I have been there since. My father got too old to run the place in the end. He had to sell. That was sad, but I think he has forgiven me. Besides, I think he rather likes the buzz of living in Paris, and my mother adores it.'

I am glad to hear both his parents are alive and well. I remember Celeste, and the day she gave me the lavender. My picture of her is still remarkably clear. I think about her daughter, Olivia. It is hard to imagine she is dead.

'I was sorry to hear about Olivia.'

He looks across the strand for a moment to the distant blue hills, their contours lumpy and uneven. Silence sweeps between us. He walks over and sits down next to me on another boulder.

'Yes, that was hard. It broke my mother's heart.'

Cleo comes bounding towards me. She drops a large polyp of black seaweed at my feet. I pick it up and throw it into the air. She chases after it.

'And you?' Pascal asks. 'Did you marry?'

I nod.

'I see,' he says. 'Children?'

'One. I'm not married any more.' I feel suddenly cross. How dare he ask if I am married or not? 'Not that it is any of your business,' I add hotly.

'*Pardon*, sorry.' He turns away from me and looks out to sea. I stare straight ahead, embarrassed I have been so rude. The land curves around us on either side, like two protective arms trying to hold the water in as it bleeds away to infinity.

'And you?' I ask abruptly. 'Did you marry?'

'Yes,' he replies softly. 'But I am divorced now, we never had children.'

So he did marry Violette, the love of his life, as Olivia called her. Yet it hadn't worked out. He was divorced. I feel a little surge inside me and I try to quell it. I pick up a large round stone and cup it in my hands, feeling the weight of it, trying to hold myself down. I listen to the sea, the waves rippling against the shore, and the squall of the seagulls around us. My heart pounds in my chest, but I am speechless. I don't know what to say. Pascal coughs, and then he turns towards me, but still I can't look.

'Dear Barbara, can you forgive me after all this time?'

I am pulled towards him, and when I look at him his eyes are topaz against his dark skin. I recognise him, a deep soul connection, and I know I still love him after all these years. It makes me furious. My whole life I have been waiting to meet a man I would feel the same way about as I did with Pascal, and I never have. He squandered my love, young and unsophisticated as it was. He threw it away.

'Why are you here, Pascal?' I ask him harshly.

'I brought Matilda.' His brow furrows, and I can see a faint blush beneath the dark skin of his cheeks.

'No,' I repeat, coldly. 'Why are you here?'

A slight breeze lifts the hair off my shoulders. My bare feet are pressed against the hard rock, its surface smooth and warmed by the morning sun. I look desperately out to sea. The sun has gone in for a moment and the water has changed from blue to silvery grey. It looks like there is a dark line slashed across the horizon.

Pascal coughs again and then he speaks slowly, as if he is thinking carefully about every single word he utters.

'I have been looking for you for a long, long time.'

I say nothing. I do not believe him.

'I found you once,' he continues, 'not long after everything happened. You were in London. I saw you in the street in Brixton. You were waiting for a bus. I was about to go over to you but then I saw you were pregnant and I thought I had better leave you alone. I thought you must have a boyfriend or a husband, and I was very ashamed.'

'No!' I utter in horror. I put my head in my hands and look down. I stare at the wet sand, at a little crab scuttling sideways. I am pulsing with hurt at this revelation.

'What is it? What's wrong?' Pascal asks in a rush.

'It was *his* baby,' I moan.

'Oh my God!' Pascal leans forward. 'I only found out a few months ago what John did to you. Matilda told me. I . . .' He seems unable to speak and tries to touch me but I shift sideways. Yet I feel different. He is able to mention the rape and I no longer feel guilty. I feel a wave of power within me. I look up at the sea glittering with iridescence from the reappearing sun. My voice is charged with anger.

'What about Violette?'

'Violette?'

He looks puzzled.

'Yes, Violette, your fiancée in Montpellier, who you married,' I spit at him, bitterly.

He laughs suddenly breaking the intensity of our discussion and its dark content. His face is creased with laughter lines around his eyes and just by looking at him I begin to trust him again.

'Oh my bloody sister! She told you Violette was my fiancée?' He laughs again.

'What's so funny?' I ask crossly, yet at the same time I feel my temper subsiding, and a little seed of hope taking root.

'Violette, bless her soul, now long dead, was an eighty-year-old painter I used to visit, who lived in Montpellier. I used to stretch her canvases for her. My wife was called Nadine. I didn't meet her until at least five years after you. By then I had given up on the chance I would ever see you again.'

Five years. He waited five years, yet I will not let him off that easily. I plough on.

'You betrayed me. You told John Finch what I said to you.'

He is serious again. He reaches forward, picks up a stick and digs it into the sand.

'I know. I didn't believe you. I told John, it's true. And now I

257

know what happened next.' He pauses, and sighs. I hear it in his voice, his guilt. 'I can't tell you how much I regret speaking to him. If I had known what he did to you I would have killed him.'

He slams his hand down on the sand. I watch little sparkling grains push between his fingers. I bring my knees up to my chest and shiver. But I have to tell him this. He has to know.

'I was a virgin,' I whisper.

'Oh, Barbara.' His voice aches with pain, for me.

We look at each other, and I know what he is thinking. He is thinking about a night in a hotel in Arles which never happened, and what might have been.

He reaches over and takes the stone out of my cold hands, and holds them in his. They are warm and pulsing with life; little particles of sand rub between our flesh. I hold his eyes and my heart is lifted by his gaze.

'Can you forgive me?' he asks me again.

I remember the day in the sand dunes and how this man made me feel, and how no one, not even my husband, had ever made me feel like that again.

Pascal keeps looking at me, while at the same time he lets go of my hands and pulls something out of his back pocket.

'I found this the other day. I wanted to show you,' he says eagerly.

He hands me a folded-up piece of paper. I open it, and I have found her again. It is a drawing of me, the day on the sand dunes. I thought he had been making a nude study of my body, but the picture is just of my face. I look at the eighteen-year-old girl, her eyes bright with promise, her little turned-up nose spattered with freckles, her long locks of thick wavy hair framing her pointy face, and her lips curled into a cheeky pixie smile. She is the girl with the open heart, untouched and innocent.

I look up into Pascal's brilliant blue eyes. I feel buoyant, held by the sincerity of his expression.

'Yes, I forgive you.'

Cleo runs up to me and pushes herself between our two rocks. We both stroke her. I pat her head, and Pascal her rump. Gradually our hands get closer and closer until our fingers knot together in the soft black fur on her back.

Acknowledgements

Thank you to Vicki Satlow for helping me start this book, and to Marianne Gunn O'Connor for her inspiration and belief. Thank you to Imogen Taylor for her constant guidance as an editor, and to all at Pan Macmillan, especially Trisha Jackson, Emma Giacon, David Adamson and Liz Cowen, and to Cormac Kinsella at Repforce. Thank you to Sally Nelson, who travelled with me to the Camargue and helped me with so many different aspects of the book; and to Sue and Dick Reed, who made us so welcome in their home in France. Thank you to those who read the manuscript in its early stages and gave me such valuable feedback and support: Monica McInerney, Kate Bootle, Donna Ansley, Pat Lynch, Alison Walsh, Sinéad Nic Coitir and Alice Barry. A big thank you to Joy Terekiev and Cristiana Moroni at Mondadori in Milan. Thanks also to Bernie McGrath, Eileen Blishen, Ciara O'Hara, Miriam McCabe, Tina Quinn, Page Allen, Synnøve and Hanna Bakke, Doireann Mangan, Carol O'Connor, Denis Boyle at Meath Arts Office and all at the Tyrone Guthrie Centre in Annaghmakerrig. Thanks also for the love and support of Fintan Blake Kelly, Barry Ansley, Helena Goode and Corey Ansley. And thank you to my angels for their guidance. This book is dedicated to the memory of my dear hound, Chlöe – RIP.